Old Dogs

Also by Ron Schwab

The Lockes
Last Will
Medicine Wheel
Hell's Fire

The Law Wranglers
Deal with the Devil
Mouth of Hell
The Last Hunt
Summer's Child
Adam's First Wife
Escape from El Gato
Peyote Spirits

The Coyote Saga
Night of the Coyote
Return of the Coyote
Twilight of the Coyote

The Blood Hounds
The Blood Hounds
No Man's Land
Looking for Trouble

Sioux Sunrise
Paint the Hills Red
Grit
Cut Nose
The Long Walk

Old Dogs

Ron Schwab

Uplands Press

OMAHA, NEBRASKA

Uplands Press
1401 S 64th Avenue
Omaha, NE 68106
www.uplandspress.com

Publisher's Note: This is a work of fiction. Names, characters, places, and incidents are a product of the author's imagination. Locales and public names are sometimes used for atmospheric purposes. Any resemblance to actual people, living or dead, or to businesses, companies, events, institutions, or locales is completely coincidental.

Ordering Information:
Quantity sales. Special discounts are available on quantity purchases by corporations, associations, and others. For details, contact the "Special Sales Department" at the address above.

Uplands Press / Ron Schwab -- 1st ed.
ISBN 978-1-943421-52-7

To my sister, Lana Schwab Criner.

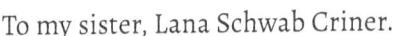

"There is no friend like a sister in calm or stormy weather."

Christina Rossetti

Chapter 1

JACK WILLS SAT in the sturdy rocking chair perched on the roofed veranda that ran along the entire front of the two-story limestone house, one foot propped up against the oak railing. The porch rail was chipped and worn from years of service as more footrest than hand support for Lucky Five Ranch headquarters occupants and their visitors. The house stood alone, save for the outback privy, on a low butte overlooking the employee residences, outbuildings, corrals, and other structures vital to ranching operations.

The flat top of the butte stretched slightly more than seventy yards with the house located at the east end and a growing cemetery to the west where several of the original Spanish residents rested along with cowhands or relatives of those who had worked the land over the years. Jack had no relatives planted there, not if a man only counted blood kin, anyhow. He was the last of his line. Nonetheless, he took the path that veered off the walkway to the cemetery tract weekly to visit the place and keep it weeded and clean. The native grasses he let grow, but he saw it as his job to fight the buckbrush, cedars, and thistles that were always trying to move in and take over.

The butte's summit lay less than ten feet above the lower ranch yard, but the house had been strategically located on high ground years back as a defensive measure against Comanches, Kiowas, and other raiders. From the south side of the butte, a rocky slope dropped gradually to the lower building site, and flat limestone rocks had been used to construct a solid stairway and a walkway to the veranda.

Sundown would not turn down the heat of a blazing Texas sun for several hours yet, but the porch roof offered plenty of shade, especially since the front faced southeast. Jack reached down and raked his fingers lazily through Thor's silky hair. The dog slept soundly on the two-layer cowhide rug next to the chair. The big coal-black dog of indeterminate breed, like his master, had given up rabbit hunting and was content these days to let somebody else search out meals for him. Most of the time, he ordered beef.

Jack lifted the telescope to his eye again and focused on the dust swirl down the North Concho River valley he had been following for a spell. It was a rider, pushing the horse beyond good sense. He could not say he had not done the same with a Comanche war party on his tail but never when his life was not at stake. He did not see anyone chasing this rider. Whoever it was would hit the fork in the trail soon, turn left to Tess Wyman's small spread or rein right to the Lucky Five. If the rider headed for Tess's, he would send one of the hands over to be certain she did not have trouble riding in. On second thought, he might just ride over himself. He was past due to pay Tess a social call.

"What the hell you looking at out there? I don't see nothing." It was his longtime friend and saddle partner, Rudolph Kilgore, who was seated in another rocking chair on the opposite side of Thor.

"What do you think spyglasses are for, Rudy? They let a man see things he'd otherwise miss."

"So, what are you seeing?"

"A rider moving fast. Just hit the fork. Looks like we got company for supper."

"Maybe they ain't friendly."

"We'll find out in about ten minutes. I'll go warn Josephina that she and Consuelo should plan on another guest." He lifted his legs off the railing and eased out of the rocker, careful not to jar his back. Once he got to moving, he would be fine. Nothing he could do about spending most of his seventy years in the saddle or all those nights sleeping on the hard ground. The lead slug still nested near his lower backbone did not help a whole lot either.

Rudy called after him, "Jack, is Jordy eating with us tonight?"

"Yeah, he said he would be up. Just got back with a crew rounding up strays."

"What?"

Jack did not repeat his reply and entered the house. Jordy was Jordan Jackson, a twenty-five-year-old cowhand, who had been raised by Jack since the age of ten and lived in the house when he was at ranch headquarters, which generally was less than half the time. Rudy called the young cowhand a working fool who didn't know when to call it a day. But Rudy had helped raise Jordy, and Jack knew his old partner was proud of the man who would be foreman in another three or four years when Rusty Dobbs intended to move to Kansas to be nearer his daughter and her family. Jack sensed that Jordy felt the burden of proving his worth given his special relationship with the boss. He had already proved it as far as Jack was concerned.

When Jack returned to the veranda, the slim and wiry rider was starting to hitch a strawberry roan mare to the hitching post in the yard below the house. The horse did not seem to be suffering greatly but was breathing heavily and frothing some at the mouth, igniting the rancher's anger. He started to say something when he saw Jordy walk up behind the rider.

The lean, sinewy cowhand, who easily passed the six-foot mark without his boots, towered over the visitor, "Can I see to your horse, ma'am? Appears to have had a hard ride. Let me get her to some water and wipe her down a bit. A little grain be okay?"

The rider lifted the front of a low-crowned hat and looked up at Jordy. "I would appreciate that. Her name is 'Dancer.'"

Jordy took the reins from her hands and turned away, leading the tired mount toward the stable, but Jack saw him give the newcomer quick scrutiny.

A young woman. What in blazes?

She looked up at him from the bottom of the stone steps that led up the slope to the house. "I'm looking for Jack Wills," she said.

"I'm Jack Wills," he replied. "Why don't you come on up? We've already set another plate for supper, and Consuelo's fixing up the spare room for the night."

She bound up the steps, ignoring the sturdy handrail that had been installed a few years back mostly for the benefit of Jack and Rudy. When she reached the landing in front of the porch, Jack stepped back so she could join them there. He saw Rudy searching his trouser pockets for his choppers and, finding them, slipping them into his mouth, something he only bothered to do for female company or at mealtimes. Jack tipped his hat when she stepped onto the porch, and she pushed her own higher on her forehead revealing lightly bronzed skin and long sable hair tied back in a ponytail. He guessed her to be several inches over five feet tall, a head turner to any male but a blind man. He waited for her to speak.

"My name is Sierra Wills," she said.

The natural response would have been to ask if she was a relative, but he had none that he knew of. "Pleased to meet you, Miss Wills. The geezer sitting on the rocker is Rudy Kilgore, and the fella snoozing on the floor is our watchdog, Thor."

Rudy remained seated and lifted his hat just enough to give a hint of his bald pate. "Howdy, ma'am," he said. "Welcome to Lucky Five."

Thor slept on, but Jack figured if the animal had sensed a threat, he would have been up and poised by his owner's boots. He was certain that Thor's hearing wasn't much better than Rudy's, yet the dog seemed to hear when he wanted to or whenever he sensed danger. Jack had to admit his own hearing missed a thing or two these days, but he had convinced himself it was far better than Rudy's. Of course, they argued some about that.

"Is that all you've got to say?" the lady who called herself Sierra Wills said, her tone a bit snippy, he thought.

He had always been slow with a reply, tending to choose words carefully, especially when speaking to strangers. "Ma'am. You are welcome here. You have been invited for supper and offered a room for the night. If you would care to state your business, I'd be glad to oblige with some more conversation."

"You did notice that we share a last name?"

"Well, yes, it seems we do."

"Did it occur to you we might be related?"

"No, ma'am. I have no blood kin." None that would carry his name, anyway. His youthful exploits did not rule out the possibilities that a Kiowa or Comanche woman had nurtured his seed to bloom. And there had been other short-lived romances during his time with the Texas Rangers and, before that, his roaming years following the war for Texas Independence. He had been no saint and was still uncertain if he regretted that.

"You do have blood kin. I am your granddaughter."

Chapter 2

"WE WILL TALK about this after supper," her grandfather had said, after Sierra informed him that she was his granddaughter. He was a stone-faced man, and she had seen neither shock, rejection, nor acceptance in those searching hazel eyes that seemed to be sizing her up for veracity.

Jack Wills had escorted her into the house and introduced her to Consuelo Cortez, a pretty Mexican girl who appeared several years younger than her own twenty. Consuelo was obviously fluent in softly accented English, but she was thrilled when she found that Sierra spoke near flawless Spanish, and the two easily jumped into a conversation of language hopscotch.

Consuelo led Sierra into the large kitchen, where she met the young woman's mother, Josephina, a short, buxom woman who embraced her with a welcoming hug. Josephina was also bilingual but struggled not to stray from English and tendered a big smile when Sierra shifted the conversation to the woman's first tongue. The aroma in the cooking area reminded Sierra that she had not eaten since breakfast.

Consuelo led her through the house, the elegance of which contrasted to the drab exterior. It was decorated Texas style with obligatory mounted buck antlers and steer horns fastened to the walls of the large sitting room and above the wide fireplace built of dark gray stones that she guessed to be granite. A buffalo hide rug was stretched out in front of the fireplace. The furniture pieces, even several rockers, were upholstered in leather. The coffee and lamp tables were all crafted of rugged oak.

A large dining room off the kitchen would serve a dozen guests, she figured. She was awed by the paintings that adorned the walls, mostly landscapes with Southwestern settings but several portraits of Indian and Mexican faces, one an ancient Indian with deep wrinkles carved in brow and cheeks.

Consuelo showed her through a door off the sitting room into a room that took her breath away: a library that she estimated was easily twenty-five feet long and fifteen feet wide. One of the walls had bookshelves from floor to ceiling the length of the room. And there was

nary an empty space. At one end of the room was a roll-
top desk and chair and an oak filing cabinet, indicating
that the room doubled as an office. A round table with
four captains' chairs was not far from the desk, suggesting it might be conference space. There was a stuffed
leather chair and padded rocker sharing a lamp table at
the opposite end of the office area, and a Navajo rug covered much of the oak flooring in the center of the room.
Smaller rugs were scattered about the seating areas, and
there was a woodstove near what she thought of as the
reading chairs and, of course, more paintings decorating
any unused wall space.

"I don't believe this. The academy in San Antonio
didn't have a library this big. Why on earth does he have
all these books? He's just a rancher, an old Ranger from
what I've been told. He spent all this money for decora-
tion?" She almost resented it when she considered the
hard times her family had endured.

Consuelo laughed. "Jack reads constantly. So does
Jordy. And the library is available to anyone on the ranch.
Some of the books—not many—on those shelves are
mine, mostly novels, to be shared with any who are interested. In the fall, the four or five children of fulltime
ranch hands will gather here for school. Jack will hire a
tutor, who will live in one of the cottages for the school

year to teach the children. My family has been with him since the beginning, over fifteen years now. I received my education here. We worship Jack Wills."

"You mentioned Jordy. Who is he?"

"He is like Jack's son. Jack found Jordy when he was ten and took him in. He came here at almost the same time we did. I think of him as an older brother. I have a younger brother, Juan, who can be a pest, but then I remind myself that I have two brothers and a sister who are buried in the ranch cemetery. That makes me glad to have that pest." A shadow of gloom crossed Consuelo's face for just a moment, but her smile returned quickly. "But I should take you upstairs and show you your room. Follow me."

Returning to the sitting room, Consuelo nodded toward the open staircase that led to the second floor. They climbed the stairs where they entered a short hallway that provided access to four doors that Sierra assumed led to bedrooms.

Consuelo said, "The larger bedroom to the left is occupied by Jack . . . and Thor. That old dog won't let Jack out of his sight. And it works both ways most of the time. The first bedroom to your right is Jordy's, and the next one across the hall is the guest room, where you will be staying."

Consuelo led Sierra into the guest room, which had a single window opening to the east and like the remainder of the house was furnished with oak pieces. The white, plastered walls were decorated with a few more original paintings.

Sierra said, "Very nice. Mister Wills has a beautiful home."

Consuelo said, "You call him Mister Wills. But you have the same last name. If I am being too forward, say so, but are you related? He didn't say."

Sierra said, "You would naturally be curious. I am his granddaughter. But I don't think he believes it. Not yet."

"But he always says he has no blood relatives. He calls all of us here his ranch family. My Mexican grandparents are all in heaven. I think of Jack as my grandfather. And how can you be his granddaughter if he does not know it?"

"We have not seen each other until today," Sierra replied. "It is complicated. I do not know the entire story, but I am certain he is my grandfather."

Consuelo said, "You have his eyes. Hazel, I guess they call it. The color changes with the light. Right now, they are a greenish-grayish brown. Jack's eyes look more greenish in sunlight. I have never seen a person other than Jack with such eyes."

"They are also my father's eyes. My mother was mestizo, her eyes were dark brown like yours," Sierra said.

"I wondered. Your skin is lighter than mine, but I guessed there was blood other than Anglo running in your veins. We are mestizo also, as are most Mexicans, mixed bloods descended from Indians and Spanish or other Europeans. Many whose bloodlines come only from the Spanish invaders take care to announce that their blood runs pure."

Sierra said, "Yes, I encountered that sometimes when I attended the Riverside Girls Academy in San Antonio. Some of the girls did not hesitate to make clear that their Spanish descent placed them in a superior station, but not all were like that. It never bothered me, though."

Consuelo said, "I wish we could talk longer, but I must help Madre with supper. You will find a pan and a pitcher of water on the vanity with a bar of lye soap and some cloths if you wish to clean up a bit. The chamber pot is under the bed. There is a bathtub in the tub room next to Jack's bedroom, but you would not have time to use that before supper. My brother, Juan, will heat water and fill the tub later if you like."

"That would be nice. I must smell like a pig after two days in the saddle."

Consuelo smiled. "Jordy has been out a week. You won't be any competition for him."

Chapter 3

FTER JACK TURNED the visitor who claimed to be his granddaughter over to Consuelo, he returned to the veranda and reclaimed his rocking chair. He reached down and scratched Thor's floppy ears, and the dog looked up at him with his soulful yellowish eyes. "We're just three old dogs sitting here," Jack said.

"Yep," Rudy said. "Ain't teaching us no new tricks. But I remember most of the old ones. That's plenty. You gonna tell me about this granddaughter? You never said nothing about kids. Got to have a kid to have a grandkid the last I knew."

Jack knew that curiosity was killing the old fart. Old? Rudy was two years younger than himself. He guessed the age business was sometimes a matter of perspective. He rarely thought of himself as being older than Rudy.

Jack waited for a spell to answer. Rudy would hear no more than half of what was said anyway, and he would either have to repeat it or Rudy would fill in the blanks to suit himself.

Finally, Jack said, "I don't know what she's up to. We're going to talk after supper."

"She's going to tell us at supper?"

Jack did not reply.

The sun was starting to drop behind the hills to the west when Jordy Jackson came up the steps to the house, carrying the saddlebags and bedroll he had taken from the young woman's strawberry roan mare. The sandy-haired young man was tanned by the spring sun but would be darker before summer was out. Jack worried that Jordy didn't take more time off. He was too serious, not much for serious drinking and only occasionally chased women.

Jack did not think Jordy had ever visited the girls at Mabel's Heaven or Tobe's Tavern in San Angelo, but, of course, a man who looked like Jordy would not be pressed to pay for such commodities. There were a good half dozen local gals trying to capture the North Concho Valley's most eligible bachelor, and Jordy had likely talked his way into the bloomers of several. Jack wished Jordy would find one to marry before his seed took hold in one that he might not want to spend his life with. He was confident the young man would do the honorable thing if faced with such a situation.

Jordy stepped onto the porch and said, "I assume the young lady is staying the night. Where should I take her stuff?"

"I'd just put it down outside the spare room's door if it's closed," Jack said. "Otherwise, put it just inside the door."

"That filly is Jack's granddaughter," Rudy said.

Thanks, Rudy, Jack thought. Damned old gossip. Has to be first with the news.

Jordy furrowed his brow and looked at Jack. "I thought you didn't have any kin."

"That's what I always figured. Lady claims to be my granddaughter. I can't imagine how that would be, but I'll hear what she's got to say after we eat."

"Filly's going to tell her tale at supper," Rudy chimed in.

Jack turned to his old friend and added some power to his generally soft-spoken words. "She is not going to say a word about being my granddaughter at supper and neither are you. Do you understand? You keep your damned mouth shut about it or you can start taking your supper at the chuck house with the hands. Can you hear me?"

Rudy shrugged, "No reason to get your feathers ruffled, Jack. Ain't my fault you spat your seed along the trail someplace. So, we're going to get together and palaver with the young lady later, huh?"

"*We* are not. *I* am," Jack said. "And you are going to be the last to hear the story."

Rudy rendered a toothless grin and cackled. The old devil knew how to rile him and seemed to take the task of agitating Jack Wills as his main job on the ranch these days. On second thought, it had been that way since they met a year or two prior to the Texas Revolution where they had fought at the Battle of San Jacinto and taken part in the capture of Santa Anna. They had partnered in one way or another ever since.

Jordy broke into the fussing. "She's sure a pretty thing even after a long ride. I'd like to see her gussied up in female garb. She had been riding that roan a little hard, though."

"Yeah, I noticed," Jack said.

Jordy said, "You don't seem very excited about the visitor."

"I will just hold off the dancing till I hear what she's got to say and find out who she really is and what kind of game she's playing."

"Well, I'll run her things up to the room. Maybe I'll get a chance to talk to her some or get a better look."

Chapter 4

JORDY SLUNG THE saddlebags over his shoulder, picked up the bedroll and went into the house. When he reached the top of the stairs, he noticed that the door to the guest room was ajar. He tapped softly on the door.

"Come in."

When he entered, he saw that the young woman who claimed to be Jack's granddaughter was facing the vanity mirror, combing out her long, black hair. She turned to face him as he waited uncertainly in the doorway.

"Oh," she said, "I thought you were Consuelo."

He grinned sheepishly. "Nope. Connie's in the kitchen. I'm Jordy. I took your horse, but I thought you might want your saddlebags and bedroll."

She looked at him with appraising eyes—Jack's hazel eyes. "Uh, can I put these someplace?" he asked.

"The bed would be fine. Thank you. I have a change of clothes rolled up in the bedroll. And thanks for looking after Dancer. I rode her too hard today, but I wanted to get here before dark. She's still just a filly, but I wouldn't have considered leaving her at my place."

"She's fine. I rubbed her down and grained her some. She's got a stable stall with water and fresh prairie hay." After dropping his cargo on the bed, Jordy backed away. "If I can get you anything else, I'll be in the room across the hall till supper. Connie will call us."

"You sleep in the house?" Sierra asked.

"Yep. Me and Jack . . . and Thor. Consuelo, her parents and brother have their own house in the flats at the bottom of the butte. They have the biggest of the stone cottages Jack built for Lucky Five hands and muleskinners and families. Rudy has a place in the flats but takes meals at the house. He could have taken a room here, but he likes his own space. Doesn't like all the stairs either. The other single guys live in the bunkhouse and get fed at the chuck house nearby."

"How many cottages do you have here?"

Jordy pictured the cluster of homes in his head. "I guess there would be nine in all. I'll show you tomorrow if you like. It's like a little town out here. Discourages the

Comanches from pestering us, but most of them are going to Fort Sill now, so that problem's about done."

"What do you do with so many hands?"

"Well, I said muleskinners lived here, too. The Lucky Five has a freight hauling business that headquarters out of San Angelo. A lot of the waggoners double as hands during round-up and hands get called into the freighting enterprise when ranch work slows down. That way they have year-round jobs. Appeals to family men."

"I had no idea my grandfather was such an entrepreneur. Lucky Five. Where does that name come from? Do you know?"

"Oh, yeah. Rudy will give you the long version of the story if you ask. The ranch was a Spanish land grant, but all the Spaniards who tried to settle it got killed by Comanches or, if they were lucky, got run off. In 1846, the year after Texas became a state, Jack met up with the grant holder in Austin. Jack was a Texas Ranger then. The owner was offering the place for sale at fifty cents an acre. That was $10,750 more or less for the 21,500-acre grant. Jack had half of what he needed squirreled away. He's always been careful with his money. Not tight, just careful. Anyhow, he tried to get Rudy to go halves with him, but Rudy didn't have the money and didn't want to own anything anyway. He will tell you that property is a burden."

Sierra said, "That can be true sometimes."

"Yes, I suppose that can be the case. Anyway, Jack found a bank in Austin that would loan him the rest and take a mortgage on the grant. He went to meet the owner and close the deal and another fella shows up at the same time and matches the offer. The seller could have conducted an auction, and Jack wouldn't have been able to come up with another dollar, but the seller was a man of his word. He said they would settle it with a roll of the dice. Highest total wins. Five dice. Other guy rolls and comes up with twenty-four total. Jack rolls and gets all fives. Jack buys a ranch that forms a wedge between the North and Middle Concho rivers. That's how Lucky Five came about. If you hadn't noticed, the brand consists of five dots as they would appear on a face of a dice."

"But he was still a Ranger after I was born. That's what Papa said."

"The ranch was nothing but grass, buffalo, and Comanches for the next fourteen or fifteen years. He had chances to swing by and look it over at least once a year, and he sketched out plans for buildings around the site of this house that was built by the first Spanish settlers—or what was left of it after the owners got burned out by Comanches or Kiowas. He didn't move onto the place until just before the War of the Rebellion. He would have been closing in on fifty-five years old then. It was shortly after he picked me up. That's enough of the story for now."

"But how did you come to be with him?" Sierra asked.

"If you stick around more than a day or two, I'll tell you about it."

"You sound like Jack Wills is going to kick me down the road."

"Not Jack. He's the kindest, gentlest man I know. He has a long fuse, but he is not buying your granddaughter story, not even near to it."

"And what about you? Do you believe me?"

"I've got no basis to say yes or no. It doesn't matter one whit to me. All that matters is what Jack decides. Whether you are or not, you have got a reason for playing the granddaughter card. I will be interested to find out what it is."

Chapter 5

THERE WERE MORE diners at the supper table than Sierra had expected, nine in all: Jack, Rudy, Jordy, Rusty Dobbs the foreman, herself and the four members of the Cortez family. Josephina and Consuelo set the food on the table but joined the group to eat like members of any family might. Consuelo's father, Enrique, spoke English albeit with a thick accent and engaged in conversation about the day's accomplishments and tomorrow's plans. It appeared that he was responsible for repair and maintenance of the ranch buildings and corrals. Fourteen-year-old Juan was attentive and spoke little but ate ravenously and did not appear uncomfortable with the adults. It was obvious they had all shared many meals at this table.

Jordy had pulled back a chair for her when she entered the dining room and then sat down beside her. She ignored the odor of cow manure and stale sweat he sent her way, wondering if he noticed her own unpleasant scent. At least he made her feel less self-conscious.

Jack had introduced her by name to those she had not already met, offering no other explanation. Dobbs, a short slender man in his late fifties or early sixties had started to ask about the kinship, she thought, but a negative shake of Rudy's head had apparently warned him off.

Rudy's bald head was a distraction. The knotted flesh at the back of his scalp and a lobster-red strip down the middle, which he had not revealed with the tip of his hat earlier, was raised with proud and scarred flesh that reminded her of a rooster's comb. He must have suffered a terrible accident years ago, she concluded. He was certainly a talkative sort and never allowed silence to take hold for more than a few seconds. She liked him. He was friendly and funny, although she suspected the others had heard his stories more than once.

When Rudy had walked into the dining room, she saw that he limped some, but the gnarled wooden cane in his hand seemed more style than necessity as his stooped form moved with a strong gait. The gray whiskers that covered his cheeks and chin suggested he was a weekly shave man and nearing harvest.

Jack mostly listened to the others, nodding and smiling agreeably. When he spoke, it was to ask about ranch or freight operations, and she came to understand that the supper gathering was in no small part a business meeting.

She hoped her appetite did not appear unladylike, as she asked for additional helpings of roast beef, fried potatoes and mixed vegetables. Jordy smiled at her when he passed the serving platter. "Save room for Josephina's cobbler. I sneaked in the kitchen earlier. Apple tonight."

"I haven't eaten all day," she said. "I have room for cobbler. I fear I've been eating like a—"

"A cowhand," he said. "Nothing goes to waste at this table. Thor will clean up the remains, and he's already had a few servings of beef." He nodded at the big dog waiting patiently in the corner of the room, watching the diners intently and wagging his tail, starting the begging with hungry eyes.

She spoke to the Cortez women. "Josephina and Consuelo, I haven't eaten this well for months. Everything is delicious. Thanks so much."

The women beamed and Consuelo replied, "You are welcome. We hope you will be at this table for many more meals."

Sierra noticed that Jack did not smile.

Sierra felt stuffed after she finished the hot cobbler. She was wondering when she would have her confrontation with Jack Wills when he answered her question. He pushed back his chair and stood. It occurred to her for the first time that, in a rugged way, he was a handsome man, crow's feet wrinkles accentuating the eyes they shared, straight nose, thin lips. He stood erect, and she noted he was not quite Jordy's height but might have been in his youth, certainly not as muscular and broad shouldered as the younger man but not frail, either. Clean shaven and a full scalp of wiry, salt and pepper hair, more salt than pepper, though. Time had been kind to this man's appearance. Good. He might be useful to achieving her objective.

"Join me in the library, Miss Wills," Jack said softly.

Chapter 6

JACK AND SIERRA sat at the round table in the library. Without request, Consuelo had brought them each a steaming cup of hot coffee as soon as they were seated, leaving quickly and closing the door behind her. It was quiet as a tomb in the room, Jack sipping at his coffee before he spoke to the young woman across the table.

"You claim to be my granddaughter," he said.

"I am your granddaughter," she replied. "My late father was your son, John Thomas Wills. Everybody called him 'J. T.,' but you wouldn't know that. You didn't stick around long enough to find out."

Jack's face did not change expressions, but she had shaken him a bit. His own baptized name was John Thomas Wills. "Your mother?"

"Rosa Martinez Wills. She died ten years ago."

"And who was your father's mother?"

She gave him a disgusted scowl that did little to diminish her beauty. "Please don't play dumb with me. Emily Wills. Emily Cooper Wills. The woman you deserted over forty years ago. She was the mother of the child you abandoned."

He remained silent while he tried to sort out the statements she had made. There were pieces of truth there. He had been married to Emily Cooper. They had met in the late twenties on a wagon train organized by Stephen Austin when Austin was recruiting settlers to Texas and the area was still part of Mexico. Jack, whose parents had both died before he was sixteen, had given up on being a Tennessee farmer and latched onto a job escorting wagon trains for Austin in 1825. It did not seem possible. A half century ago. He had just turned twenty.

Three years later, he met a buxom girl with chestnut-colored hair and blue eyes traveling with one of the trains he was escorting. Emily Cooper drew the eyes of most of the young men on the train, but she flirted mostly with Jack. Her roots were in Virginia, and her wealthy father, Cyrus Cooper—probably rightly so, Jack now figured—was convinced Jack was not a proper suitor for his daughter and made no bones about it, likely fueling the fire between the two. Jack's brains resided below his belt in those days, and he owned a horse and saddle and the clothes on his back, not much else. In hindsight, old Cyrus could not be faulted for wanting something more than a broke kid for his daughter's husband.

After a courtship of two months, and upon arrival in Texas, Jack had spirited Emily away and married her before an old wagon master friend who claimed to have authority to marry folks. Jack had never been sure if their marriage was legal, but he would have never got beneath Emily's skirts without a wedding. And his pizzle was in a hurry.

"I was married to Emily," Jack said. "We had no children. The marriage lasted less than two years. I was gone most of the time working on assignments for Stephen Austin, and later Sam Houston, preparing for the revolution. Emily stayed in a little community, now known as the town of Huntsville."

"You had a baby together and you walked away and left them. Never came back, Grandma Emily told me. My father never met his dad. You never met your son."

"When was your father born?"

"You don't even recall your own son's birthday?"

"When was he born?"

"The tenth day of March 1830."

He tried to roll back the years to that time. He had been home in the one-room log and sod shack that Emily hated so much for several months during the spring of 1829, and she had reluctantly given in to his lustful approaches as often as weekly during that time, always making clear the inconvenience he was causing. It was late June when he was summoned by Austin again, and when he had informed her, she calmly told him not to bother coming back. She had written to her father, and he was coming to pick her up before Independence Day. She would be getting a divorce. Jack had swung by two months later, and she was gone. If her best friend knew where, she was not telling. Anyway, the date of J. T.'s birth made his paternity possible.

"Where does your Grandma Emily live these days?"

"In heaven. She died almost six years ago in Austin. Papa was with her."

"How old did she say J. T. was when I left?"

"You don't even know that? Maybe I should not have bothered to come here."

"How old?"

"You abandoned them on Papa's first birthday."

The sinking feeling in Jack's stomach made him feel weak. Sierra Wills carried a bundle of lies with her. But critical parts of the story made sense. And her hazel eyes were undeniably Wills. He had to see this tale through, but he would not dispute any of it, not now, anyhow. Attacking Emily would make Sierra defensive and serve no purpose, perhaps make him seem even more despicable. He had learned over the years that some lies were best left untouched.

"Tell me about your father," Jack said.

"He hated you."

"I guess that's a start."

"He was raised in Austin. Great Grandpa Cooper was an investor there. Just outside the town, he had a plantation and lots of slaves. Papa was embarrassed about the slaves as he got older, but he didn't want for anything when he was growing up. He loved horses, and he learned all about them from the slave who was stable manager on the plantation. He was even taught about breaking horses, although he said Grandma was terrified that he would be hurt."

"They lived on the plantation with his grandfather?"

"Yes. Great Grandma was sickly. Grandma Emily was the matron of the house, you might say."

"She did not remarry?"

"No, of course not. She said you were the love of her life. She never divorced you. Unless you divorced her, you became a widower when she died. Or if you married someone else without divorcing her, you became a biga-mist. Grandma thought that was more likely."

"I did not remarry. But I want to know about your father."

"He was a good man. Kind. Hardworking. And he loved his horses. That was his dream. To breed and raise horses. But he wanted to do it on his own. At twenty he left the plantation to work on the estate of one of the Spanish patrons, Manuel Garcia, who lived nearby, and worked mostly with the horses. He liked that the patron had no slaves. He met Mama there. She was mestizo, and Great Grandpa Cooper was not pleased when Papa married a Mexican who was not of pure Spanish descent. Grandma Emily did not like it either, but she grudgingly accepted Mama into the family because she did not want to lose Papa. They never became close, though."

"And after they were married, they remained on the Garcia estate?"

"Yes. I was born there. So were my brothers—both of them."

"You have brothers?"

"Had. They died shortly before I was born. Ages two and three. Smallpox. They are buried at the hacienda."

Jack tried to convince himself that Sierra Wills was a storyteller, an outright liar, but too many pieces of her story rang true. It was highly unlikely Emily would have remarried for anything but money. She had hated the marital bed, and her interest beyond things material had been nil during their time together. She had always loved romantic novels. He wondered if their brief courtship had been the product of an inexperienced woman's fantasy and a young man's lust for a pretty female, doomed to destruction by their venture into reality.

Sierra yanked him back to the moment. "You are not with me. Sometimes your silences make me nervous."

"I'm sorry. Tell me the rest."

"What little I remember of our time on the estate brings happy memories until the war came. Papa opposed slavery but was convinced the South would eliminate that curse in due time. That is what he told me later, anyway. He served in a cavalry unit, of course, mustered out as a colonel. Mama took ill during the years Papa was absent, and I spent much of my time with Grandma Emily whose house was only three miles down the road. Finally, Mama died of consumption two weeks before Papa came home from the war. I was almost eleven by this time, and I had no notion that the worst hard times were in front of us."

"Did your father remain at the Garcia estate?" Jack asked.

"No. We returned to the plantation for a time. The slaves were gone, and his help was needed there. Great

Grandma had died, and Great Grandpa Cooper had no money, only his landholdings. Then the Yankee carpet-baggers came, and within two years the land was sold for back taxes. Great Grandpa hanged himself from a rafter in the barn the day the sheriff and his deputies came to remove us from the property."

Jack said, "I missed those years. I left the Rangers, and Rudy and I came out here a year before the war started. Out in the middle of Comanche country, the war and the worst of the carpetbagger years pretty much passed us by."

"You were lucky," Sierra said.

There was much more to his story but telling it would serve no purpose. "So, how did you end up in the North Concho Valley?"

"When Papa realized the land would be lost, he rented a few hundred acres from the old patron—my grandfather—that had an old log house and a rickety barn on it and moved the half dozen or so horses that remained on the plantation to that place. He also salvaged a buckboard, some tools, and a few mules. We took what furnishings we could use to the log house, and Grandma Emily settled in with Papa and me there. That is when Papa started his own horse herd, and he was happier than I had seen him since he came home from the war. But Grandma hated it.

She cried almost every day. She just wasn't cut out for that kind of life. I felt sorry for her."

Jack thought, *Yeah, it is tough without slaves and servants and all of life's essentials.* He would never voice those sarcastic words, though. "So now you are settled on Garcia's rent ground. You are still near Austin. That's a long way from here."

"Grandma's death made Papa restless. She just wasted away, lost her will to live, I think. Papa was ready for a new start but had to wait several years. He managed money well, and Señor Garcia owned a thousand acres about thirty miles east of Fort Concho and San Angelo. It had sat idle for years because of the Comanche threat, and it was not enough land for a big cow ranch, but plenty for fifty to sixty horses. Garcia sold him the land for eight dollars an acre and took a mortgage back. We still owe seven-thousand of that, and the San Angelo Bank holds a four-thousand-dollar lien on the horse herd."

"Too much," Jack said. "With other expenses, you could barely pay the interest."

"Papa had twenty mares and two good stallions by this time. He headed out this way with two Mexican vaqueros, leaving me in Austin to finish schooling at the girls' academy. I threw a fit, but he didn't budge, insisted I would never regret an education."

Jack was stunned. His son had been living within thirty-five to forty miles of the Lucky Five. "He didn't know I lived nearby?"

Sierra sipped at the coffee that had little warmth remaining, giving him a dose of his own silence before she spoke. "He knew. I think that is why he grabbed the offer Garcia made. He said someday he was going to face you down, whatever that meant. But first he wanted to prove he could make a good life without you. All those years, he always knew where you were living when you were not out with your Texas Rangers on a mission. Grandma Emily kept a scrapbook of newspaper clippings, showed him the story of you being one of the heroes of San Jacinto. You were famous, you know, as a Captain in the Texas Rangers, mostly as a Comanche fighter bringing back white captives. Some of the stories called you Comanche Jack. But you reported to Austin dozens of times at Ranger headquarters and never had time to visit your son."

Jack ignored the barb. He could see how it would look to someone who had not been told the truth. "You said your father is dead. When? What happened?"

"One year ago, next month. June 8, 1874 to be exact. I had been back a year when Comanches raided. Our little three-room house was a stone fortress. Barred windows, rifle ports. We always kept a three-day water supply inside in case of siege. But a war party caught Papa coming out of the stable. There were only a half dozen raiders, but they put two arrows in his back as he raced for the house. The vaqueros dragged him in, but there was nothing to be done. He was gone in an hour, along with his dreams."

It was more than Jack could get a hold on. In less than an hour his son had been born and died. A person who had lived forty-four years not knowing he had a father who would have loved and cared for him and fought like hell to have been a part of his life. Emily had bested him, but it was their son who was the instrument of whatever game she had been playing. He was surprised that tears did not come, but how does a person grieve for the loss of someone you have never known? It was like reading a tragic story, leaving you sad but not inconsolable.

Chapter 7

"I AM SORRY about the death of your father. I will likely have more to say, but I need to think about what you have told me," Jack said.

"You don't believe I am your granddaughter, do you?"

"I do believe you are my granddaughter, Sierra, and you are always welcome here. There is a home for you in this house if you choose."

Sierra found herself surprised and unsettled by Jack's words. Her visit to the Lucky Five had been her own roll of the dice, a gamble that she might solicit the help of this legendary man who had deserted his family. "Thank you," she said.

Jack said, "But you did not come here just to prove you are my granddaughter, did you? That was the first step."

It was time to lay her cards on the table. Not much got past this old man. "No, I came for more than a family reunion. I need help. After Papa died, I stayed on at our little horse ranch. We just finished the probate to get everything in my name. I had to let one of the vaqueros go, but the other stayed on, and we took care of the herd that consisted of about thirty mares and half that many fillies. There were four stallions. A few of the mares had colts at side. Most are due to foal early summer."

"A nice-sized herd."

"Turkey Creek runs through our place, so water isn't a problem, and we adjoin a lot of open and unclaimed range. The Comanches are surrendering and heading to Fort Sill, so Indian troubles should be ending."

"But?"

"A week ago, Comancheros hit the Turkey Track Ranch—that's what Papa called the place because of all the turkeys in the woods along Turkey Creek that leave tracks all over the ranch. And it makes a simple brand: a vertical line with two more lines branching off near the top. Anyhow, there must have been fifteen riders. They swept through like a whirlwind, and all we could do was watch. Thankfully, they didn't come near the buildings. My strawberry roan filly and a few other horses were in the stable. My wrangler, Angel, followed them for three days before he gave up and returned home. In the meantime, I made a day's ride to talk to the Army at Fort Concho. They couldn't, or wouldn't, help. A captain there said they were short of troops because they were escorting surrendering Comanche bands to the reservation. He thought it was a civilian matter anyway. Said I should contact the Texas Rangers. That would take weeks."

"That's true enough. A lot of money on those hooves."

"At $500 or more for a good stallion, $250 for the bred mares and another $300 for mares with foals at side, $200 for a filly, then add on some premium for top notch quarter horses, and we're looking at $15,000 to $17,000, enough to clear the debt and then some. The ranchland gets foreclosed without the horses, and I will still owe the bank."

Jack rubbed his chin. "Horse rustling makes more sense than cattle. Cows are bringing between twenty-five and thirty dollars these days. With the Comanches going into the reservation, I guess the Comancheros are expanding their business enterprises. You're sure they were Comancheros?"

"That's what Angel said. I wouldn't know a Comanchero from anybody else."

"Stands to reason, I guess—that many men. What direction were they headed?"

Sierra said, "Angel told me they were driving the herd southwest into the Chihuahuan Desert country."

"Likely Lookout Canyon. It's a Comanchero hideout. Sort of a headquarters, although the Comancheros don't have a central command as such. They are just a collection of no-goods in different bands who took on the Comanchero name because of their dealings with Comanches. They started out as respectable traders, but that changed over the years when the tribes became a market for guns and liquor. The canyon is a place they rendezvous and re-supply. There are some buildings there, several trading posts, stables, that sort of thing."

"Is it a place they would take horses?"

"Absolutely. There are all kinds of dead-end offshoot canyons where horses could be penned off."

"Where do they sell the horses?"

"Army. Ranches. Some go to Mexico. Are the horses branded?"

"Yes. A small turkey track on the neck."

"It would take some time to alter brands, and they couldn't market the entire herd at once. They would worry that word is out about a theft that large. The good news is that they will likely hold the herd until things cool some."

Sierra said, "You sound like you've seen this canyon."

"I've been there once with an outfit of Rangers. We were trying to recover farm and ranch children taken by Comanches and traded to the Comancheros."

"What would the Comancheros do with them?"

"Take them to Mexico to sell them as slaves or, more often, to bordellos."

"Did you rescue the children?"

"No. And I lost six men. Not my proudest day."

She sighed. "I see." She was starting to resign herself to losing the horses and the ranch. She did not even know why she had come to this man in the first place.

"If I am right about the location of the horses, we will do better this time. We will need tomorrow to prepare. I plan to pull out the next morning."

"You are going to help me?"

"I hope so."

"I am going with you."

"I figured as much."

"Thank you . . . What should I call you?"

"Jack will do."

"Would you care if I call you Grandpa Jack?"

"That's okay if it suits you."

"Thank you, Grandpa Jack."

Chapter 8

RUDY WAS ALWAYS telling him he was plumb weak north of the ears when the two men fussed. His old partner would say that chasing down horses in the Chihuahuan Desert was conclusive proof.

When he walked into the sitting room, he was not surprised to find that Rudy and Jordy were sitting in stuffed chairs nursing half-full glasses of whiskey, Thor sleeping at Jordy's feet. The three-quarters full Jack Daniels bottle on the table between them told him the drinking had been purely social. They looked up expectantly when he entered the room. Jack claimed his rocker across the coffee table from the two.

"Would you like a drink, Jack? I'll get a glass," Jordy said, starting to rise from his chair.

Jack waved him off. "No, thanks, Jordy. My stomach would pay for it this late." Spirits were rare for him these days, especially evenings. Alcohol seemed to burn a hole in his gut anymore. Of course, a lot of years had passed since he had been a serious drinker. Maybe he had not hardened his innards to the stuff. Look at Rudy. He was unfazed by booze of any variety, and God knew Rudy had drunk enough for two men over a lifetime.

"Well?" Rudy said. "I been staying sober to hear your story."

"What story?"

"The girl. Sierra."

"Consuelo's helping her get a bath ready in the tub room upstairs."

"Damn it, Jack. Is she your granddaughter or ain't she?"

"She is." Jack said, his voice a near whisper.

Rudy leaned forward from his chair, resting on his cane. "What did you say?"

Jordy turned toward Rudy and, speaking loudly, said, "Jack said that Sierra is his granddaughter."

"How can that be? Can't have no granddaughter without a kid."

"I had a son. Comanches killed him a year ago."

"You never told me about no son. You always said you didn't have no kin."

"I didn't know."

Rudy looked at Jack, his head cocked to one side, obviously waiting for an explanation. Jack was not in the mood to talk about the son he never knew. The appearance of Sierra and the story she brought with her were surreal, and he could not get a handle on it all. It could not be true, yet he had no doubt that it was.

Rudy said, "You ain't talking, are you?"

Jack sighed. "Sorry, Rudy, not tonight. Not about that. Here is something to chew on overnight. I am going to take back fifty-some horses from Comancheros at Lookout Canyon in the Chihuahuan Desert. Leaving the day after tomorrow. We will need two or three good wagons from the company and a volunteer crew of nine or ten men. I need men who can handle a gun, maybe some of the ex-buffalo soldiers on our payroll. I will offer a hundred-dollar hazardous duty bonus. Jordy, you pick the men and tell them the deal. Keep at it until you've got enough takers. Rusty will stay at the ranch, and he and Rudy can run things while we're gone. I'd like you to come with me, if you're willing."

"I had already signed on," Jordy said.

Rudy said, "I can't hear so good. But I picked up enough to know you're about to out-stupid that scarecrow out in Enrique's garden. You've finally dumped what was left in your brain."

"That could be, but you don't have to worry yourself. You'll be sitting here lazing in the breeze on the front porch."

"Like hell I will. You ain't leaving me behind. You'll need somebody that can handle a gun running the chuck-wagon. Try to get Bram Potts to come with us and we'll keep you fed."

Jack said, "You were with me the last time I visited Lookout Canyon. Do you remember what happened then?"

"I sure as hell do. I'm wondering if you do."

Chapter 9

J ACK SET HIS library rocker next to the table that offered the best kerosene reading lamp. His wire-rimmed spectacles were propped on his nose, Hawthorne's *House of the Seven Gables* rested in his lap, and Thor's head rested on his stockinged feet. He had been sitting with Thor in the room for better than an hour savoring the quiet companionship of his friends that lined the wall. A nice cool breeze drifted through the open window. A perfect night for a good book, but he had not read a word. The thoughts that rampaged in his mind had torn him from his reading mission.

Rudy had left abruptly an hour earlier, pissed with Jack's failure to contribute to the conversation. "I'm just sitting here talking to myself," he had complained.

"Tell me something new," Jack had replied, lamenting now that he had been so testy with his old friend, who could not help that he was born to snoop and talk.

Jordy had departed earlier when Consuelo informed him that Sierra had vacated the tub room and that Juan had filled the tub for his bath, exhorting the young cowhand that he should take advantage while the water was still warm. Bathing was complicated in the house but more luxurious than most homes on the Texas prairie, which had to settle for an outside barrel, if not a nearby stream. Water had to be heated on the downstairs woodstove and carried to the second-floor tub room off the hallway that led to the bedrooms. The cast iron sink and clawfoot tub were connected to a pipe that drained to a gully that cut through the backyard, and a mirror above the sink afforded added convenience for grooming and shaving.

Jack pulled his timepiece from his pocket. Almost ten-thirty. Past his bedtime, but fat chance of sleeping tonight. There was a light tapping at the door. "Come on in," he said.

Jordy, wearing an old cotton shirt draped over his baggy white undershorts, stepped in. "Are you okay, Jack?"

Jack set his book aside. "Sit down." He gestured to the chair on the other side of the lamp table. "Just trying to sort some things out. Not doing much of a job of it."

Jordy picked up the book. "House of the Seven Gables. My favorite of Hawthorne's."

Jack said, "Only one of his I haven't read. I've started it at least three times, but it's a slow starter, and I seem to get distracted by other books. It's at the top of my list to read before I cash in."

"You've got some time."

"A man never knows. I'll bet my son, John Thomas—J. T. they called him—thought he had years to live when he got up the morning the Comanches hit their place. You know your string's running out when you get to my age, though. I don't worry about it. Hell, I might have twenty hours or twenty years, but I've had more than most. I haven't been cheated out of time. Maybe that's why us old farts don't worry all that much about the end coming. We've had our turns."

Jordy said, "I'm sorry about your son, Jack. But I've got to say I am confused about this and the sudden trip we're making to the Chihuahuan Desert."

"You're entitled to know what's going on. I have been whipping myself for not telling Rudy. I get so damned impatient with him anymore. He only hears half of what

I'm saying and won't close his mouth long enough for me to repeat it. I've had no better friend over the past forty-some years, and he's always had my back. Saved my life more than once."

Jordy chuckled. "And told me how he did it at least a dozen times."

Jack gave a small smile. "Yeah, but the stories grow with the years. He's changed them so many times, I can't remember what really happened myself. Anyhow here's what Sierra told me."

Jordy listened while Jack told him about his conversation with Sierra, refraining from any interruption. Jack noticed that his foster son's eyes glistened with the tears Jack had not summoned when J. T.'s death was mentioned.

Finally, Jordy asked a question. "And you never explained to Sierra that you didn't know about J. T.? That Emily was leaving you?"

"I didn't see the point of it. She likely wouldn't have believed me and would have thought I was defaming her grandmother."

"You should have stood up for yourself, Jack. That's what you always told me to do with liars."

"Maybe I will later when I find the right way to say it. Anyhow, that's pretty much the story. I wanted to ask her more about J. T., but I didn't think the time was right for either of us. It is a strange feeling when you can't see the face of your child in your mind. I've been sitting here thinking about what might have been different in my life if I had known about J. T. I'd have quit the Rangers, so I would've been nearby even if Emily and I couldn't stick it out as husband and wife—and the chances of that were slim to none."

Jordy said, "I wouldn't have been your foster son then. I'd probably be dead or on the way to the reservation with a Comanche band, if you and your Ranger company hadn't shown up at our burning wagon. My folks and little sister were already dead, and I was just lucky to have crawled to the ravine while they were doing their looting and maiming. I can still hear Ma screaming while they took her. But they knew I was around. They would have found me if you hadn't showed up. Then you took me in and left the Rangers. Rudy, too. And you brought me here and raised me up, gave me another dad, and an uncle, too. I am lucky this Emily didn't get ahold of you. A lot of folks are. This ranch would not have been. The jobs would not have been here and the caring for and schooling of the ranch and freighting families."

"You are overstating my influence a mite, Jordy. But it is strange how every day we make what seems an insignificant decision at the time or take a little turn that changes the course of our lives and maybe those of countless others. And we don't know—and they don't either— what event triggered it all."

Jordy said, "And now Sierra's shown up here. Things are going to be different than if she had not. I wonder if it is going to be good different or bad different?"

Jack said, "It might be some of both."

Chapter 10

JACK ENDURED A fitful sleep that night. It had nothing to do with his nightly battle with Thor for an equal share of the bed. He simply could not turn his mind away from the quest to recover the stolen horses and the stunning revelation, delivered by a previously unknown descendant, that he had sired a child many years ago. These thoughts struggled for his attention, none ever truly winning out.

He dropped off to sleep several times to be awakened soon after with an urgency to relieve his bladder. Three or four times nightly these days, he pulled out the chamber pot to deposit a weak stream or, sometimes, mere droplets of piss. And even Thor could not make it through the night anymore without a trip outside to water the grass. Tess had given Jack a powder concocted partly from yucca plant that helped noticeably, improving the flow when taken early evening with a glass of water and cutting his unwanted awakenings considerably. But damned if he could remember to take it half the time, and tonight the powder had failed to make the task list. His supply of yucca powder was about depleted, and he would resupply when he saw Tess in the morning—if he remembered.

He was first to rise as usual, beating the sun by a good half hour. He put some tinder and a few small logs on some lingering coals in the cookstove, hoping they might ignite and provide Josephina with a fire and warm stove when she arrived. He lowered himself to his hands and knees and commenced blowing on the coals, yielding nothing but smoke for several minutes before a flame erupted and curled around the tinder. He closed the stove door, grabbed the seat of a chair for leverage and slowly got back to his feet. When he straightened, he heard his back crack and hoped he would not be starting their journey with a gimpy back. His back would not reveal the answer till the next morning.

He started to pump some water in the coffee pot, but the handpump gave him nothing but air at first. Finally, it took hold, and the water came. He should have Enrique check the pump and see if it needed work. He heard movement behind him and tossed a look over his shoulder. Josephina walked in with her usual smile, bubbling with an enthusiasm Jack could not muster yet.

"Why, thank you for starting the fire, Boss Man," she said. "That will earn you hotcakes and sausage this morning. Are you hungry?"

"As a matter of fact, I am. I'll go shave." He nodded toward Thor, sitting in the corner. "I think Thor will be more interested in what you are doing, so I'll leave him for company."

"I told him last night I had saved back some scraps for him. That's what he's waiting for."

Jack met Jordy coming down the stairs, clean shaven and attired in a fresh shirt and denims. "Breakfast ready?" Jordy asked.

"Josephina is getting started. I was going to shave first."

"Wasting your time. Your granddaughter has taken over the tub room."

"I hadn't thought about that. Don't recall we've ever had a woman in the guestroom. That could take some getting used to if she sticks around a while."

Jordy said, "It won't matter for a spell. Where we are headed, there are wide open spaces. Room for everybody in the creek if you can find one. While you are waiting, do you want to talk about the crew and wagons?"

"Might as well."

They went into the library and sat down at the table. Jordy pulled a folded sheet of parchment from his shirt pocket and spread it out on the table for Jack to examine. "I have started a list of supplies we will need. I'll check with Rudy about food for the chuckwagon. Pots and pans would already be stashed in it. I thought I would talk to Bram, and if he's willing to go, he and Rudy can take the wagon into town today and get supplied up."

Jack said, "Tell him we're going to use two or three mule teams on each wagon and will be moving fast, so they will need to anchor the load."

"Three teams?"

"I'll leave the number to Tige Marshall. We've lost enough time as it is. I would like to do twenty-five miles a day if we can. I'm going into town to visit the Lucky Five Freighting station today to be sure they can round up enough mules for the wagons we're taking. I hope we have two of the long Studebakers available, especially the one with the false bottom. I'm going to hide some extra weaponry in the storage space."

"You don't see much chance of just cutting out the herd and making a run?"

"Can't be done."

"What do we need the Studebakers for? They will slow us."

"Trade goods. We're going to be traders, maybe Comancheros ourselves if we need to."

"I'll take your word for it. I've been thinking about the men. I'd like to recruit Tige Marshall and let him pick two or three of his ex-buffalo soldiers. I will leave it to Tige, but I would like to have Abel Burke and Nick Iverson with us—maybe Roper Hawley. He was in Tige's outfit, and in a fight he's the equal of two or three men."

"I like that idea. But Juana might object, and they have the two kids to think about." Tige was a former Army Sergeant and natural leader who, with his wife, Juana, managed the freight business. Not yet thirty, the handsome mulatto, born a slave, was hard working and ambitious.

"He's itching to get out of the office, and we couldn't have a better man riding with us. The handsome devil will sweet talk Juana and get cut loose for the mission."

Jack said, "Okay, who else?"

"Swede Larsen as a mule skinner for one of the Studebakers and Irish O'Toole for the other. For wranglers and night-hawks: Possum Crowell and Mitch Eagle Eyes. Mitch could do some scouting for us. If a wagon breaks down, Swede can fix about anything."

"Good choices." The wranglers worked mostly in the ranching enterprises, as did O'Toole and Larsen, and their absences would leave Rusty Dobbs short-handed. Spring round up was past, however, and Jack figured Rusty should be able handle the day-to-day essentials for several weeks with the two hands that remained.

"I'm going to check in with Tess on the way to town. If she invites me to stay over tonight, I'll likely take her up on it. If I don't show up, Thor will want to sleep with you."

"I don't have any better offers. Is he coming with us?"

"Yep. He couldn't keep up afoot these days, but he can ride on the wagon seat of one of the wagons. You take care of things on this end. I'll arrange the wagons and talk to Tige and the town folks. Meet me at the station in San Angelo about eight o'clock tomorrow morning with the chuckwagon and the ranch crew. Have everybody toss their personal gear in the chuckwagon for now."

Jordy asked, "Are you going to explain to Rudy about your granddaughter?"

"I'd take it as a favor if you would do that. You can tell him anything I told you."

"Thanks for nothing. And what about Sierra? You're just leaving her here?"

"Yep. I'm not up to talking to either her or Rudy today. Let her help you put the parade together."

"Jack," Jordy said, "when I was a kid, you would have told me I was running from my responsibilities."

"I ain't no kid. And I'm not running. I'm just delegating."

Chapter 11

J ACK, ASTRIDE HIS bay gelding, passed the turnoff to San Angelo and continued along the wagon path south toward Tess Wyman's place. He wanted to be in town by ten-thirty, so this would be a quick stop, just long enough to wangle an invitation to return later. He and Tess had been whatever they were for over ten years now. He still could not put a tag on their relationship. Friends and comfortable companions, always. Lovers, sometimes. Jack thought they were too old for him to call Tess his girlfriend, and lady friend sounded too stuffy. He guessed it didn't matter. They would just stay good neighbors.

He had never formally proposed marriage to her, but he had suggested it, testing the waters two or three times over the years. The last time, a few years back, Tess had laughed and said, "There's not room for both of us and

Thor in the bed. Let's not spoil a good thing." There was some truth to what she said. If Jack were in the bedroom, Thor would whine outside the door all night until he got in. It would be damned hard to relegate his canine partner to a rug, and the dog would not sleep with Jordy if Jack was in the house. But they would have figured out something.

When he rode onto the imaginary line that separated Tess's little six hundred acre spread, he caught sight of twenty-five or thirty Lucky Five cows grazing there. They did not require fences between their places, since Tess's property, except the garden near her house, was all grassland, and the Lucky Five leased her acres. The tract was initially a part of the Lucky Five grant, but Tess had acquired it some ten years earlier as a part of Jack's private treaty with the Kwahadi Comanches.

Tess was half-blood Comanche by reason of her Comanche mother's marriage to Jacob Wyman, one of the first white traders to deal with the Indian tribes long before Texas became a Republic and later a state. Her mother, Knows Healing, was a medicine woman renowned among the Comanches for her treatment of illnesses and injuries, often via her medicines concocted of various plants.

The marriage had been unique, because Knows Healing continued to reside with her people, but Tess and her brother, after they reached school age, lived with their white grandparents and attended school during fall and winter. They saw their father only infrequently since his trading required almost constant travel. Thus, Tess, then known among the Comanches as "Healer's Daughter," and her younger brother, Jeffery, also known as "Two Tongues," were raised in two cultures and, adaptable as children usually are, moved easily between them.

Tess, during the time she resided with the Comanches, was an apt student of her mother's skills and apprenticed at her side. Two Tongues eventually joined his father in the trading business, his mixed heritage and bilingualism being an asset as they traded with the tribes. The fact that he was bilingual was particularly helpful in dealing with Comanche bands. He eventually married a white woman and left the Comanche world with only occasional visits to bring his children to see their grandmother who steadfastly remained Comanche.

Tess, on the other hand continued to move between the two cultures, never marrying but spending more time with the Kwahadi as her mother aged and needed her help. Tess received a modest inheritance from her grandparents when they died and maintained a bank account in the small town where they had lived. She also held a half interest with her brother in a farm the grandparents had owned.

The Kwahadi and many of the other bands had come to rely on Tess's skills, but after the death of her mother, she had desired more physical comforts than she found in a Comanche tipi. She worked out a compromise. She would find a location still largely ruled by the Comanches, build a house, and be available to those who chose to travel there. The North Concho Valley was the logical location for her residence. The location she chose was a short ride to the Middle Concho River to the south, and the bottomlands along the two rivers abounded with plant life to harvest for her medicines. Her home would be near enough to nomadic Kwahadi routes that her Comanche friends could procure such herbs and shrubs that she might request from other sources.

The only downside was that the military was planning a fort nearby and a white village was already springing up in anticipation. The trading post, however, less than five miles distant would solve her concern about procuring food and other supplies. Once the location had been identified, Tess had approached the rancher who claimed the land and negotiated purchase of a tract at a nominal price. Jack Wills's incentive had been that the

Kwahadi would cease their raids and stealing of his cattle and warn off other bands from his range. The rancher paid a fee of five steers annually to the Kwahadi for the protection, a fraction of the annual losses he had been incurring as a result of Comanche theft. More importantly, ranch hands and their families had begun to enjoy a level of security previously unknown at ranch headquarters.

When Jack nudged his mount around a bend in the trail, Tess's house appeared, nestled at the base of some hillocks that rose gently from a prairie alive with new greening grass and a sprinkling of early spring flowers. The north and west sides of the house were shielded by a cedar windbreak. The house was a simple rectangular structure, constructed of limestone quarried from Jack's first excavation of an otherwise useless half section nearer San Angelo, which had turned into a profitable venture.

Juana Marshall handled bookkeeping chores for all the enterprises, but several years earlier, Jack had asked Jordy to review financial reports with her semi-annually, so he might become better acquainted with the business side. He had recently observed that the ranching operation always showed a small loss or a profit that was razor-thin, and that the other side of operations subsidized the ranch. Jack had just smiled and said, "Yep, that's a cattle-man's life."

Jack dismounted and tied the bay at the hitching post in front of the house. He would not be here long enough to justify putting the horse up in the small stable south of the house. The front door opened even before he stepped onto the covered porch, and he was welcomed by a wide perfect smile backdropped by a woman's copper-tinted face. Tess Wyman's snow-white hair was tied back, and she wore a red cotton shirt that fell over faded, blue denims along with ankle-high moccasins that did not have many walks left in them. To Jack, this woman, not quite bony but slim and wiry, was a stunning creature to behold.

Tess waited for Jack to cross the porch, and when he opened his arms, slipped into them and held him close before planting a quick kiss on his lips. "I've missed you," she said, tugging him into the house.

"It's been only three days, but, yeah, it's been too long."

"Can you stay a while?"

"I'm on my way to town, so this stop will have to be a short one. Coming back, though . . ."

"You could come for supper?"

"At least."

"Are you suggesting you might stay the night?"

"If I had an invite."

"Since when have you needed an invitation? You know you are welcome here anytime—or all the time, for that matter. I will plan for you for supper and overnight. Now come in the kitchen. You at least have time for coffee."

"Yep. Of course, that means I'll have to water a tree on the way to town."

"They are your own trees. You can take your pick. Are you needing some of the bladder powder?"

Jack sat down at the table in her tidy kitchen while Tess retrieved two mugs and the coffee pot on the woodstove. "I will need some powder. I'm leaving for a spell tomorrow. Probably be gone several weeks."

Tess's brow furrowed as she set a mug on the table in front of Jack and poured coffee in it. "You are trying to be too casual. This is serious business. Tell me about it." She sat down across the table from him, reached her left hand out and took his.

Tess was a toucher, Jack thought. He had grown up without the memory of a female's touch, his mother having died before his third birthday. The women he had known, including his only wife, had never been the touching types. He liked that part of Tess. But he could not think offhand of anything he did not like about her.

"It's a long story," he said, "but I'll give you a nutshell version and tell you more tonight if you want."

He told her about the appearance of his granddaughter and her request. She listened attentively and did not interrupt. When he finished, she said, "You told me that you were married years ago. You thought she divorced you. How do you know this Sierra is your grandchild?"

"Her story fits. She's got my eyes and some of my family looks. And she is sure as hell convinced of it. Why on earth would she pick an old fart like me to come to for help if she didn't think I was her grandfather?"

"The old fart is something of a legend in this part of Texas, it's not so farfetched that she heard you lived out here and thought she would rope you into helping her recover the horses."

"She knows too much about Emily that rings true."

"How do you know Emily didn't have a relationship with another man? Maybe that's why she sent you away."

Jack gave a wry smile. "Not Emily. She crossed her legs so tight it took a pry bar to get to her love nest."

"That's not very nice," Tess scolded. "I suppose you tell people I'm a slut, since I'm so easy."

"I don't tell anybody anything about us . . . except that we play checkers till we're about to drop. They look at this decrepit old man, and I think most believe me, all but Rudy. He's always pushing me for details."

"He knows you too well. Anyway, Jack, I would be lying if I said I am excited about this adventure you are planning. I love you, and I'll be worried sick while you are gone. But I can see there would be no changing your mind. I'm glad your granddaughter and you have met, and I'm so sad about your son. You must be devastated about that."

"It's so strange, Tess, I never knew about him. It is like this person they called J. T. is just a dream, and he's a cloud floating around out there. I don't even know what he looked like. And I'm half afraid to wake up and find out he was real."

"You will probably wake up someday, Jack." She squeezed his hand and released it.

Chapter 12

TESS WATCHED JACK Wills ride down the wagon path that branched off the main trail to her place. Oh, if they had met each other forty years ago when Jack was thirty and she was thirty-two. They had missed so many years. But she supposed it was hard to say about such things. Perhaps, each would have been a different person then, and they would not have been ready to connect. It was possible, she supposed, that they had met at the time that was perfect for love to blossom.

She smiled. There were only a few secrets she had withheld from Jack over the years, having cut most of them loose a bit at a time, just as he had done. But he did not know her age. He had given up the guessing game a few years back, but he had always estimated her age at least ten years younger than the actual figure. She did not delude herself, however, that Jack would do anything but underestimate. He was too much a gentleman to do otherwise.

This latest venture Jack was embarking on worried her. Most Comancheros lacked any kind of moral compass, and they were known as fierce, reckless fighters. In many quarters, the threat of Comancheros in the vicinity struck more fear than the word that Comanches were nearby. They pillaged, raped and killed with abandon. If Comancheros came, a rancher was fortunate if all that he lost was a cattle or horse herd.

She consoled herself that Jack's easygoing calmness and quiet nature often hid a keen mind that quickly made decisions and knew exactly what he was going to do and why. And he would never brag about his successes. She had found that a man who constantly reminded others of his own brilliance generally came up short when it came to brains. She consoled herself that Jack already had a plan. He was incapable of not having one. But no one else would know what he had in mind until he was darned well ready to tell them.

Tess started to reenter the house when she saw two riders moving her way from the direction of the Middle Concho. As they crossed the prairie and drew nearer, she recognized the rider astride a sorrel. It was She Who Speaks, the young female interpreter and unofficial counselor to the war chief, Quanah. The other rider was smaller, likely a child. When they rode into the yard, Tess waved and walked out to greet them.

She Who Speaks dismounted, raised her hand, and pressed her fingers against Tess's. "Healer's Daughter," She Who Speaks said.

"She Who Speaks," Tess responded. "What brings you here? I thought your band would be at Palo Duro Canyon."

"We will go there soon. There was hope that we would find buffalo here. It was not to be."

They spoke English, because She Who Speaks was fluent in at least five languages including Spanish and Comanche. She had been taken captive when she was thirteen or fourteen years old when her Jewish parents were killed on their journey across the Texas prairie. German and Yiddish had been her first languages, the young woman, now in her mid-twenties, had told her on another occasion. Tess, of course, was fluent in Comanche but struggled with her Spanish. This young woman seemed to move effortlessly from tongue to tongue. Her language proficiency and ability to adapt had probably saved her from sale to Comancheros and ultimately a trip to a Mexican bordello.

Tess looked at the child, a boy of nine or ten years, she guessed. He seemed well enough.

She Who Speaks said, "Quanah asked that I bring Little Hawk here for your help."

"What seems to be the problem?"

"He has a growth on his back."

Tess did not consider herself a surgeon. She was a mere collector, producer, and dispenser of remedies derived from herbs and other plants with medicinal properties. She feared she could offer no more than sympathy. Speaking Comanche, she addressed the boy. "Little Hawk, please dismount, and we will go into my house, and I will look at your back."

The skinny, dark-eyed boy looked at She Who Speaks, who nodded approval, and he slid from the horse's back. After hitching the horses, the visitors followed Tess into the house. Her four-room abode included the kitchen, a parlor with a fireplace, and a bedroom, but the largest room was what she called her medicine room off the kitchen. It was a light-filled room with three windows, two long tables, side by side with space in between for the user. Cupboards and counters claimed most usable wall space.

Tess led She Who Speaks and Little Hawk into the medicine room and directed the boy to climb onto one of the sturdy tables. "Would you take off your shirt?" she asked.

Little Hawk complied, pulling a dirty buckskin shirt over his head and placing it on the table. Tess was horrified when she saw the emaciated form beneath the shirt, every rib outlined against flesh stretched so tight it appeared a bone might break through at any moment. She looked at She Who Speaks, and speaking English, said, "He's starving."

"The soldiers have killed most of our horses, cut off supply sources. They killed twelve hundred horses at Palo Duro Canyon last fall, you know."

"I heard."

"It has been effective military strategy for the Army. Starvation is driving us to the reservation."

Tess said nothing and gently grasped the boy's bony shoulders and turned him so she could view his back. A fist-sized ball was located at the middle of his back. She probed it gently with her fingers. Firm, but there were soft spots. "Is it painful?" she asked.

"No," he replied.

The answer did not tell her much, since a Comanche boy likely would not admit pain. "I am sure it is an abscess. I can open and drain it, but I am certain someone in the village could have treated this. Did you come here for some other reason?"

"I told Quanah I would speak with you. Please, take care of Little Hawk, and I will explain."

Tess gathered up a tin pan and clean rags and took a sharp skinning knife from one of the drawers. She asked the boy to lie down on his side. "It may hurt at first, but it will be over quickly," she informed him.

She Who Speaks spoke as Tess searched the abscess for the most desirable target. "We are aware that you are close to Mister Wills. The Kwahadi have promised not to take his cattle, and The People want no trouble with white ranchers. Quanah has asked if you might approach Mister Wills for permission to cut out twenty steers or unbred heifers from his herd. The People must be fed to have strength to travel. We have no money now, but Quanah does have funds he can access after we arrive at Fort Sill. The price of the cattle will be paid to Mister Wills. I will help Quanah with the financial arrangements."

Tess sliced the soft peak of the abscess and blood and puss erupted like lava from a volcano. Little Hawk did not flinch. Tess squeezed the still half-full pocket, catching what she could of the fluid in her pan. "I will see Jack later today and make the arrangements." She was confident that Jack would not reject the proposal. "Come back tomorrow and bring warriors to drive the cattle. How far are you from here?"

"About five to seven miles west."

Tess plucked what she had been looking for from a glob of pus. "A thorn. My guess is it came from a locust tree. I will apply a poultice, but it is best to allow this to drain. I will give you the powders you need to mix the medicine for the next week."

She Who Speaks said, "I cannot thank you enough."

"Remember, I am of The People, also. I do what I am able. Now, before you depart, you will both join me at the kitchen table. You will not leave here without a good meal. And I hope you will return with the warriors tomorrow, so we can talk some more. I so rarely see a woman to chat with anymore."

Chapter 13

JORDY WAITED ON the veranda for Sierra to come out. Their conversation at breakfast had been polite but a bit cool. He could tell she was not pleased by Jack's absence. Of course, Rudy's big ears had not encouraged a casual conversation. At least he had had an opportunity to fill the old Ranger in on more of the story about the previously unknown granddaughter and her late father. Not to his surprise, the tale had just whetted Rudy's appetite for more details. Jordy had decided he was finished with the subject as far as Rudy was concerned. He was turning Rudy back to Jack.

He had promised Sierra a tour of ranch headquarters while they arranged for the journey ahead. Ordinarily, he would have looked forward to such a tour with a pretty, young woman, but he was still uneasy about her role in the ranch family, and she had been alternately charming and snappish. Jack had taught him to withhold premature judgment about folks, and that was where he stood.

Sierra stepped through the doorway, with the front of her wide-brimmed hat pulled down her forehead to ward off the morning sun. Her hazel eyes, shaded by the hat brim had a grayish-brown cast today, he noted. The previous night in the lamplight, he had thought they had a more greenish tint. Jack's eyes played those tricks, too. She wore boots and britches that were nicely snug from his viewpoint, so he figured she was prepared for horseback if they took the notion.

They did not start the tour off on a happy note. "I was annoyed that Grandpa Jack wasn't here for breakfast," she said. "We just met, and he takes off like a scared rabbit."

Jordy took it somewhat positive that she referred to Jack as "Grandpa." She and Jack would be the last of their blood, so maybe she did not want to cut that string whatever grudge she held. "You signed Jack up for a big chore. He's in town putting everything together." *If the horny old geezer wasn't in Tess Wyman's bed*, Jordy thought.

"I guess I should just be glad he agreed to help me."

"That's progress," Jordy said.

"You don't think he should do this, do you?"

"No."

"I don't think you like me much," she said.

"I don't dislike you."

"Weasel words."

"Let's get moving," Jordy said. "We have things to do today. Things to see." Thor was snoozing on his old buffalo robe. "You coming, Thor?" The dog looked up at him with sallow, sad eyes and then slowly got to his feet and stretched lazily.

"He doesn't show much enthusiasm," Sierra said.

"He's pouting because Jack's not here. Thor puts up with me, but I know I'm not his first choice as a companion."

With Thor trailing behind, Jordy and Sierra headed down the steps that led to the level ground where the other ranch buildings had been erected.

"Thor," Sierra said. "The name doesn't fit somehow. Isn't Thor some kind of Greek god or something?"

"Norse. God of thunder and lightning, associated with storms, according to Jack. He showed up on the porch one night in the middle of a terrible storm. He was drenched and shivering, only a few months old. We never could figure out where he came from. Jack said Thor must have dropped him off. That's how he got his name. It was about twelve years ago, not more than three years after Jack took me in. He said he was keeping the pup for me." Jordy chuckled. "Well, Thor and I played together sometimes, and we got along fine. But if Jack was around, the dog trailed after him."

As they walked out onto the flat ranch yard, Sierra said, "Last night, you promised to tell me how you came to be here."

"I'm just another stray Jack took in. Most of the hands on this ranch are strays of one sort or another, wandering aimlessly till Jack gave them a place to root. Even old Rudy. He's a strange duck, and I don't think a lot of men—or women—wanted much to do with him. But he latched on to Jack and has tagged along since they first met during the revolution. I think folks stick with Jack because he treats everybody the same, no matter where you come from, what your color is, or even if you are a little bit loony. The only thing he won't excuse is whining about the cards life has dealt you. He would say get off your ass and find a different game or learn how to win at the one you are playing."

"You think he is God, don't you?"

"I think he is human, but I don't know if God made a better man."

They walked in silence toward a row of stone dwellings along the back fringe of the ranch yard. The houses were constructed in a variety of shapes and sizes, a few small rectangular structures, several L-shaped. The house setting downslope from the headquarters residence was a two-story structure, smaller than Jack's house but spacious, nonetheless.

Jordy said, "The larger house nearest Jack's is occupied by the Cortez family. You will see a set of steps near the back that provide easy access to Jack's. The cottage next to it is Rudy's. Consuelo and Josephina look after that house, too, so the place doesn't turn into a pigsty."

She seemed to be only half-listening. "I've lost you," Jordy said.

"I'm sorry. I did hear you. My mind keeps wandering off. I'm confused, I guess."

"What do you mean?"

"This Jack Wills you have told me about is not the same Jack Wills I have been hearing about all my life— the man Grandma and Papa always told me about. This sounds nothing like a man who would totally abandon a one-year-old child."

Jordy said, "He did not. Never. Jack said he never knew anything about a baby. Your grandmother sent him away before he was aware that she was with child. When he returned, she had disappeared. He didn't know where she went. She knew he was a Ranger, though, and Texas Ranger headquarters was in Austin. Your grandmother could have left word for him there anytime. Jack would have found some way to be a father to J. T., probably left the Rangers."

"So he says."

"No, he did not say. I figured out the rest myself. I don't know the fine details. But that is how it had to be. You will likely never hear that excuse from Jack. That's not his way. Now, I will show you the barn and stable. I should be able to find some of my recruits around there."

Sierra said, "I am going to talk to Grandpa Jack about this tonight."

"I doubt it. I'm betting Jack will be staying over at Tess Wyman's place tonight. He will meet us in town in the morning."

"Why on earth would he stay at that woman's house when we've got this trip in front of us?"

"Tess is a special woman. They've been seeing each other for a spell."

"Some young man-trapper, I suppose," she said.

Jordy smiled. "Tess would likely be flattered at that remark. But she is a handsome woman." He decided to tease her a bit. "And males and females of a certain age still got needs, you know. I imagine Tess can still light a fire in Jack's furnace."

Sierra squeezed her eyes shut. "Stop. This is disgusting. I don't want that image in my mind. He is my grandfather, for God's sake."

There was a heavy silence between them as they crossed the yard toward the huge barn and twenty-horse stable that sat side by side with a connecting passageway between the structures. The wide barn door was open, and they found Rudy with a gangly towhead inventorying pots and pans in the storage boxes that lined the outside of the chuckwagon bed. Jordy noticed that Rudy had forgotten his cane this morning and was moving around as if he had shed twenty years.

Rudy looked their direction as they approached the barn, made a quick turn, fished something from his pocket and raised it toward his face. Fixing his mouth for female company, Jordy supposed.

"Howdy, Miss Sierra," Rudy said, lifting his battered sombrero and displaying his mutilated scalp—he had favored sombreros for as long as Jordy had known him. "Didn't expect to see you again so soon, but it's a pleasure." He gave her a big smile featuring his tobacco-stained, store-bought teeth.

"Just 'Sierra' will do."

Donning his sombrero and nodding toward the young man loading the chuckwagon, Rudy said, "This here is Bram Potts. He'll be helping me keep folks fed."

Bram was noticeably nervous, Jordy thought. He suspected Bram had not had much experience with pretty, young ladies or any women, for that matter. "Hello, ma'am," Bram said, "Pleased to make your acquaintance."

"Thank you, Bram."

Rudy said, "Jordy, you got the guys from the ranch crew lined up yet?"

"We're working on it this morning. Do you really think any of the boys would turn down a call for help from Jack?"

Rudy shrugged, "Suppose not. I don't remember who you're looking for. Irish was one. He's breaking horses. Him and Mitch Eagle Eyes. I think Mitch was supposed to go, too."

"And Swede Larsen and Possum Crowell. They're both on ranch duty this week. Jack was going to get the rest of the crew from the freighting company."

Rudy said, "Swede's over in the blacksmith shop as usual helping Enrique replace a wagon axle. Possum's with Rusty and Pete Collins, checking the east herd for calving cows and new calves, riding along the North Concho, most likely, maybe a half hour out I'd guess. I could have Bram run them down if you like."

"No, I wanted to show Sierra some of the range anyhow. We'll saddle some horses and head out that way after I talk to the guys here at headquarters. Before we go, I'll come by and drop Thor off if you'd keep him company while we're out."

"Aw, you know he's going to bitch and whine about being left behind."

"We won't be gone long. Thor just can't take a long run like he used to."

"I suppose when we go, the old mutt's going to be riding in the chuckwagon with me."

Jordy spoke under his breath to Sierra, "It's best to have all the old dogs together."

"You talking about me, kid?" Rudy said, head cocked and one eye squinted shut.

"I was telling Sierra that Thor likes to pal around with you."

"My hearing might be off a mite, but I can still tell when you ain't telling the truth. Don't matter none. You'll be old someday, too, if you're lucky. Then you'll get your comeuppance."

Chapter 14

JACK'S FIRST STOP in San Angelo was at his lawyer's office. He thought of Frank Bell Russo as just a kid, too young to be giving a man Jack's age advice. Then, he remembered Frank had been his law wrangler for a half dozen years, ever since Fort Concho was built adjacent to the town and triggered a serious boom and was probably not far from forty years old. Funny how time changed a man's perspective.

It did not matter. Jack liked and trusted the man with sea-blue eyes and a handle-bar moustache. Russo had a head of thick black hair, wore a vested business suit that Jack thought would roast a man during a hot Texas summer, but he supposed Russo would feel naked without it. The lawyer was on the short side but trim for a townie.

"You are proposing a lot of changes," the man on the working side of the desk said.

"Yep. And I need them by the middle of the afternoon. I'm leaving these parts in the morning."

"You are not planning on dying, I hope."

"Nope. Just prepared. Don't start adding up your probate fees yet."

Russo gave him an annoyed look. The lawyer was a serious sort, and Jack thought he needed to work on his sense of humor. Maybe that was just something a man either had or did not.

"We've got a typewriter now—a new Remington got here on one of your freight wagons last week. My law clerk has figured out how to work it, but it's still slow going. You're going to have the first will we've put out on it. You will have the fanciest will in Texas, and we won't even charge you extra for it. Come back at three o'clock."

Maybe Frank Bell Russo had a sense of humor after all.

After leaving the lawyer's office, Jack went to the Lucky Five Freighting office. The small frame building was dwarfed by the mammoth stable and warehouse behind it. When Jack first heard the government had acquired land for an Army post, he had quietly purchased a 160-acre tract abutting the property and immediately started building freighting facilities and corrals. A potential competitor complained that Jack had procured a license to steal with his location next to the post. Lucky Five had a near monopoly on government freighting, so Jack could not deny that things had almost turned out that way.

Jack entered the clapboard office building and was greeted with Juana Marshall's welcoming smile. "Jack, what a nice surprise. I was just thinking you were about due to show up in town." Juana's smile seemed perpetual, and it was difficult to be with her more than five minutes and not surrender to her persistent optimism. A visit with Juana would quickly break one of the black moods that for no explainable reason had been clutching him on occasion lately.

"I can only go so long without seeing you, Juana. I needed a day brightener."

"Okay, Jack. Turn off the charm. You are here on serious business. I can tell," she said. She motioned at the little table behind the counter, where she often sat down with customers. "Sit down. I have coffee on the little woodstove in the cave."

He pulled back a chair and watched Juana as she disappeared behind the curtain that separated the front office area from "the cave," as Juana called it for its single narrow window that left it dusky at best on sunny days. It was essentially a storage room with floor to ceiling shelves, the contents of which were known only to Juana. Jack had no desire to know.

Juana was a multi-generation Texan of Mexican ancestry, a year or two past twenty-five, who had migrated to San Angelo from San Antonio when Fort Concho was being constructed after the War of the Rebellion. Her parents had established a restaurant featuring Mexican food and drinks, where Juana still managed the bookkeeping and inventory. She had a head for numbers and a solid education which she was putting to use teaching Tige and their two small children to read, write, and cipher.

Jack admired Juana's quick mind, and she was such a pretty thing, on the short side and not petite, but busty with curves where they should be on a woman. Flawless, bronze-tinted skin, only a shade lighter than her husband's. Tige had walked away with a prize when he won Juana's heart.

His mind was still wandering when Juana placed two filled pottery coffee mugs on the table and sat down across from him. He looked up and saw she still had that ever-present smile, but her dark eyes were questioning.

Jack said, "I need to talk to Tige, but I was hoping I could speak with you first."

"Tige is with some skinners in the stable. They have some loads going out from the fort this afternoon. We're short-handed today, so he was going to help with the feedings and such, too. He won't be back anytime soon."

"I hope the two big Studebakers are available."

"I'm sure they are, but I will check my logbook to be certain."

"I have a mission that could be dangerous. A man of Tige's talents would be useful."

Juana's smile became tentative. "Tell me about this mission."

Jack rendered a fifteen-minute version of the story. "I will tell you more sometime, but that's the gist of what this is all about."

Juana said, "I think that is enough for now. You must feel overwhelmed and excited at the same time. A grand-daughter dropping into your life. I cannot imagine. But why did you come to me first? Why not Tige?"

"If you don't want him to go, I won't say anything."

"He would find out what you were doing anyway and be upset you did not include him. And I think you need him. Besides, Tige is longing for adventure, and he does not require my permission. Talk to him."

"Jordy is going with us. Rusty will be running the ranch, but you will have to handle the money. You have authority to sign drafts or deposit funds that show up. Rusty will stay in touch with you."

"I adore Rusty. We won't have any problems. You just take care of my husband . . . and yourself."

Jack found Tige Marshall in the stable supervising and helping with stall cleaning and feeding the mules and horses. The company owned over thirty wagons and was the lifeline that brought most of the food and other supplies to both Fort Concho and the town.

The financial challenge for the business was, as Juana frequently reminded him, that too many of the wagons left empty. Loads both ways were needed to turn a good profit, especially when the company had well over one hundred mules and draft horses to keep fed with hay and grain produced on the Lucky Five river bottom lands.

Tige was preoccupied with explaining something to two young Mexican stable hands Jack had not seen before, new workers he assumed, although his appearances at the stable were infrequent. When the two departed to perform whatever task Tige had assigned, the man whose muscle-sheathed shoulders and arms threatened the seams of his cotton shirt turned and saw Jack. His face lit up and offered a generous smile as he stepped toward Jack with an outstretched hand. They exchanged firm grips, but Jack knew that the freighting manager had spared his employer the full strength of his hand's grasp.

"Good morning, Boss. Ain't seen you about for a spell."

"You might wish I had stayed away longer when I tell you what I'm here for."

Tige, who was a few inches taller than Jack, appraised Jack with his dark eyes, and his smile disappeared. "I hope I'm not losing my job."

"Nope. I just want you to take a leave of absence to help me chase down some Comancheros. There will be a hundred-dollar bonus for every man who signs on."

"Ain't needing no bonus for that kind of fun. Gotta tell you, Boss, I've been itching for some real work."

"You haven't even asked me for particulars."

"Boss . . . Jack, I'm an old Army sergeant. I don't ask questions when the general talks. I just do."

"Well, I'm not your general. But I did get your general's approval."

Tige smiled knowingly. "I ain't surprised. You don't want to cross Juana. I can be spared, but she can't, if you was to tell the truth."

"I would be lost without either of you, and you should know it by now. Here's the story quick-like. I had a gal show up, who claims to be my granddaughter. I am convinced she is. Comancheros stole over fifty horses from her place, and she wants me to get them back. I said I would do it. They are likely at a place called Lookout Canyon out in desert country."

"I've heard of the place," Tige said. "What do you want me to do?"

"Recruit three of your buffalo soldiers who aren't out on a wagon run."

Tige said, "That would be Roper Hawley, Abel Burke, and Nick Iverson. Good men, and I can't think of much any one of them wouldn't do for a hundred dollars. Consider it done."

"I want to take two of the big Studebaker wagons, including the one with the false bottom. Attach the bows and put the canvas bonnets on. I want an assortment of guns and ammunition in the false bottom. Do you still have Miss Molly?"

"Yessir."

"Invite her along, too."

"I wouldn't leave without her."

Jack said, "We're going to be traders. I want the wagons filled with trade goods. Canned foods, blankets, bottles of liquor, anything that you think such folks as Comancheros might buy or trade for."

"Maybe some things women might take a liking to. They will have women there."

"Good idea. I'll leave that to you. Take what you can from our warehouse. Get the rest from the general store or wherever you can find it. Juana will pay the bills."

"She will damn well want a list of everything that's coming out of the warehouse," Tige said.

"Whatever keeps her happy. Rudy will be bringing the ranch chuckwagon. I think some mules from here should be traded for the ranch critters. A single team would probably work, but I will leave that to you. The Studebakers may need three teams, but, again, that's your decision."

"You didn't say how many days we have to get ready."

"We're pulling out tomorrow. Noon at the latest."

"Somehow, I figured as much."

Chapter 15

I T WAS NEARING five o'clock when Jack reined the bay gelding that he called "Pokey" into Tess's yard. He dismounted and led the horse to the little stable. The mount was the same age as Thor and had earned its name for lack of speed. Jack had raced him twice at a Fort Concho fair, earning last place each time before retiring as a racehorse. But Pokey was gentle as a lamb and durable as a camel in the heat. Besides, he thought of the horse as a friend, and at Jack's age he did not need a bucking bronc anymore. His back and butt were aching from what little riding he had done today.

Tess entered the stable while Jack was pitching some hay from the stack at the far end of the stable into the bay's stall. "Appears that you've got him brushed down and ready for the night," she said.

"Yep. Brushed down and an extra bucket of water in the stall."

"You're riding Pokey on your trip into the Chihua-huan?"

"He'll do fine. He's got a good ride or two left in him. He's barely middle-aged for a horse . . . unlike his rider."

"I've got a tub of water in the washroom. I was checking to see if you're ready for a bath. I will pour some hot water in to warm it up."

Jack said, "Smells good out there. You must be cooking outside tonight."

"It's hot enough in the house. I don't need the wood-stove going. Besides, cobbler works best in a Dutch oven with coals on the lid and under the bottom."

"I'll be right in."

When he left the stable carrying his possible bag, Jack walked around to the back of the house. He paused a moment to inspect Tess's stone fire ring. The wood had burned down to a bed of coals, but the Dutch oven sat on a broad flat rock outside with a sprinkling of coals scooped between its stubby legs and twice as many on top. Tess's forked supports for the pointed iron spit that rested against the stone rim rose from the crackling coals. There would be beef roasting as soon as he took his bath. That was all the incentive he needed to get the bath out of the way.

He opened the back door and stepped into the enclosed porch or "mudroom," as Tess called it. A blue-painted tin tub sat in the middle of the room that was just off the kitchen. A wood stove for winter warming sat in one corner and most of one wall was blocked by two rustic cedar tripods with ropes strung between them for hanging clothes. The tub also doubled for laundry duty and was an oval-shaped convenience that always made Jack think of a coffin, although he was not able to stretch out in the thing.

Scrawny Tess could about swim in it. Well, maybe not. He smiled, remembering the time they tried to share the tub a few years back. He had settled in the tub and Tess had climbed in and awkwardly, back to him, sat down between his legs to allow Jack to scrub her back. Jack had leaned over to reach a scrub brush on the floor outside the tub, and his weight shift toppled the tub, dumping the occupants and a tubful of water on the floor.

Jack and Tess still laughed about their bath sharing attempt, but neither had ever proposed another such frolic. The effort was not without its rewards, though, as Jack recalled that night in bed as one to aspire to. He still teased Tess sometimes about that night of the triple poke, although she insisted that he had dreamt one. Maybe so, but a man should cling tight to the best of his memories, illusory or not. It was not long after that he started having pizzle trouble.

Tess was pouring a bucket of steaming hot water in the tub now. "I think this should do you," she said. "Strip down. I hope you have clean underwear in your bag."

"I do, ma'am. I know you don't like to dance with cowmen who don't put on clean underwear."

"I don't care a whit about dancing, but I don't want a man with dirty underwear in my bed."

"I can't remember ever wearing any underwear beneath the sheets with you, clean or dirty."

"Just get your clothes off and get in the tub. I'll scrub your back and maybe give old Medicine Stick a swipe or two if you behave yourself."

Medicine Stick was Tess's nickname for his pizzle. Her suggestion triggered a stirring in his loins, but Medicine Stick did not spring up like he would have in the old days. Still, he was confident that Tess would take care of any problems.

The sun had not set yet when they sat at the kitchen table finishing the cherry cobbler, Jack's favorite. Everything had been his favorite, the roasted beef chunks, potatoes fried with skins on, and baked beans with chopped bacon pieces. Simple fare, and that was his style, however, he noticed that Tess had become increasingly quiet as their playful banter ran its course.

"You seem to be taking on a mood," he said. Jack knew a mood when he saw one, having to deal with his own more frequently these days. He was not quite as easygoing as many of his friends and acquaintances thought. "I told you I was fine with the deal you made with She Who Speaks. You can talk for me anytime."

"I know. I'm not thinking about that. I'm selfish, Jack. I don't like you going off like you are planning. We haven't had enough years together."

"We would never have enough years, Tess. Even if we had met forty years ago."

"You will watch out for yourself, won't you?"

"I've been watching out for myself through all kinds of trouble for fifty years. Some of the Rangers used to call me 'Careful Wills.'"

"You're giving me tall tales again, but I have been thinking about these precious years. My life is changing, Jack. The Comanches are all headed to Fort Sill. By summer's end, there will not be a Comanche around these parts. They won't be coming by for medicines and treatments anymore. It will be easier for me to make some changes in my life. While you are gone, think about that question you have asked me off and on over the years. If you ask me when you get back, I won't put you off. You will get an answer loud and clear." She slid her chair back and got up. "Now, I am going to put some things away, and I'll finish cleaning up in the morning. It's near our bedtime, and you need rest for tomorrow."

"I didn't come by for rest. I came for your company and maybe a little extra if you're feeling like it and got some pizzle potion handy."

Tess said, "I am going to put your potion and the other medicine in a small glass of water for you to drink. No coffee or you will be up half the night. Now why don't you run outside and pee, and I'll have everything ready when you get back."

When Jack returned, he found Tess had left the kitchen. He drank the glass of water that had turned greenish from the medicines. He looked in the bedroom and discovered her there, naked and lighting the bedside lamp in preparation for darkness that would soon descend. She preferred the flickering flame and soft glow of a lamp when they made love, and they were both comfortable with their mutual nakedness.

Tess lay down on the sheets, watching him with her seductive eyes while she waited. He undressed, pleased that his pizzle was already awakening. He joined her on the bed, wondering if he would be crippled in the morning.

"Your back's hurting from saddle time, isn't it?" Tess asked.

"Only a mite."

"I'll do the heavy work tonight," she said, rolling toward him.

Her fingertips took control of his flesh, and he pulled her head toward his and gave her a lingering kiss. "I love you, Tess Wyman," he said.

"Ah, but will you say that after you have had your way with me? By the way, Medicine Stick is powerful tonight."

At sunrise, Jack woke up alone in bed. He got up, dressed, and followed the tantalizing smells to the kitchen. Biscuits, eggs, and bacon were waiting, and coffee was brewing.

Tess met him with a quick hug and kiss. "I knew breakfast would get you up."

Jack dropped into a chair at the table. "I'm so damn sore this morning, I don't know if I can step into a saddle."

"You don't have to on my account. You can just stay right here. I won't make you repeat last night for a spell."

"Don't tell me I was dreaming, but I could swear the middle of the night, we had another ride."

"You weren't dreaming, lover. We had a double." She placed a plate with bacon and fried eggs in front of him. "Biscuits are in the covered pan. Honey jar is beside it."

"I'll be damned. You must have put in an extra dose of the pizzle potion."

Tess sat down across from him and took his hand as he was reaching for a biscuit. "Jack, I have a confession."

"A confession? Don't tell me you've got a husband somewhere I don't know about."

She smiled. "No, nothing like that. It's the pizzle potion, Jack."

"What about it? I'm not going to drop dead from taking too much, am I?"

"Not quite. Jack, the potion is just a half spoon of sugar and ground dandelion leaves."

"What do you mean?"

"Your problems were all in your brain. You had a few difficult nights and set your head to thinking it was all over. I just told you the potion would solve the problem. In a way, I guess it did, the notion of it anyway. But Medicine Stick was still on his own, doing just fine once your brain left him alone."

Jack squeezed her hand, released it and reached for a biscuit. "You've got a devious side, Tess Wyman. I will have to watch out for that."

"Are you still going to ask me a question when you get back?"

"I am. And I am counting on you to have the right answer."

Chapter 16

THE FIRST DAY on the trail had been disappointing to Jack. Miles were just guesses in this country, but he calculated that they had traveled no more than fifteen miles of the estimated 150 or more they needed to cover to reach Lookout Canyon. The first day out tended to be slow, he reminded himself. A wagon party rarely departed as early as planned, with last minute changes in supply needs, shifting of wagon loads for better balance and the like. They had moved out of San Angelo at nearly eleven o'clock, several hours later than he hoped but earlier than he had been prepared for.

Tige had decided that a single mule team would be more than adequate for the chuckwagon and that double teams would be sufficient for the Studebakers. They had a string of four extra mules on a reata in case of injury to an animal or for relief of tiring critters. A team could be added to a wagon if necessary.

Chihuahuan Desert country lay to the southwest and Lookout Canyon lay within its mapped boundaries. They would be traveling along the fringes for several days, and water and grass would be in short supply early on. The Chihuahuan did not fit the image of endless sand that most folks thought of when a desert was mentioned. It was a vast territory covering most of West Texas and parts of northern Mexico, southern New Mexico Territory and southern Arizona Territory. Small mountain ranges broke up some of the area, and other parts were rough with canyons, arroyos and rock formations. In sandy and valley areas, creosote bush dominated, and yucca and mesquite thrived in foothill edges. There was water if a man knew where to find it, occasional streams and waterholes, even rivers like the Pecos and Rio Grande. In some places decent grasslands stretched out as temptation that would likely bring cattlemen when the tribes were moved to reservations. The Comanches would be gone soon, but many Apache bands had not surrendered yet and occasionally still found their ways into West Texas.

Jack had ridden Pokey till midafternoon when his painful back mandated a change. He had claimed a seat on the chuckwagon with Rudy where Thor had been riding, forcing the big dog to climb into the covered wagon bed to resume his napping. Thor had not been that much of a sleeper in his younger days, Jack thought. He worried that his old friend was ailing, but he ate well enough and seemed to summon up energy when he had some motivation. Not unlike himself, he guessed.

Rudy was a born mule skinner, and he obviously relished running a team again. He had promised to teach his assistant, Bram Potts, the fine art on this journey, but that would wait till he wore down some. For now, Bram rode horseback within earshot of the wagon.

"Ass is getting sore," Rudy said. "When we gonna pull in for the night?"

"Within an hour. Mitch is finding a water spot up ahead. Needs to find a place with grass for all these critters."

"You ain't had a serious talk with your grand-gal yet. I been watching. You ain't said more than 'howdy do, ma'am.'"

"Nope."

"Ain't it about time?"

"We'll talk some when it works out. It's none of your concern."

"That ain't true. I got to put up with your damned crabbiness when you're putting things off that need doing. It would be easier for everybody if the two of you would act more friendly. I don't think she knows what to make of you. Time to get acquainted, so she can find you ain't quite as mean and nasty as you seem."

"That's a compliment?"

"Best I can do right now."

Jack found himself royally pissed at his old comrade-in-arms, but he had to admit there was a spoonful of truth in what Rudy said. He had been standoffish. She was not his enemy. My God, Sierra Wills carried his name and was his own flesh and blood.

Soon after, Mitch Eagle Eyes rode up to the chuckwagon and Jack asked Rudy to rein in the mule team. Mitch, a half-blood Comanche, sidled his horse up to Jack's side of the wagon seat. Jack had not found anything yet at the ranch that Mitch could not do, but he knew that the wiry man loved horse work, so whenever feasible Jack paired him with Irish O'Toole, the ranch's unofficial horse wrangler. Both good men, but in his judgment, he kept on nothing but. Nobody headed down the road for better wages.

"Hey, Boss Man," Mitch said. "If you don't mind pulling over early, I got a camping spot a half hour up the trail. Clear stream, some shade and a fair amount of firewood scattered about."

"We'll take it. I'm thinking we might want to head off more westerly tomorrow. We can talk about it tonight. Any idea who is following us?"

"Figured you seen him. I circled around and got a better look. Just one man. If he's Comanche, he ain't much of one. I could walk up in full light on naked prairie and cut his throat, and he'd never know what happened. Darker than me, though. Might be Mex. Hard to say."

"Comanchero?"

"Could be. Some got cunning. Most don't know shit from wild honey. He'd be with the last."

"We'll leave him alone for now, maybe bring him in for a talk if he is still with us in a few days."

"Just tell me if you want him dead."

"I will. For now, just lead us to your campsite."

Mitch nodded, wheeled his horse around and headed back up the trail. As Rudy nudged the mules forward again, Jack's eyes followed the rider as he disappeared into the sun. He dressed like an ordinary cowhand except for the calf-high moccasins he wore. Jack thought Mitch should be near forty now. The half-blood had scouted for several years with Jack's Ranger outfit before joining Jack on the exodus to the ranch some fifteen years earlier.

Mitch kept his tongue tight about his past, but that was not unusual for Texas men. Jack had pieced together this much, though: Mitch was the child of a Comanche warrior and a captive white woman. He had lived with Comanches during early childhood but was young enough when his mother was ransomed that he was taken with her from the village, albeit not likely without a struggle. He would have been Comanche by that time. It did not matter. With horses to recover, Mitch Eagle Eyes had been an obvious choice for the mission.

"You didn't tell me somebody was following us," Rudy complained. "How long you knowed that?"

"Picked him up when I was still mounted, a few hours out of San Angelo. He was on that ridge to the southeast. I can't read without my spectacles, but I do fine with the distance. No cause to get anybody stirred up."

"Well, I'm stirred up you didn't tell me."

"You're not happy unless you are stirred up about something."

The wagon struck a pit in the trail that nearly bounced Jack off his seat and shot a sliver of pain up his lower back. He looked over at Rudy. "Did you do that on purpose?"

Rudy responded with one of his twisted toothless grins.

Chapter 17

JACK WAS GLAD the little caravan had pulled off the trail early. He tried to climb down from the chuckwagon gracefully, but grace had vacated his stiff and aching bones. His feet hit the ground, and he straightened slowly. It annoyed him that Rudy, the old fart, was moving faster than he was, directing orders rapid-fire to Bram about setting up the chuckwagon for supper and getting a fire started. First day out. Jack figured he would work out the creaks after another day or two on the trail.

He retrieved Pokey from behind the chuckwagon where the gelding had been hitched after Jack's dismounting. He led the horse to the stream for a drink and looked around the site while he waited. A shallow but fast flowing stream. Clean as a man would find in this part of Texas. They would collect the horses and mules downstream and replenish water supplies well above the critters.

As Mitch Eagle Eyes had promised, firewood was ample. A healthy stand of willows sprinkled with hackberry trees lined the stream, and the grass varieties should appeal to the mules and horses, not lush growth but adequate. Equine eating opportunities would be sparser as they moved on, but starvation was not a likely threat this time of year.

Jack led the bay along the stream's edge toward a broad stretch of grass that followed the tree line, where Irish O'Toole, Possum Crowell, Mitch and, surprising him, Sierra, were attaching rope lines for four or five animals each to the trees. Other ropes attached to halters and tied to the line would give enough slack for grazing.

When Irish O'Toole saw him, he finished a hitch in the rope he was working on, waved at Jack and walked his way with a broad smile on his dark face. "Hey, Jack. I'll take Pokey." He took the reins from Jack's hand and caressed the horse's soft muzzle affectionately. Irish spoiled Pokey rotten.

"How is the young lady doing with the horses?"

"Just fine, Jack. She knows horseflesh, mules included. If she stays around, I'll have to look over my shoulder to be sure she doesn't take my job."

Irish, the son of a Negro slaveowner and his mulatto wife, had enjoyed a tutored education exceeding that of most Southern whites. He could read and write proficiently and was a well-spoken man in his early thirties. He resided in one of the Lucky Five ranch houses with his wife, Rose, and their two sons. Rose had been born a slave on the O'Toole Texas plantation, but from her coloring, Jack surmised that a fair amount of white blood ran in her veins. It baffled him sometimes why some thought it important to identify folks by race. It didn't take but a few generations for most people to have a little bit of everything in their blood.

As to Irish's history, Negro slaveowners were not commonplace, but they appeared with enough frequency that they were not a particular curiosity either. Regardless, the outcome of the war had impoverished Patrick O'Toole's family as well as those of his white neighbors. The nickname? Jack had never asked about the source but supposed it was somebody's idea of a joke based upon the seeming incongruity between Patrick O'Toole's name and the color of his skin—and it was likely there was an Irishman somewhere in his background.

"Your job's safe, Irish. If she stays around, she will be bringing a big horse herd with her and along with it more horse work than you ever dreamed of."

"I like that notion, Boss. We could make some money with horses at the Lucky Five."

"Sierra gave me some numbers that made me think about that. Whether she stays or not, you and I need to talk about the horse business when we get back to the ranch. Maybe we could partner up on something like that."

"You're talking about my dream, Jack. You have been letting me foal a few of my own mares on the side, but I've got ambitions. I'd love to stick with the Lucky Five, but something is calling me. Maybe the call is coming from right there on the ranch."

"We will talk."

Jack thought that Irish led the horse off with some extra spring in his step. He had a lot of good folks working with him in his businesses. Sure, he would like to help them do better, but he came out best if he gave them the opportunity in Lucky Five ventures.

Rudy was already cooking when Jack returned to the campsite, jabbering like a magpie at poor Bram, who apparently had learned to shut out the noise and was obviously fond of his supervisor and mentor. Jack decided to take a stroll upstream before supper call. He needed some thinking time where he could talk things over in his own head. Besides, he feared that if he sat down now, they would have to retrieve one of the mules to pull him to his feet. Crazy old man. He should have known better than to take off on a fool's quest like this. He had a notion to turn the party around and head back to the ranch in the morning.

Chapter 18

SIERRA WAS A bit nervous about her grandfather's request that she join him near the trees south of the Studebaker wagons after supper, but she was glad he was going to break the taciturn silence that had governed whenever he was in her proximity. He was a strange man. He did not talk much, but when he did, everybody listened. Not because they feared him, though. The people who worked for him—no, worked with him—respected him, maybe loved him. They were more like a big family in the camp, bickering sometimes and occasionally disagreeing vociferously, but an attack on one would be an attack on all.

She guessed that Jordy and these people on Jack's payroll had somehow melded into a family, and she found herself a little jealous and resentful that his blood kin had been denied that relationship. Jordy's love for the man and the admiration and affection of all those others for Jack Wills made no sense to her. This was not the man her father and grandmother had hated so. Piece by piece, she was putting together someone quite different.

When she approached the trees, she saw Jack sitting on a stump, staring in the direction of the setting sun. Thor, of course, was sprawled on the ground at his friend's feet.

As she drew nearer, Jack, without turning his head, said, "Pick a stump and have yourself a seat."

Sierra found a half-dozen choices where travelers had downed good-sized trees years earlier. She claimed the one nearest to Jack some five or six feet distant. He swung around and faced her, leaning forward with forearms resting on his thighs, fingers entwined. His eyes fastened on hers like he was looking for something there. He nodded with what she took as approval of some sort.

"Tell me about J. T.," he said.

"There is so much. What do you want to know? I've told you some things."

"I want to know him better. What did he look like? I wish I had a picture."

"At home, I have daguerreotypes taken in his dress Confederate uniform. I think I told you he was a cavalry colonel. If the house is still standing when I get back, I will dig the daguerreotypes out and bring them for you to look at. But he looked a lot like you. His hair was black, starting to get a few strands of white when he was killed. Like you, he wasn't inclined to hair on his face—no moustache or chin whiskers."

Jack asked, "Was he short? Tall? His mother's people were on the short side."

"Oh, Papa was tall. A little taller than you are. I suppose about Jordy's height. On the skinny side but muscled in the arms and shoulders," Sierra said.

"I know he loved horses. He was obviously a hard worker and a man who tried to better himself. Was he a reader?"

Sierra smiled, "Everything he could get his hands on. That is why he insisted I go to school. But we didn't have any kind of a fancy library. Just books stacked on the floor along one wall of his bedroom. He liked Poe a lot."

"Depressing stuff but hard to set aside once you start. So your father hated me? I hope he didn't let that run his life. Hate's not a good burden to carry. Closes your mind to possibilities."

"It was always there, but he didn't talk about it all the time or anything. Just when he got moods, and that wasn't often. He laughed a lot, enjoyed simple pleasures. His happiest days were when Mama was alive. He loved her more than anything, and she loved him. I never heard a cross word between them. They were like a mule team, always working together to get where they were going."

"So he had bad times in his life, but he saw good times, too?"

"Oh, yes. He told me more than once that you've got to have bad times to know what good times are. Then, it is not so hard to recognize the good times when they visit. Treasure the simple joys, he said." She nodded toward Thor. "Like a loyal dog at your feet."

Jack smiled, "J. T. Wills was a wise man."

Sierra said, "He was. But I have got to know something. You have not directly answered an important question."

"Try me. I'll see what I can do."

"Did you leave Grandma Emily when Papa was one year old?"

"No. I did not know your grandmother was with child when we parted, and I did not leave. I was sent away. It seems likely she did not know she was carrying a child at the time."

A storm raged in Sierra's head. Was it possible that her father lived out his life with a false belief? That her beloved Grandma Emily had planted a lie and let it grow unabated? She found herself trembling as she spoke. "Are you saying my Grandma was a liar?"

Jack said softly, "I won't say that, Sierra. I am telling you my part of the story. You will have to sort the truths out yourself. And ask yourself if it matters now. What's done is done."

"Let's just say she lied," Sierra said. "Why? And if she did, why did she let it go on for all those years?"

"A person tells a lie, and they become a prisoner of it. The only key out of that jail is the truth, and that brings embarrassment, sometimes deep shame or the fear of losing something or someone you hold dear. I carry a few lies on my back, and they don't get lighter with the years. Still, I guess it is just easier to live out the lie sometimes."

"Maybe for the liar," Sierra said, "but not for the lie's victims."

"Depends on the lie, I guess. Sometimes, the truth would be too late anyhow."

"You almost sound like you are defending Grandma Emily."

"I'm not defending anybody. I've got enough trouble figuring out what's going on in my own head these days. I'm not about to guess what went through somebody's mind nearly a half century ago. Like I just said, what's done is done."

"I'll tell you more about Papa. You should know about the good times and the things he loved to do. You will be proud of the man and how he dealt with life."

They talked until long after darkness cloaked the desert-prairie with only a star-studded sky casting a warm glow over the earth. Jack asked few questions. He just listened quietly, smiling and nodding his head when something pleased him. Sierra found herself calling up memories long since buried, cheered as if meeting old, treasured friends. Why is it, she wondered, that it is so much easier to remember the bad than the good?

Finally, she noticed that others had already crawled into bedrolls around the campsite. Those that had not were laying out their ground beds. "I've been rattling on so much," she said, "I hadn't noticed everybody was going to bed."

"It's been nice, Sierra. We'll try to make a habit of this. We're past due for catching up."

"Where are you sleeping tonight, Grandpa Jack?"

"I see nobody's under the nearest Studebaker. I thought I would roll out my blankets over there."

"Do you mind if I roll mine out near yours?"

He stood up, and she noticed he winced and grabbed the overhanging branch of a hackberry tree to steady himself as he got to his feet. "I would be honored," he said.

Chapter 19

JACK WAS IN a dead sleep when Thor's low growling awakened him. The dog had been curled up on top of a portion of the blankets Jack left for his furry friend. Usually, the dog crowded Jack to the edge of his blankets, leaving him encased like a wrapped mummy. Thor stood now, though, his eyes focused to the south.

Jack scooted out of his blanket cocoon and tossed a glance to the other side, where Sierra slept in her blankets a few feet away. She appeared undisturbed. He slipped on his boots and picked up his gun belt before sliding out from under the wagon bed and stumbling to his feet. He knew better than to disregard Thor's warning, and he had to water the cactus anyhow.

He took several steps away from the Studebaker to get a clear view of where the horses and mules were strung out. He could make out the shadowy images of two guards watching the remuda. The animals were gold on a journey like this, and an old horse soldier like Tige Marshall would post double guards even in country considered safe. He was not certain who was posted with the horses, although he thought one might be Irish. Mitch Eagle Eyes would likely be his relief. The other was a tall man, likely Roper Hawley. Neither appeared to be aware of any threat.

"Okay, Thor," Jack said, "show me."

The dog slipped into the trees along the stream, and Jack followed, moving stealthily but worried that he would alert a visitor if they had one. With Thor in the lead, they moved slowly along the streambank for several minutes. Suddenly, the big dog stopped. Jack's eyes followed Thor's gaze. Fifty to sixty feet downstream, a man stood half-hidden by the trees. He held a rifle in his hands, and his attention was directed away from the stream, in the direction Jack estimated the remuda and guards would be. Jack edged into the cover of the trees and watched while he considered his next move.

If he hollered, the man would run. Jack would prefer a captive, so he could ask some questions and find out what the stalker was up to. A human and animal head count could have been made from the safety of hills along the way, so he was looking for something more. The man turned in Jack's direction and started walking his way. Jack would be forced to make his presence known soon. He slipped his Peacemaker from its holster, and when the visitor was no more than twenty-five feet distant, Jack stepped from the trees.

"Stop where you are and drop the rifle," Jack ordered. His finger was wrapped around the trigger, ready to squeeze if the man gave a sign of using his own weapon.

The stranger obeyed, and the rifle clattered on the rocks. There was movement to his right across the stream, and Jack whipped his weapon toward the sound.

"Just me, Jack."

It was Mitch Eagle Eyes. Yet another man appeared behind the visitor. Jack recognized him as Roper Hawley, who had been with the remuda. He was one of Tige's buffalo soldier hires for the freight company, by far the tallest man in their party, his body and legs stretching so long they made the big sorrel gelding he always rode look like a child's pony.

Jack turned his attention to the stranger and stepped nearer to him. A paunchy man wearing a Plainsman hat pulled low on his forehead, Jack could not make out much of his face, which was shielded not only by the darkness of night but by a shaggy, black beard.

"What's your business, mister?" Jack asked.

"Just looking. No harm intended. Thought I might beg a cup of coffee."

"After midnight?"

The man shrugged. "Never hurts to check. I wouldn't of woke up nobody if I didn't see somebody at a fire."

He had a slight accent that suggested Spanish lineage, possibly an Anglo father and Mexican mother which was a common pairing in the Southwest. "You could have approached our nightriders instead of sneaking up like a fox looking for chickens. What's your name?"

"Smack."

"What' your full name?"

"Just Smack."

"That's what we'll put on your marker then."

"What marker?"

"For your grave, if we've got time to dig one."

Smack pushed his hat back, and Jack could see his eyes now and the fear that resided in them.

Smack said, his voice not so confident now, "I ain't done nothing that deserves a hanging. You can't do that."

"We can do that. A lot of men who didn't deserve it have been strung up. That man behind you. His name's Roper. He's our hangman. Keeps a rope on his saddle with the knot already tied."

"What kind of people are you?" Smack asked.

Jack could see he was being taken seriously now, and he had a hunch about this man. "I guess I can tell you since you won't live to tell anybody. Have you ever heard of Lookout Canyon?"

"Maybe."

"Yes or no. Or we'll get the hanging done and get back to sleep. Roper, why don't you go get your rope, and we'll get this done."

Hawley said, "Sure enough, Boss. Ain't had this kind of fun since the old cottonwood tree at the Lucky Five." He disappeared through the trees.

Smack said, "Yeah. Yeah, I know Lookout Canyon. Been there."

"Well, that's where we're headed. We've got wagons full of trade goods, all kinds of foodstuffs, guns, whiskey, and some gold bullion we can't get rid of north of the Rio Grande without questions being asked. We want to do business with the Comancheros."

"I can help," Smack said. "I'm with the Comancheros. I do scouting work for them. That's why I was here—to see if you were worth a raid. I saw you loading up in San Angelo this morning. Figured you wouldn't have all these men if you didn't have a load worth attention."

Jack said, "And once you confirmed it, you were going to contact a band of the vermin and sic them on us?"

"Just tell them what I saw. But no need if you're headed for Lookout Canyon. You let me go, I can ride ahead and sort of blaze a trail for you . . . let them know you're good folks and that you'll be along with goods to sell or trade. See that they treat you like friends."

"You would really do that for us?" Jack wanted to beat the hell out of the miserable bastard, but he figured he did not have anything to lose by playing the game. He could not lynch a man, never did have the taste for it. And they did not need the nuisance of a prisoner to watch over. There was a chance the guy might help them get through the figurative gate, which was objective number one. At the least, if Smack did what he claimed he would, they might avert an attack along the trail.

"You let me go, and I'll get my horse and head out tonight. I ain't one to forget a good turn. I promise."

Jack figured Smack's word was worth a pile of cow shit, but he replied, "Git, before Roper gets back."

Smack didn't need to be told a second time. He wheeled, splashed across the stream and crashed through the trees and brush toward a knoll above the camp.

Mitch leaped over the stream, and Roper emerged from the trees, and they both came up to Jack.

Roper, towering over both of the others, said, "Figured you was joshing the feller, Boss. And I sure don't have no hangman's noose on my rope. Don't want nothing to do with folks on the other end of a rope. I seen two of my people mob-lynched. It's a sight that sickens a man's soul."

Jack knew about that. He had been too late to stop a few hangings when he was a Ranger and had come across the aftermath. Worst, though, was when he had been helping a sheriff hold off a mob trying to take an accused killer of a woman from a rickety jailhouse. They had been overrun, and both the prisoner and sheriff had been hung from the big oak "hanging tree" on the town square. He had been spared because of his Ranger badge and a fear of the wrath of the Texas Rangers when they learned one of their own had been a victim.

As it turned out, the prisoner had been innocent, and one of the leaders of the mob, the woman's husband, had been the killer diverting the blame to his wife's illicit lover. Jack had at least brought the husband to justice in the aftermath, but the man got off with a prison sentence. The prosecutors declined to file charges against any participants in the hanging because they thought they were doing their civic duty. He hated mobs to his very core whether the objective was a lynching or any other act to overrun a man's personal freedom or property outside the structure of the law.

Jack sighed. "I'm going to see if I can grab some shut-eye, gentlemen," Jack said, suddenly realizing he still held his Colt. He pressed it into his holster and walked away.

When he returned to his bedroll, he was glad to see that Sierra still slept. He removed his boots and gun belt and tossed his hat aside and slipped into the blankets. He felt Thor lie down on the bedroll's edge and press against him, and Jack reached his arm out of the blanket and stroked his friend's head. The shuteye he wanted to grab never came. His mind was wrangling with decisions to be made before breakfast and thinking about the son he never knew.

Chapter 20

SIERRA HOPED THAT she was not annoying Grandpa Jack. Since their talk last night, she was finding it difficult to have him far from her sight. She was wanting to know this man and somehow fill the gap of all those years she and her father had missed. Grandma Emily had given birth to a lie and carried it to her grave. Sierra had not a scintilla of a doubt that Grandpa Jack had told her the truth. It was consistent with all she was learning about this man. He had not known he had a son all those years.

She wondered how that knowledge might have changed all their lives. Certainly, Papa would have seen much of his father. Would Grandpa Jack have stayed on with the Rangers? Would he have purchased the Lucky Five or even had the opportunity? Would her father still be alive? Would she have even been born? She supposed she could write pages of questions and "what ifs." So many life stories changed by a single lie. It boggled a person's mind.

They had finished a breakfast of bacon and hotcakes swimming in molasses efficiently put together by Rudy and Bram. The two were a good team, she thought, and obviously had an affection for each other that was belied by Rudy's grumpy, growling manner with the young man. She was also learning that Rudy was far from the senile old man she had first judged him to be. She would not be surprised to learn that his seeming unsophistication was largely an act, a ploy of sorts to cause others to underestimate him. She was confident that Grandpa Jack did not.

The mule teams were being hitched to the wagons now, and Sierra stood beside Jack while he talked to Jordy, Mitch Eagle Eyes, and Tige Marshall. "I think we head due west on the old Butterfield stage road, pick up the Comanche War Trail and go through Castle Gap to Horsehead Crossing. That's the only place I know of we can cross the Pecos River with these wagons. The riverbanks are too damned high and steep from the north side of the Pecos as I recall. Tige, you spent some time at Fort Stockton. You must have ridden along the Pecos."

"Yeah, maybe five years back with a detachment of Tenth Cavalry not long before I mustered out. I don't know where else we'd cross. I didn't like Castle Gap much. It's a perfect place for ambush, and the Comanches left a lot of dried out bones from horses and mules that died there during their attacks on travelers and the Army. We can cross easy enough if the river ain't running high because of spring thaws from mountains to the north."

Jack said, "With the tribes going to the reservation, Comanches shouldn't be a problem. Those few bands that refuse to go in are not likely to be stirring up trouble right now."

Tige said, "The crossing is about fifty miles northeast of Fort Stockton. The Comanches are going in, but Apaches are known to come this far west. Some are at San Carlos in Arizona Territory, but soldiers at Concho tell me it's almost a game for those devils to jump the reservation every so often, and there are bands that haven't even thought about going in."

"We won't be going south. Once we cross the river, we will head northwest along the river's course for a day, then head west for another day, maybe two, till we reach Lookout Canyon." Jack turned to Eagle Eyes. "Do you know that country, Mitch?"

"Never been there. I've heard of the Comanche War Trail, but I was a kid when I left the Kwahadi band. I don't even remember that much Comanche language. I always ended up with scouting jobs because I kept my Kwahadi name."

Jack said, "What you didn't learn with the Comanches, you made up for with the Rangers."

"They'd have never hired me on if they guessed how little I knew."

"Well, you're our scout. We will hit the trail we're looking for an hour west of here, I'd guess. It should take about three days to Horsehead Crossing. Main concern is water. When I was down this way with the Rangers years ago, water was hard to come by on this stretch. But that was in early August. Your job is to locate water."

"I'll find water and keep an eye out for surprise company."

The group broke up and Jack walked toward the Studebaker where his saddled bay was hitched beside Sierra's red roan. Jordy's horse was tied to the other big wagon, and he moved up on Sierra's other side.

"Who's driving the wagons today?" Jack asked Jordy.

"Bram and Rudy will switch off on the chuckwagon, of course. Swede will handle one of the Studebakers, and Tige plans to skin the other."

"Good. I need to chat with Tige a spell. When I take a break from the saddle, I'll join him on the wagon seat."

Mitch Eagle Eyes had disappeared by the time the party headed out, with Jack and Sierra, astride their mounts, taking the lead, followed by the three wagons. Irish and Roper lagged at the rear with the spare mules and horses, and Abel Burke and Nick Iverson, two of Tige's former buffalo soldiers, each took a side and rode some distance out on the wings of the procession, keeping their eyes out for the unexpected. Jordy had fallen back, but Sierra had lost track of him.

The procession reached the old stagecoach trail less than an hour after they pulled away from the campsite. When they moved onto the well-packed wagon tracks of the broken trail, Sierra could tell they picked up the pace significantly.

During the ride to the trail connection, nary a word had passed between the two. Sierra thought it was something else she shared with her grandfather, the ability to tolerate extended silences, even savor those moments. She wondered where his thoughts were, though. Probably strategizing recovery of the horses, she supposed. Jack satisfied her curiosity when he sidled his mount nearer to hers.

"Your Grandma Emily was a pretty thing," he said. "We just didn't know what love was, either of us. We hardly knew each other, and the bug just hit us both when we were susceptible. I never struck her—or any woman, for that matter. I didn't quarrel with her. I just went quiet. But I never did try to understand her and never figured out what would make her happy. So, instead of facing up to our differences, I ran, found every reason to take jobs away from home and left her a lonely woman."

Sierra said, "Don't blame yourself. I loved Grandma, but she was a person who saw my father and me as possessions as much as family. She wasn't somebody you ever got close to. She had opinions, and life was easier if you didn't challenge them."

"I'm just saying," Jack said, "that for respectability's sake, she had to acknowledge she had a husband. She could not really admit to J. T. that she had never told her husband they shared a child. If she had, she knew that would have brought me back into her life in some fashion. And that was the last thing she wanted. That's why she concocted the story. Don't be hard on her. I likely deserved what I got."

Sierra added, "I don't think so, but regardless, Papa did not deserve what he missed out on."

Chapter 21

NEAR HIGH NOON, they paused to rest the mules and horses near a limestone ridge that erupted from the coarse dirt and sand some distance off the trail. There was a spring flowing from the rock that left a pool of clear water before racing away and disappearing underground. Canteens and water barrels were filled before mules were unhitched and all the animals were led to drink. It was time consuming, but the riders and muleskinners worked in shifts, and everyone got bacon sandwiches from the leftover breakfast meat and ginger cookies Rudy had stashed away before departure.

The country was getting rougher now, rockier and hillier away from the trail. Sierra sat on a stone beside Jack as they ate, Thor sitting with his head propped on Jack's knee, begging for half of his master's lunch.

"We were going to higher ground as we moved west," Sierra said.

"Yeah, we are on a plateau that extends for miles in all directions. Castle Gap is kind of a passageway where the plateau splits and opens for a mile or more to let us down to the Pecos and Horsehead Crossing. The gap runs four hundred or more feet below the top of the walls above it. The south wall is called King Mountain and the north wall is called Castle Mountain. Of course, they don't have peaks and height like usual mountains, but you will see the that the two sides have different characteristics."

"I feel like I'm on a vacation excursion, but I know I am not."

His face did not change its expression. "Nope, you are not."

Jordy rode up and dismounted. She had restrained herself from asking about his whereabouts. He led his mount toward them. He appeared calm enough but businesslike. Jack said nothing, just nodded at him.

"I did like you suggested," Jordy said. "I rode back and made a half circle around our back trail. Nobody following us, but I went to the top of a knoll and saw a cloud of dust—had to be riders—to the northwest. It didn't look like they were coming our direction, but we are on sort of a parallel course."

Jack said, "Could mean nothing."

"Or it could mean something."

"Yep. Rudy's got a sandwich or two saved back for you, and some cookies."

Sierra got up and stepped toward Jordy and grabbed the reins of his horse. "Let me water Buster while you get something to eat."

"Thanks. I'll take you up on that." He surrendered the reins and headed for the chuckwagon.

Buster was a large buckskin stallion, and Sierra had been admiring the magnificent animal since their first encounter. She rubbed the horse's neck and shoulders. "Oh, so muscled and strong. You are meant to be a stud."

"Already picking his mares, aren't you?" Jack said.

She turned to Jack. "Do you think there is any chance Jordy would sell him?"

"Nope. Might rent him. Service would have to be at the Lucky Five, though. Jordy won't let the horse out of his sight."

"How old is he?"

"Five-year-old, as I recollect."

"I'll think on this." She led Buster away to the pool near the spring. The stallion would be a perfect stud for Dancer, she thought. Her roan mare would turn three soon, and it was time for breeding. If Sierra could get

Dancer bred within the next month or two, the mare could foal late spring or early summer. When she recovered the herd, she would approach Jordy about mating their horses. She had some other mares that had been unbred at the time they were run off, but one of the herd stallions may have since done his duty.

When she led the buckskin back to where she had left Jack, she found that Jordy had returned with a sandwich and cookies wrapped in his kerchief and that both men were now standing and appeared to be engaged in serious discussion. She heard Jack say, "I don't like the coincidence," when she walked up.

"I'll hold your horse while you finish eating," she told Jordy.

He nodded appreciatively while he took a big bite of the sandwich.

Jack said, "I'm going to ride with Tige a spell. I'll talk to you two later."

When Jack walked away with Thor at his heels, Sierra saw that he was walking stiffly with something of a tilt. "Grandpa Jack looks like he's hurting," she remarked.

"Yeah, his back gives him trouble these days. He does okay when he can nurse it along. Too much time in the saddle really hurts him. A wagon seat isn't that much better, but you won't hear him complain about it." He grinned. "Rudy does enough of that for both of them."

Sierra did not smile. Second thoughts about the mission had already been gnawing at her. When she had gone to the Lucky Five for help, it had been with a sense of entitlement. That had dissipated as she came to know her grandfather. The reality of the danger that lay ahead had come home to roost, and she was beginning to wonder if this was a fool's errand. Good people might die during a perhaps futile attempt to recover her horse herd.

Chapter 22

JORDY TOOK JACK'S place at the head of the party and was pleased when Sierra nudged her mare up beside him. He had encountered only a few opportunities to speak with her since leaving the ranch. He was forced to admit, however, that he enjoyed her company and found her fascinating once he got past his initial hostility toward the quest that he felt she had coerced Jack into with the guilt card. Truth was, though, Jack likely would have done the same for a stranger who came to the Lucky Five for help. Jack had a simple philosophy he had declared over the years, "Don't hurt other folks and don't take what's theirs." Those who broke that rule were inviting John Thomas Wills to spoil their party.

Sierra edged her mare to within talking distance from Jordy and his buckskin. They were still on something of an uphill climb, which slowed the mule teams with the heavy wagons behind them. Sierra half hollered to be

{151}

heard above the clattering mule and horse hooves and the rattling of wagons. "Jordy. I'm embarrassed to say this, but I have been having second thoughts about this venture. What do you think Jack would say if I told him I want to call this off?"

Jordy could not believe what he was hearing, and it miffed him more than a little. "He would say, 'Fine. I'll have a few of the men take you back to the Lucky Five. You can wait there till we bring those horses back.' That's what he would say, or something near to it."

"I just don't think this is worth men dying for."

Jordy said, "This isn't about you anymore. Jack doesn't tolerate murderers and thieves. You just gave him an excuse to have one last go at the bad guys. Maybe you held out the carrot, but I think Jack and Rudy have been itching for this chance. They just didn't know it. Anyway, it is too late to call off the dogs. I guarantee it."

He could tell from the grim look on Sierra's face that he had not given the answer she was looking for. He continued, "Sierra, whatever happens, it's not your fault. These are all grown men here. Most have been in one kind of combat or another before. They have no illusions about the risks. But they're glad to follow Jack to hell and back to finish this job. That goes for me, too."

She pulled the horse away, and they rode in silence for the next several hours.

Chapter 23

JACK SAT ON the wagon seat next to Tige with Thor wedged onto the flat wagon entry step behind the seat, so Jack's hand could dangle over the low seat-back and give due attention to scratching the big dog's ears. The wagon followed Jordy and Sierra, who were well ahead, engaged in serious conversation it appeared. Jordy still seemed wary of the new granddaughter, but he had softened considerably since her first appearance. The young man sure kept his eyes on the young woman's butt when she walked by and apparently approved of what he saw.

His eyes continuing to roam the surrounding land-scape, he spoke to Tige. "I think we will have to take both wagons into Lookout Canyon. Not the chuckwagon, though. After we get through Castle Gap, I'm going to send Mitch Eagle Eyes out to scout the canyon from the rim, see if he can locate the horses and get a rough count on the Comancheros. The horses are likely being held in one of the dead-end branch canyons. The canyon is likely two or three miles long, and the west outlet isn't wide enough for a wagon to pass through. I want to send Irish, Mitch and Possum in to help Sierra identify and separate out and hold her horses, although we will take any other critters that choose to come along."

"You are letting your granddaughter go in?"

"No choice. First, I couldn't stop her. Second, those Comancheros would like nothing better than to get hold of that young woman. She should be with some of the men." He shuddered at the thought that Sierra might be taken by these animals.

"There will likely be guards at the outlet. Not many, maybe, but a few to give warning of any attack from that end," Tige pointed out.

"They will have to be taken out," Jack said.

"I will send Roper along," Tige said. "I will tell him to protect Sierra. He would die before he would give her up, and he is worth three warriors in a fight. I am worried, though. All our weapons will be under the false floor in this wagon if they disarm us at the entry."

"If they do, when the wagons stop, we will bail out and take cover under your wagon," Jack said.

Tige said, "I'll need to stick with this wagon and keep Abel close by. Swede's muscle might come in handy."

"Rudy and I will stay with the other wagon. Jordy, too. I thought we would leave the chuckwagon and extra mules and unneeded horses a mile or so back with Bram and Nick Iverson there to give us cover if we're on the run. Bram can shoot with anybody, but his targets have always been deer or other creatures for a meal."

"When the slaves were freed, Nick made his way north and joined up with a colored company during the war and then served as my corporal when we fought Kiowa and Comanches. He will keep Bram steady and know what to do if unexpected trouble comes. He won't like being told he might miss the real action. But he's still soldier in his heart. More than I am."

Jack was silent for several miles as the wagon bounced down the trail. He took off his hat and wiped his shirt-sleeve across his sweaty brow. Was it the burning sun that had unleashed its fury this afternoon? Or raw fear? He placed the low-crowned hat back on this head, tugged it low on his forehead, and reached back to stroke Thor. The dog licked his hand as if he understood his human friend's worries.

"We don't have near enough men, do we?" Jack said.

"By Army regulation standards, no. Of course, some officers didn't worry so much about that when they sent buffalo soldiers out, but we fooled them more than once and came back to the post alive."

"Tige, something I never mentioned to Jordy. If I come out of this slung over the back of a horse, wrap me up in my blankets, hold your noses and get me back to the Lucky Five for planting."

"Boss, you're giving me the shivers talking like that. I ain't heard you go on like this ever," Tige said.

"One of my moods, I guess. I've got to get back alive. I'm going to ask a special lady to marry me."

"You are? It's got to be Miss Tess."

"Yep."

Chapter 24

SOMEONE HAD BEEN watching from outside the camp the past two nights, and the presence had caused Jack fitful sleeps. Thor's low growling had awakened Jack shortly after midnight both nights, and he and the dog had walked the camp and checked with the remuda guards, who assured him they had neither seen nor heard anything that triggered alarm. That had not been comforting because he considered Thor's judgment regarding such matters far superior to that of any human.

The only trees on the gravelly landscape were small and spindly. A few rock formations might offer cover, but the ground was mostly bare. It would not be difficult for Thor to smell out the observer. Still, he was reluctant to order the old dog to ferret out the source of concern, for it might place his furry friend in danger, and chances of catching the invisible intruder were slim. After an hour or so, Thor had calmed both nights, signaling that the watcher had gone. It had to be an Indian, Jack decided, to slip in and out so quietly. And, if there had been more than one readying an attack, Thor would have raised a bigger fuss.

With a steaming tin cup of coffee in his hand to wash down morning biscuits and greasy gravy that did not settle so well on a fragile stomach these days, Jack walked a wide circle around the camp with Thor at his side. A female voice came from behind him. "Did you lose something?"

He turned and saw Sierra hurrying his way. He had two tagalongs these days. Not that he minded. It was a good feeling. The young woman had quickly moved from being just the granddaughter of his blood to taking up residence as the granddaughter of his heart. From his relationship with Jordy, he had learned that the latter was more important than the former. Jordy was the son he had been fortunate enough to know and love.

"Looking for tracks," Jack said as Sierra caught up with him.

"What kind of tracks?" she asked.

"Likely Indian. Thor has been hearing or sensing somebody out here the past two nights. We've been up to check but didn't turn up anything."

"I didn't hear you get up and I've been bedding down within five feet of you two every night."

"You are what we call a dead sleeper. Good thing to be unless you are on guard duty."

Thor growled and trotted toward a creosote bush less than twenty feet away.

Jack said, "Thor's found something for us." The dog reached the bush, sniffed, lifted his hind leg and pissed. He looked back at Jack and waited.

"It might have been nature's call," Jack said, as he and Sierra joined the black dog.

"No," Sierra said, "I see prints in the sand. Very faint."

Jack was not picking up the sign, so he let himself down on his knees for a closer look, mentally cussing his failing eyesight. "Damned if there aren't. Moccasins. Devil got in plenty close. This bush isn't much for hiding, but some Comanches and Apaches can hide ten feet away on bare ground in full sun."

"Grandpa, I won't swallow that."

"Twenty feet maybe. I'm getting as bad as Rudy. I wonder if lying is contagious?"

"So what was he doing here?" Sierra asked.

"Scouting us out. But why? Looking to steal some horses? Worse? That's what I'd like to know. And who? What tribe?"

He clambered back to his feet with a grunt when a stab of pain struck his lower back.

"Are you okay, Grandpa?"

"Just need to walk out a few kinks." He headed back to the wagons where the mule teams were being hitched.

Sierra said, "Jordy's been saddling our horses."

"Yep. I do appreciate that today. He can be a handy feller to have around. Can be a pain sometimes, too, when he treats me like an old man. I let him know when he oversteps, but he just chuckles. The worst thing about getting old is when folks treat you like it."

"You aren't old, Grandpa. You're just catching your second wind."

He reached over and placed his arm about her shoulders and gave her a gentle squeeze. "I knew there was something I liked about you, young lady."

When the wagons were ready to roll out, Jack ordered the drivers to hold up a bit. He had his eyes on the swirl of dust moving their direction from up the trail. He figured it was Mitch Eagle Eyes, but he was riding fast in contrast to the usual easy trot of his mount's pace.

Jack mounted Pokey and nudged the gelding up next to Tige and Jordy, who were astride their horses and engaged in conversation next to the front wagon. "Mitch isn't sparing the horse much this morning," he said to the two men.

"No, Jack," Tige said, "a man rides like that, he's either carrying good news or bad news. Ain't likely the good kind."

Jack sighed. "Not likely."

The three men waited pensively until they saw the outline of an ant-sized horse and rider emerge from the dust and grow as their forms drew nearer to the wagons. Shortly, Eagle Eyes reined up in front of them. Jack waited for the scout to speak.

"Don't like what I'm seeing, Boss."

"And what are you seeing, Mitch?"

"Apaches. One anyhow. But he ain't likely a loner. About missed him. He was laying face-down in the grass fifty feet off the trail. He looked dead, but if I'd veered off to check him out, I'd be the dead man. I turned my horse around and beelined it back here."

Jack said, "Probably the same one that's been checking on us the past few nights. How far to Castle Gap? Can't be long."

"I didn't get that far, but in the distance, I saw the rises you call mountains. We're less than three hours away I'd guess."

"If they want to take us down," Jack said, "that's where it will be. The devil himself designed that place for ambush. We need to talk about this."

Chapter 25

JACK COULD SEE no sign of Apaches as they approached the so-called mountains that rose above Castle Gap, a stark split in the plateau on which they journeyed that led them to the Pecos River. The uprisings of earth along each side of the gap seemed more like giant mesas than mountains, he thought, with their flat tops and steep sloping walls.

Regardless, from his visit years back, he knew the walls would be an impressive sight when they took the trail that cut between them. But this was not a scenic vacation to West Texas. If an Apache war party were waiting, their trek to Lookout Canyon could be in jeopardy. Much of the threat would depend upon numbers. Rudy had suggested any war or hunting party this far east in their ranging territory would likely not consist of more than a dozen to fifteen warriors. Jack tended to agree.

Tige and his three buffalo soldiers had split off soon after Eagle Eyes reported in, two headed for Castle Mountain on the north side of the gap and two riding south toward King Mountain. Swede and Possum were driving the Studebakers now, and Bram was handling the chuckwagon. Rudy sat beside Bram on the seat, a Sharps rifle cradled in his arms and his double-barreled shotgun with Thor on the deck behind him.

Irish brought up the procession's rear with the string of spare mules. Mitch Eagle Eyes and Jordy rode some distance ahead of the mules with Jack and Sierra lagging back beside Swede and the front wagon.

Jack looked over at Sierra who appeared surprisingly calm as they approached the entrance to the gap. "You said you can handle that Winchester. Have you ever killed a man?"

She looked at him with her hazel eyes appearing almost grass-green in the sun's glare. "No, and I'm not wanting to, but I can do it if I have to. You can count on my gun."

"I will. I'm hoping any Apaches are looking for easier prey, but they might be lured by the mules and horses. A passel of mules would feed a band for quite a spell."

"They would eat the mules?"

Jack said, "The mules would be a delicacy to them, and the critters are food they could herd back to their village, which is likely along the border between New Mexico Territory and Mexico. Makes sense. They would not have pack animals to haul that many deer or buffalo carcasses, let alone preserve them for that amount of time. They need food on the hoof, cattle or mules. Hunting parties are changing their targets these days. If they saw our trade goods, they might like to take a wagon with them, but that would slow them down a lot and leave a distinctive trail."

Sierra said, "I am just hoping they had second thoughts."

Jack nodded ahead to the opening of the gap. "We'll know soon enough. Keep your eyes open and let me know if you see anything. Remember, we're not going to try to outrun the Apaches. The drivers will pull up the wagons at first sight. When the fighting starts, we will drop off our horses and take cover under the wagon. I'm guessing they will hit us about halfway through the gap, if they strike. They will want all our animals in the trap and then they will plug the ends if they've got enough warriors."

They headed into the gap and Jack looked up at the bluffs towering over them. The rim of the south wall was lined with limestone, but cedars cloaked much of the lower slope below the rim, offering cover for any would-be ambushers. The north slope was mostly stone and shale-covered, broken up with clusters of huge boulders and intermittent stands of sagebrush, yucca, and mesquite, also providing ample hiding places for ambushers who were near invisible anyway.

The sides of the trail were strewn with cattle and horse bones and skulls, as were the lower slopes. He had heard of thirsty cow herds dying in the canyon just before reaching the Pecos waters, sometimes swallowed up by stampeding herd companions. Charlie Goodnight had told him once of a drive by himself and his partner, Oliver Loving, of some two thousand steers and cows to Fort Sumner in New Mexico Territory some ten years back. It would have been on much of the trail Jack's party had taken, and there would not have been nearly enough water for one-tenth of a herd that size. They had lost almost a third of their herd during such a stampede. But Charlie had made many drives through the gap since.

They were deep into the gap, the wagons rolling at a snail's pace when the roar of a rifle shot echoed through the stone walls above them. Rudy's Sharps. Jack wheeled his mount and looked back toward the chuckwagon, which was nearly twenty-five yards behind. Rudy was standing in front of the wagon seat, pointing toward the boulder-strewn north slope. Jack's eyes ranged the slope, and he spotted Rudy's near-naked target, sprawled with head downslope.

Suddenly, other heads emerged from the rocks and brush, and the Apaches, most bearing rifles, but several with bows and quivers full of arrows, raised up and began to fire. A mule screamed, and one of the critters in the front team stumbled forward and went down, dragging its teammate to its knees. The wagon, which had been slowing, jerked to a full stop, and the mules brayed and struggled in panic. "Take cover," Jack yelled, getting off a few wild shots with his Peacemaker.

He was relieved to see Sierra had dismounted and was dodging under the wagon with her rifle. Her strawberry roan mare had raced away, but that was the least of their worries. He dismounted, slipped his Henry rifle from its scabbard and slapped Pokey on the rump and joined Sierra. Soon Eagle Eyes slipped in beside him. "Jordy's buckskin went down, and Jordy slipped off. He's okay but rolled to the other side of the trail and took cover behind a pile of rocks. Told me to git. Horse got back on his feet and limped off."

He heard the Sharps roar again, so he knew that Rudy was okay. He probably took an Apache down, too. He was a crack shot, and Jack only reluctantly accepted Rudy's periodic challenge to a shooting match, knowing that even if his former keen sight suddenly bounced back, he would be destined for defeat and a month of ribbing. A crack of a rifle from the next wagon back told him that Possum was unharmed.

They were receiving a rain of gunfire and arrows now. Sierra, stretched out on the ground, was firing steadily, and Jack thought it was her slug that dropped another Apache charging down the slope.

Eagle Eyes said, "All their warriors are along the north wall. There were seventeen or eighteen, but not now."

"We can't get a decent angle from under the wagons until they get in closer," Jack said, "and then we chance the devils overrunning us."

Eagle Eyes said, "I can slip out the other side and see what I can do from behind the wagon, maybe get back to Possum and back him up."

Another mule scream told Jack a second animal had gone down. It sounded like the cry came from one of the wagons behind them. "No. You stay here. I can see Swede's feet. He's positioned near the driver's seat. You stay with Sierra. I'm worried about Irish and the string. I'm going to work my way back. I'm counting on Tige to show up with his buffalo soldiers sooner than later."

He wriggled his way out from under the wagon's south side and clambered to his feet. Swede was looking at him with sad eyes.

"What is it, Swede?"

"Number two mule, Boss. I think I shoot her. Okay? Mate dead from Apache shot. Her leg break when mate pull her down."

Jack looked at the front of the teams and saw the struggling mule. "Yes, take her out of her misery, Swede. Then, stay put and see if you can make the Apaches pay for it."

"Ja, Boss. Will do that."

He could see that Jordy was pinned down off the trail but had fair cover with the rocks. Jack wheeled when he heard Thor barking furiously from the direction of the chuckwagon. Recklessly, he headed for the chuckwagon, running past the second Studebaker where he saw another downed mule holding the others and the Studebaker in place. A wound in the animal's head suggested Possum had been forced to put the critter down. He noted Possum was ensconced under the wagon, and giving token gunfire, since the Apaches had all but disappeared behind boulders for the moment, likely readying for a rush.

Thor's barking had turned to fierce growling now, and angry screaming signaled he was in a struggle with a human adversary. Jack found himself huffing and struggling to catch his breath as he approached the chuckwagon. The racket was coming from inside the wagon. A wave of nausea swept through his gut when he saw Rudy crumpled on the ground near a front wagon wheel, hatless and blood streaming not far from his old scalping mutilation.

Bram's feet were sticking out the front wagon opening and kicking wildly as the commotion continued from within. Thor yelped, but his growling turned fiercer. Jack set his Henry down, reached for the Peacemaker and climbed upon the wagon seat. When he peered into the dusky wagon, he found Bram on the wagon floor, struggling to get upright and Thor at the other end engaged in combat with an Apache who was frantically trying to drive his knife into an enemy that had its jaws locked on the wrist of his weapon hand. Thor was blood smeared, but Jack was uncertain of the source.

Jack climbed over the wagon seat and into the bed, trying to get a bead on the Apache but his aim was thwarted by Thor's wrestling with the warrior. A quick glance at Bram told him that his need for assistance was not urgent, and he stumbled to the back of the wagon to enter the melee. As he crawled next to Thor and the Apache, the Indian noticed him and raised his head. The barrel of the Peacemaker came down like an axe and hammered the warrior's head. He still clutched the knife, so Jack launched the butt of the pistol for good measure. Thor released his hold on the wrist, the hand opened, and the knife fell onto the floor of the wagon bed.

Jack turned back to Bram whose shirt was blood soaked. "You take a bullet?" he asked.

"No," Bram said, "knife cut. Not deep. Thanks to Thor. This Injun come from nowhere, took Rudy and was on me before I could get my rifle to my shoulder. I fell back in the wagon, and Thor was on him like a mountain cat on a deer. Ain't never heard such a racket, but that hound saved my scalp. Just help me get upright and then check on Rudy. I'm afeared the Injun done kilt him."

Not Rudy. The ornery cuss was more than a brother. He helped Bram get his feet unhooked from the back of the wagon seat and leaned him up against the wagon's sideboards. Another look at Thor found the dog panting with his tongue sticking out but propped up on his front legs, eyes alert. "Good dog," he said, "brave dog."

He went back through the wagon opening, only then becoming aware of the rapid and consistent gunfire cracking through the canyon. He looked toward the north wall and saw that the Apaches were on the run. They were taking fire from above, where Tige and Roper were pouring lead. Caught in a crossfire, the half dozen ambushers who survived were racing west along the mountain's edge toward the gap's exit, where Jack assumed a warrior or two waited with horses. They would likely circle back tonight to find their dead and wounded.

Jack eased down off the wagon seat to the ground where Rudy was crumpled up facedown. He rolled his friend over, checking first to see if he was breathing. He was. The only wound he could find was a deep gash within a lump on the left side of Rudy's head, where the blood had clotted some but started to flow again after Jack moved him. He caught sight of a stone-headed war club on the ground nearby. That must have been the weapon, and somehow the warrior had dropped it before he pulled his knife or perhaps Rudy grabbed it while he was falling from the wagon seat.

"Rudy, it's Jack," he said. "Wake up." He twisted Rudy's ear, and his eyes popped open.

"What the hell you doing, Jack, messing with my ear? Oh, shit. I got a headache that's tearing my head off."

Chapter 26

JACK DID NOT like the idea but resigned himself to spending the night in the middle of Castle Gap with the thought they would make Horsehead Crossing by noon and be across the Pecos on the west bank early afternoon. Three wounded Apaches, including the warrior who had clubbed Rudy and taken on Thor in the chuckwagon, sat glowering in a cluster on the slope. Five Apache corpses were stretched out nearby. Jack suspected all would disappear during the night. They would pos guards in the event the survivors had notions beyond r trieval of their dead and wounded, which he consider unlikely.

Jack had been surprised when Sierra assumed c mand of medical treatment, telling Jordy that she nr his help. She even carried a box with heavy suture a needles in her possible bag, which she had broug her for mending horse injuries. She was examining Rudy, Bram, and Thor near the chuckwagon, advising Jack she would look at the Apache wounded when they were finished with their own. Nobody else among their party had incurred a scratch.

Bram's wound had been a knife slash across his ribs that yielded a river of blood but touched no vital organs.

Jack watched as Sierra efficiently stitched the wound after pouring some whiskey from one of Rudy's hidden bottles over the open cut. She instructed Jordy to rip a clean sheet she had found in the wagon into strips and to wrap Bram's waist.

She moved to Thor, lying on the ground next to Rudy.

"The dog comes before me?" Rudy complained. Jack thought Rudy might be half joshing Sierra.

"Thor whipped his opponent," Sierra replied. "Besides, he shouldn't take as long."

Jack knelt beside the dog and stroked his head. "She'll fix you up as good as new, old boy. Or get you back in business, anyhow. I think we're both beyond made new."

Sierra found a cut on the dog's shoulder and shaved around the area with the razor she had commandeered from Jordy and quickly took four stitches. She added two more to a slice on one ear. The dog did not even whimper while Jack held him still for the surgeon.

"The cuts on his muzzle and below the eye will heal on their own. He'll have scars to go with all the others on his face." Sierra said.

"A story for each one," Jack said.

"Now, Uncle Rudy, your turn," she said.

"Uncle Rudy?" He was silent for a moment as if pondering. "I like that, young lady. Yeah, Uncle Rudy will do just fine. Makes me feel like family."

"You are family," she said.

Rudy beamed until she started probing his wound. Then he moaned.

She got out her suture and needle. "I haven't even started yet, Uncle Rudy."

Rudy's eyes widened when he saw the needle. "My God, girl. That's big as a damned Bowie knife. You ain't fixing to sew up my scalp with that?"

"It's the only sized needle I've got. It is for horses."

"We'll let it be. Ain't like the top of my head is a thing of beauty. The scar will fit in with the decorations that Comanche put there."

Sierra said, "It won't take more than four stitches. I promise. It will take forever to heal if I don't stitch it. Do you want screwworms to get in there? They might eat right into your brain."

"No chance," Jack said. "That's all rock fill in his head."

"Screwworms?" Rudy asked. "I thought that was a cow and horse thing."

"Flies lay the worm eggs. They'll go for anything," Sierra said.

"I wear my hat most all the time."

"I am surprised at you, Uncle Rudy. Papa would have said that you're all gurgle and no guts."

"Well, now that ain't true. I was just trying to save you some bother."

"No bother. Jordy, I need the whiskey bottle and one of your rags."

Rudy sighed and closed his eyes. "Ouch, oh," he groaned as she gently cleaned his scalp with the whiskey.

"Worse than I thought," she said. "It might take an extra stitch or two, but you'll be running blood if we don't deal with it."

Rudy scowled. "Do what you got to. You're bound and determined to stick that knife in my head. I'm guessing that 'Uncle Rudy' business was just sweet talk to get your way with me."

"No. Like it or not, you are my Uncle Rudy from here on."

She stuck the needle into the swollen flesh, and Rudy howled like a wounded wolf, catching the attention of everyone in the vicinity of the wagons. Thor headed under the wagon, and Bram got slowly to his feet. "Got to find a place to water the grass," he said, disappearing behind the wagon.

Jack had more sympathy for Rudy than he showed. That was one darn big needle, and he was glad that thing wasn't poking into his scalp. It was not a Bowie, but it wasn't a dress-making needle either. He decided he did not want to watch any more of the surgery. Hearing it would be a big plenty.

Most of the other men were engaged in unharnessing and dragging the dead mules off the road. He was glad Tige had insisted on plenty of spares, but they were down to a single extra mule now. He could not take the deaths of the critters casually, and it saddened him to leave the dead animals to the buzzards and coyotes. In a few days, they would be reduced to skulls and bones to litter the Castle Gap along with those of seemingly hundreds of horse, mule, and cattle remains that rested there. Jack figured it would be easy enough to locate human bones and skulls if a man were inclined to look. He was not.

Strange how little he worried about his own death as he got nearer to the end of the last chapter of his life. But as he grew older, he seemed to be bothered more by the deaths of others, even animals, than he had as a younger man. The dead Apaches on the hill engendered a certain remorse regardless of the fact they had died trying to kill him and his friends.

He encountered Roper Hawley lugging harnesses back to the storage pile. He waved the ex-soldier over. "Hi, Roper, you and Tige showed up just in time today. You did yourselves proud. The Apaches weren't expecting an attack from upslope."

"It was a good plan, Boss, circling around behind both sides of the mesa and coming in behind. Abel and Nick felt left out, though, with all the Apaches on the north."

"We didn't know where they would be, and we had to cover both sides."

"Anyway, I'm glad you come up with the idea."

"I didn't," Jack said. "It was Tige's plan. He's too quick to give credit to somebody else."

The tall man grinned and nodded, "That's Tige, all right. Don't care who gets the credit. That's why men follow him. I might not live to see it, but someday colored men like Tige Marshall will be generals."

"I have no doubt. There is a colored man by the name of Henry Ossian Flipper who is a cadet at West Point right now and seems to be on track to graduate. I've read about him in newspapers from back east. Maybe he will be that general."

Roper shrugged. "Maybe. Maybe not. The best we can do is grab our chances, Boss, learn all we can and work like hell to get wherever we're trying to go. And I ain't unmindful, Boss—none of us is—that you gave us that chance."

"I just hire the best men for the job, Roper, but thanks. Now I would ask a favor of you."

"Name it, Boss."

"After you drop that harness someplace, I would like for you to pick up your rifle and follow Sierra and Jordy over to the wounded Apaches she's going to tend to. I don't think they've got much fight left in them, but a man never knows. She won't be able to explain what she's trying to do, and that might spook them."

"Glad to do that, Boss. I can sign with Comanches. Should be about the same with Apaches. I'll see if I can help out some."

Chapter 27

HORSEHEAD CROSSING LAY a dozen miles southwest of the exit from Castle Gap. Jordy Jackson, astride a sorrel gelding that had temporarily replaced his injured buckskin stallion, had paused on the high ground beyond the gap and looked at the barren land that stretched out below him. He turned his head when he heard the rattle of hooves on loose rock behind him. It was Sierra.

"Have you got the trail sighted?" she asked, nudging the roan mare up beside him.

"Oh, yeah. It's a wide trail, if you even call it a trail. Jack says Goodnight and Loving have been running herds through the crossing for years, and Comanches have used it coming off the war trail for raids in Mexico. It is said the early Spaniard conquistadores crossed here and, of course, wagon trains, stages. Army—about anyone who wants to cross the Pecos in these parts. There are only a few decent crossings in West Texas, not so much because of the river but the high, steep banks."

"Is the river deep? We can swim it with the horses, but I wonder about the wagons," Sierra said.

"Jack crossed at Horsehead some years back, and he has talked to other ranchers that have used it. He doesn't seem worried about the crossing. Of course, you can't usually tell what's going on in Jack's head. But if he sees a problem ahead, I guarantee he's got a plan for it. He just won't tell us till he is ready."

"I've never seen the Pecos," Sierra said. "I have seen Texas maps, and it comes down out of New Mexico Territory like a big old wriggling snake and heads southeast till it connects up with the Rio Grande."

"I haven't seen it either. We've been driving our cattle north and east. But Jack says it twists and turns so much, you can get confused about what side of the river you are on."

"Well," Sierra said, "I guess we'll find out soon enough." She nodded toward the wagons and riders. "They're moving out. Do you suppose we ought to join them?"

No, Jordy thought, *I would rather spend the day just talking to you.* He didn't care it was small talk. He was starting to keep an eye open to opportunities to be near this enchanting young woman, who was turning out to be nothing like the spoiled brat he had initially pegged her. Sierra was not only pleasant to the eye, but she had some smarts upstairs. "I suppose we should fall in," he said. "Maybe you would take another look at Buster before we get too far down the trail."

"He should be fine, but I'd be glad to."

The buckskin stallion had taken an arrow at his shoulder point, and Jordy had learned that Sierra's presence had provided the party with the equivalent of a veterinary surgeon for their critters, not to mention her rudimentary skills with human patients. When the horse limped in with Sierra's Dancer and Pokey early evening yesterday, Sierra had offered to examine the stallion.

She had quickly excised the arrow point while Jordy controlled the horse and sutured the shallow wound that she had widened slightly with a scalpel in order to remove the barbed arrowhead. She had partially closed the wound leaving a small outlet for drainage.

When they caught up to Irish, whose string had been reduced to a single mule, two spare horses, and Buster, they untied the buckskin and led him off the trail. They dismounted and Sierra examined the wound while Jordy held the reins of their mounts in one hand and steadied Buster with the other.

"He's doing fine," she pronounced. "Give him three days' rest and he will be ready to ride."

"You are quite amazing, you know. I mean, your surgical skills. And you had the scalpel like you were prepared for all of this."

She smiled, and he suspected lighter skin would have produced a blush. She took her mare's reins, and their fingers brushed. Was he imagining that her fingers lingered a moment?

"Papa taught me about caring for the animals. As you know, out on this vast prairie there is no one to call upon to help with ailing or injured critters. Folks have got to learn to do for themselves. I have several forceps, pliers, and the like in my kit."

"Jack does most of the vet work at the Lucky Five, but Irish is handy that way. He's doing most of the castrations and routine stuff these days. Birthing, we still call in Jack, but somebody helps with the heavy pulling. I can do some of that when we're pressed, but I don't have the gift. I can't wait for you to meet Tess Wyman," Jordy said.

"Tess? That's Grandpa Jack's lady friend?"

"Yes. She's half-blood Comanche and kind of a medicine woman. Comanches and a fair number of whites come to see her for her herbal and plant remedies, and

she does certain treatments and repairs short of surger-
ies. You will hit it off. I know you will."

"And maybe I can learn from her."

"I know she would love to have a pupil."

Chapter 28

HORSEHEAD CROSSING WAS a spooky place, Sierra thought. Ruins of an old way station and outbuildings lay around a bend in the river. Horse skulls were mounted on the rotting posts that were scattered about the abandoned site. Along the riverbanks on both sides of the river were still more skulls and bones, both equine and bovine. She figured hundreds of animals had contributed, and that would not include those that had been carried off by scavengers.

The land along the slow-flowing, muddy water, which she thought looked more like moat than river, was desolate and near naked save for the usual creosote bushes, yucca, mesquite, and assorted cacti. She understood now why traffic funneled to Horsehead Crossing. Here the banks sloped gently toward the winding river, and wagons and travelers of all varieties could enter and exit the waters on each side without great effort if they could ford the waters.

Sierra stood by her grandfather, watching Swede take the first Studebaker through the current. The wagon sank nearly to the floor of the bed but moved steadily through the waters and soon the front mule team gained footing on the opposite bank and pulled the big wagon up the incline to the flat above.

Jack commented, "Looks like the big wagons won't be a problem. They're set up on springs and the beds can clear the water. The chuckwagon sits lower, but it's lighter. That's why Tige has his crew over by the old station. They're salvaging lumber to build a raft. Built right, it won't take much of one. We'll have it here for the return trip, if somebody doesn't come along and cut it loose or turn it in to firewood."

Sierra said, "How did you know we could do this?"

"I didn't for sure. No wagons to take across when I was here last, but this place is almost a legend. Charlie Goodnight told me about the wagons. Said they would be fine as long as we didn't hit rainy season, which comes late summer down this way."

The second Studebaker followed the other without incident, and she watched now as Jordy and Mitch Eagle Eyes moved the spare mule and horses across the river.

Jordy knew his horses, she thought, and he rode like he and his mount were melded. He never bragged about his prowess, however. He must have got that from Grandpa Jack. She thought of it as quiet competence. And those searching cocoa-brown eyes spelled danger for a woman in her prime. She vowed to remain on guard. The last thing she needed at this time was involvement with a man.

A short time later, Tige and his crew walked along the riverbank toward the crossing. Abel and Nick held onto ropes attached to a crude raft they were pulling down-river. When they reached the crossing, they dragged the creation through mud to prop it up against the east embankment.

"What do you think, Jack?" Tige said. "Ain't pretty, but she floats."

"I'm watching," Jack said noncommittally.

The raft consisted of two half-rotted beams with planks lashed between them about every two feet. It appeared that only the wagon would sit on the raft. Sierra wondered how they would get it across the channel which was a bit more than one hundred feet wide at this point and far from running full. The distance was not an issue, but Sierra was skeptical about dragging the chuckwagon laden raft through the mud and then keeping it afloat.

The mule team was unhitched from the wagon and anchored by ropes to the raft. Rudy and Bram crossed the river on borrowed horses, and Jack and Sierra followed to await arrival of the chuckwagon on the opposite bank. Sierra noticed that Jordy and Eagle Eyes had joined Tige and his crew in pushing the chuckwagon onto the raft, where it was anchored by multiple ropes to the beams. Irish and Jordy removed boots, shirts, and britches, tossing their clothes in the back of the wagon, and waded into the mud to lead the mules across the river.

"Why is Jordy helping with the mules?" Sierra asked Jack, as they watched from the high bank above the crossing. She could not keep her eyes off Jordy's lean, nearly naked body, scrutinizing the muscled shoulders and torso as he moved about, noticing with a lingering look that Irish, while not a big man, was also a fine specimen of manhood. In West Texas, she decided, especially on the ranches, there were not all that many men gone to fat.

Jack said, "Jordy and Irish are the strongest swimmers. Currents can be tricky. Channel's probably not more than four feet deep, but water's high enough a man can't keep his feet planted on the bottom, at least not for long without getting swept off balance and washed away downstream. And there can be tricky, deep whirlpools in any river." He was looking at her, smiling impishly, and she realized her grandfather was guessing that she had been staring at Jordy.

She tried to deflect his suspicions. "I'm fascinated by how your men go about their business so casually, undaunted by any challenge in front of them."

"Competence, persistence. Those are the kind of men I look for. You will notice that nobody sits on his fanny waiting to be told how to do something. They just figure it out and do it."

The ropes connecting the raft to the mules tightened as Jack and Irish led the mules into the murky water. With the mud sucking at the raft bottom, it resisted, and Tige and his former buffalo soldiers got behind it and pushed while holding fast to the raft with two long ropes that were to stabilize the rear as it made its crossing. When the mud released its hold, the raft leaped forward, and the mules pulled it into the water. They were moving steadily to the other side until the rear of the raft dovetailed, yanking Abel Burke into the water and launching him downriver.

Roper and Tige held fast to the other rope and kept the raft's rear from swinging into the center of the river while Abel frantically tried to hang onto the other rope that was dangling in the water. Tige yelled, "Abel can't swim."

Jordy handed his mule's rope to Irish and started swimming toward Abel, riding the current and propelling his body with strong, steady strokes. Sierra's heart raced when she saw Abel disappear underwater as Jordy approached. Then she saw the rope floating loosely, writhing like a snake in the water. Abel had lost his grip. Jordy plunged beneath the river's service where one of the countless twists in the river's course would send him out of sight, apparently around one of the steep banks.

"Mount up," Jack said. "God knows how far the river's going to take them."

"But Jordy can swim to the bank."

"He can swim with the best, but he won't quit till he finds Abel. And there's nothing stronger than a drowning man caught up in panic."

As they rode away, Sierra tossed a glance over her shoulder and saw that Roper had waded into the water behind the raft and was pulling in Abel's rope. Eagle Eyes was in the water taking over Jordy's abandoned mule, and every man's attention was on getting the raft and cargo across the river. Tige would see that the mission was carried out. That came first.

They skirted two more bends in the river before they found Jordy, still in the water but his arm wrapped about the former soldier's chest, pulling the man to a portion of dry channel just below one of the banks. When he reached dry ground, he dragged Abel from the river, dropped the man on the ground, knelt and began pumping his back, pushing him sharply between the shoulder blades intermittently. Finally, Abel began to cough, and water spewed from his mouth.

Jack and Sierra dismounted and went to the edge of the bank and looked down some seven or eight feet below. "Jordy," Jack called. "Will he be all right?"

"I think so. We need to give him some time. I didn't see you coming. Do you have horses?"

"Yep. Pokey and Dancer."

"Abel won't be walking far. He will need a ride."

Jack said, "Done."

Soon, Jordy had Abel sitting up, leaning against the rock-laced, sand and dirt bank. Abel was a short, wiry man a year or two over twenty-five, Sierra guessed. A neatly trimmed moustache adorned the flesh above his upper lip and Sierra thought him a handsome sort. He was a quiet man who generally kept to himself.

Jordy stood beneath the bank looking up at them, seemingly not conscious that he was all but naked with his soaked undershorts clinging to his body like a second skin and leaving nearly nothing to imagination. Jack went to his mount and reached in the saddlebags and pulled out a rolled-up shirt. He dropped it down to Jordy. "This is an extra. Make yourself decent."

"Sun feels good on my back, Jack. Besides, your shirt would be too small," Jordy protested.

"It's not for your back. Wrap it around your waist. There's a lady present, and she happens to be my grand-daughter. I don't want her exposed to such coarseness."

"Oh. Sure, I can do that." He unrolled the shirt and made an apron out of it, tying the arms about his waist.

It didn't matter to Sierra. The image was indelibly painted in her head, never to be erased. It was not as if she had never seen a man naked before. She could claim neither innocence nor virginity. There had been a man when she was seventeen and attending the academy in San Antonio, a handsome artist named Carlos in his late thirties who claimed to be unmarried and had employed her to be the subject of paintings commissioned by customers. The money was good and the paintings, while risqué, were not obscenely so—except for the single nude. She learned later that all her paintings had likely ended up in saloons in Texas and Mexico. Sierra liked to think they were high class venues but conceded it was not probable. She thought it very unlikely any would ever show up in West Texas, or she certainly hoped not.

She had convinced herself she was truly in love with the artist, though, and likely would have posed for a dozen nudes if he had asked. And he was a good lover, or she supposed so, having no basis for comparison. Certainly he had taught her things that had not resided previously in her fertile imagination and had created an appetite that had been previously dormant. It had all ended when the undisclosed Mexican wife showed up at the studio one afternoon and discovered the lovers naked on the studio cot. Carlos had ended up with a derringer slug in his ass, and Sierra had narrowly dodged a bullet on her way out the door. There was not a day that passed she did not thank her lucky stars she had not ended up with child. What a fool she had been. She had led close to a nun's life since that experience.

"Sierra, did you hear me?"

It was Grandpa Jack. She tended to shut out the world sometimes when she was lost in her thoughts. She was glad he could not read minds. "I'm sorry, Grandpa. What was it you said?"

He looked at her with his head cocked to one side and his eyes squinting. "Your head is someplace it hadn't ought to be. Been there more than once myself. I need you to help me get Abel up here."

"Oh, sure. Just tell me what I should do."

Jack said, "Jordy says he can lift and push Abel up the side of the bank as far as he can. Then Abel will raise his arms, and we will each take a wrist and pull him up."

"He's not a big man. We should be able to do it."

They knelt on the edge of the steep bank and leaned over while Jordy, his muscles rippling, hoisted Abel upward, the ex-soldier helping by digging his feet into rock and dirt bank. Jack and Sierra each grabbed an extended arm and inched backward, as Abel gained leverage and came over the top.

As they caught their breaths, Sierra said, "We can't get Jordy up that way. There is too much of him for us."

Jack said, "You hear that, Jordy? Sierra thinks you are too fat for us to haul you up."

"Yeah, I heard that," Jordy said.

"That's not what I said, and you both know what I mean."

Jordy said, "You get Abel back to the wagons. I can walk back up the channel. A lot of the edges are dry, and I can wade or swim some where it's not. You can probably move more as the bird flies now but allow for me to do the twists and turns. I'll meet you at the crossing."

When they got back to Horsehead Crossing, with Abel astride Pokey behind Jack, Sierra was glad to see that the chuckwagon was on the bank and all the mule teams were hitched and ready to move on. Tige and Roper helped Abel off the horse and half carried him to one of the Studebakers.

Tige said, "I assume Jordy's okay?"

"Yep," Jack said, "he'll be along shortly. He wanted to swim his way back to show off for the young lady."

"You serious?" Tige asked.

Sierra said, "No, he's not serious. He's walking along the channel most of the way. We couldn't get him up the darn bank."

"I like Jack's story better. We'll razz Jordy some about that."

Chapter 29

JORDY HAD SHOWN up at Horsehead Crossing several minutes after the others, and after slipping into his clothes and boots he liked the feel of being on horseback again except for the damp undershorts that the sun had not quite finished drying. It could have been a lot worse than chafing underwear, he figured. Jack was planted on the seat of the front wagon with Thor squeezed between him and Tige, who had taken over the skinning job from Swede. Jordy suspected the two men needed time together to strategize. According to Jack, after two nights on the trail, they should be closing in on Lookout Canyon.

Jordy was riding near the chuckwagon, keeping an eye on the two wounded cooks. Rudy had insisted upon driving the team given that Bram's stitched wound was vulnerable to the abrupt motions required in handling the mules. "I don't yank on reins with my damned head," Rudy had said.

It seemed to Jordy that Rudy had adopted Bram and was looking after the young man like an anxious father. Jordy was glad for that. Despite all his bluster and joshing, Jordy sensed that Rudy was a lonely man, rejected by others over the years for his quirks and blunt ways. That was likely why he had attached to Jack. Outcasts seemed to be drawn to Jack Wills, who was unimpressed by wealth, rank or social status. The village idiot got as much respect from Jack as the Texas governor.

"Wait up, Jordy."

It was Sierra catching up to him astride that pretty, strawberry roan mare. For some reason, he felt she had been avoiding him since the near tragedy at the Pecos. "Hadn't seen you for a spell. Wondered where you went."

"Well, for one thing, I was checking on Buster to make sure the stitches held when he made the swim across the Pecos. He's fine." She reined in beside him, and they rode in silence for several minutes before she spoke again. "Do you suppose we could make arrangements for stud service?"

Jordy chuckled and grinned. "What did you have in mind?"

"Well, I . . . what are you laughing about? Oh, no. That didn't come out right. You are disgusting. You know what I mean. This is awful."

He could see Sierra was embarrassed and flustered, and he could not help but enjoy her discomfiture. Still, he moved quickly to put her at ease. "I do know what you mean. You are talking about Buster and Dancer, I assume."

She eyed him with what he thought was feigned contempt. "You assume correctly. Buster is a fine stallion, and Dancer should be bred soon for her first foal. When we recover the herd, I have several other mares I would like to breed to Buster. Two are buckskins, so the mating should produce buckskin foals. They bring a premium."

"You would need to ask Buster, but I don't think he would object."

"You are starting to annoy me. I am wanting to negotiate fees."

"No charge. But he can't leave the Lucky Five. You would have to leave the mares or stay around until they are with foal."

"I insist on paying a stud fee, but I guess we can work that and other details out later."

"I should think so. We do have a few tasks ahead of us."

"Sorry. Papa was always chiding me for planning too far ahead. He told me I should quit getting the cart before the horse, but it is hard for me to do."

"I don't mind. I find it charming—and funny. I don't enjoy totally predictable friends, and you certainly aren't that."

"I guess I will take that as a compliment of sorts," Sierra said.

"Then, am I back in your good graces?"

"You were never out. I was just a little embarrassed."

"Don't be. Let's move ahead. I see Mitch heading this way, and he's kicking up dust. That's usually not a good sign."

They reached the front wagon shortly before Mitch Eagle Eyes arrived. Eagle Eyes reined his mount in next to Jack's perch on the wagon seat.

Jack said, "Tell me you're bringing good news, Mitch."

"Remains to be seen, Boss. Comanches ahead of us. They've set up camp along the Pecos, about where I figured we'd pull in tonight, not more than two hours away."

"We're not supposed to be at war with the Comanches right now. Most are headed for Fort Sill and the reservation," Jack said. "Quanah and his Kwahadi band were the last holdouts. Supposed to be, anyhow, but there are likely several splinter bands out there. Did you get a count?"

"No more than a dozen."

"Any sign they were setting up for an ambush?"

"No. I didn't get in too close. When I saw their sign, I staked my horse and followed on foot a spell. When I saw smoke, I found a rock outcropping not too far out and watched from there with my spy glass. Not much to hide behind in this country, and I ain't no Apache that can make hisself invisible behind a yucca plant," Eagle Eyes said. "They had a few guards posted near the remuda, but they didn't look like they had plans to move any time soon."

Jack said, "It doesn't appear they're hiding out from anybody if they've got fires burning."

"I suppose that's true enough," Eagle Eyes said.

Jordy said, "Jack, remember that dust cloud I saw a few days before we got to Castle Gap? We thought it was from riders on the Comanche War Trail. I wonder if it could have been this bunch."

"Makes sense. With no wagons to slow them down, they would have been through the gap long before us or the Apaches. But why? Long way to come for a hunting party?"

Eagle Eyes said, "From what you say about the location, we ain't going to get to Lookout Canyon without meeting up with this bunch."

"No," Jack said, "Mitch, I'd like to have you stay close by, and you and Jordy ride the perimeter while we pick up the pace some. We'll be ready for trouble, but if we can get there before dark, we'll invite those folks for supper." He looked up at Sierra. "I wonder, Sierra, if you would get the word to Rudy. He won't kick up a fuss with you if you give him the news about guests for supper."

"I'll offer to help him and Bram tonight. Maybe I can recruit somebody else, too, given our cooks are crippled up some."

Tige said, "Recruit Nick Iverson. He volunteered for cooking more often than not in our Army days. You can't do much till we see what our welcome is going to be."

When Sierra turned her mare back and headed for the chuckwagon, Jack, with the trademark crooked grin on his face turned to Jordy and said, "I'm keeping my eye on you, boy. Your flirtations with my granddaughter damn well better be honorable."

"What flirtations? She's the one who caught up with me and started talking," Jordy said, half embarrassed that Jack had noticed whatever it was that was going on between him and Sierra. "I haven't known her much more than a week. Besides, Sierra's a grown woman and of age, and I've been past that a spell, I don't see that it's your concern."

Jordy and Jack did not quarrel much, but occasionally they had a good one, and Jordy for some unexplainable reason had bristled at the jest. He was ready to take the ornery old cuss on if pressed.

Jack chuckled. "Methinks Jordy Jackson doth protest too much."

Chapter 30

"I SEE THE smoke, Tige, but no sign of a war party coming our way."

"No war party, Jack, but there's two riders in the distance."

"Damn, I don't see them. I didn't bring my specs, but I only use them for reading anyhow. It's hell getting old, Tige. Some days, I feel like I'm just wearing out piece by piece."

"Ah, come on, Boss. You can still work us all into the ground when you've a mind to. No man I'd rather ride the river with, that's for sure."

"I thank you for your kind words, but my parts are telling me something different. Anyhow, I can make out your riders now. It looks like Mitch has seen them and is coming in. He doesn't speak much Comanche, but he can help some."

Tige said, "I could get Roper up here. He can sign with the best."

"Might do that, but let's wait and see how it goes."

As the riders approached, Tige said, "Boss, the big, bare-chested one looks like an older warrior, but I would swear the one with the war shirt and britches is female."

"Strange, if you're seeing right," Jack said.

Several minutes later, the Comanches reached the wagon, each with a hand upraised in the peace sign. And, indeed, one was a young woman, a pretty one.

Jack was momentarily taken aback when the woman spoke, "Jack Wills?"

"Yes, ma'am. I am Jack Wills."

"I am She Who Speaks, friend of Healer's Daughter, the woman you know as Tess Wyman. This is Growling Bear, the senior warrior with our party and Quanah's emissary."

The young woman's English was flawless, spoken without a hint of accent. Jack knew some of her story, though, from his conversations with Tess. She Who Speaks's first language had been German. The child of Jewish emigrants, she had been taken captive when Comanches killed her parents and quickly added Comanche to her growing list of languages. Comanche elders had recognized the value of someone with her gift and pressed her into interpreting duties. As Quanah, himself only in his mid- to late twenties, rose to power as Kwahadi war chief, she had gained his confidence and become his personal interpreter and a counselor of sorts.

"We are here as friends," Jack said. "I have a treaty with the Kwahadi, and we have been at peace for many years, even while others of our peoples war."

She Who Speaks said, "I know this. And I know of your mission. I have spoken with Healer's Daughter who suggested we might strike a bargain and become allies."

"Now, that sounds interesting. Why don't we set up camp next to yours? My cooks will prepare a supper and you can be our guests. After that we can talk."

She Who Speaks turned to Growling Bear and spoke Comanche to the warrior, who had thus far been silent. He smiled and nodded approvingly and replied to her at some length.

The young woman turned back to Jack. "Growling Bear accepts your invitation and welcomes you to camp with us. And, yes, we shall talk later. He also says that we can roast the doe one of our warriors shot today near the stream that feeds the river."

Jack said, "Lead the way."

Chapter 31

HE KWAHADI WARRIORS at first appeared uneasy when the wagons from the Lucky Five rolled
in, staring at the strangers and keeping some
distance from the newcomers as if an invisible barrier
separated the encampments. Soon, however, Eagle Eyes
and Roper strolled over to the clusters of warriors and
began conversing with Roper's signing and Eagle Eyes's
limited Comanche vocabulary. It was not long before the
Lucky Five party and Comanches were intermingling
freely and finding ways to talk. Several Comanches knew
a smattering of English that helped the dialogue.

Sierra had just finished helping Rudy set up the Dutch
ovens filled with biscuit dollops on hot coals. There was
no doubt that Rudy was in command of the meal, and he
had instructed Nick Iverson to watch the bean pots and
start the bacon frying soon. The deer carcass had been

butchered and chunks of venison roasted on the iron spits that Rudy stocked. Several warriors were turning some of the spits, and Sierra was pleased that meal preparation had turned into a communal project.

"Just keep an eye on the biscuits," Rudy admonished. "Them is dessert and main course. Fill a man with good biscuits and jam, and he overlooks burnt meat or dried-out beans. 'Course I don't know how Injuns are for biscuits, but I'm guessing they won't turn them down."

Sierra stood back to let the ovens work their magic for a spell when she saw the pretty Comanche woman approaching. She guessed that the young lady was about her age or no more than two or three years older. They had not yet met, but Jack had told Sierra a bit about She Who Speaks and her background. While she appeared Comanche, She Who Speaks did not carry a drop of Comanche blood.

Sierra stepped toward She Who Speaks and extended her hand. "I am Sierra. I have been anxious to meet you."

The Comanche woman accepted her hand and offered a warm smile. "I have wanted to meet you, also, but the older gentleman seemed to be keeping you busy."

"Yes. He is stern taskmaster, but he is more bark than bite. He is a good person and would die for my Grandpa Jack or me."

"Your Grandpa Jack is a legend among the Comanche bands and greatly respected, and Tess Wyman—known as Healer's Daughter among The People—loves him very much. She is the reason we are here."

"I don't understand."

"You will come to know Tess and love her. She feared for Jack's life when he left on your journey to recover the horse herd. I was at her house with an injured boy the day previous. She asked if warriors from our village might help and suggested we might incidentally turn a good deed to profit."

"What do you mean?"

"The soldiers have slaughtered most of the Comanche horses. Our lives have been dependent upon the horses, but their destruction was key to starving The People to the reservation. Tess said we could help Jack Wills and run off Comanchero horses to take to the reservation with us. The peace agreement says we can keep whatever horses or other goods we take to the reservation with us. It does not restrict the source of such things."

"How do you know all of this?"

"The agreement was on paper in English, which, of course, The People ordinarily would have been unable to read. Quanah had me read the document and explain it to him."

"You sound like a lawyer of sorts."

"I have hopes that such might happen."

"How long have you been with the Comanches?"

"Over ten years. I was fourteen years old when my parents were killed by Comanches. We were separated from our wagon train, and I was taken as a captive. My father was a physician. We came from Germany to America and lived in New York for several years before my father's wanderlust sent us west. We were Jews, and Yiddish and German were spoken by our family before we came to America, but in New York I learned about my affinity for languages, and I had English books to read, of course, so that helped. I suppose the language skills saved me from a bordello in Mexico or worse. I even acted as an interpreter when the despicable Comancheros came to trade."

"So you speak four languages?"

"Well, I learned to speak a rudimentary Spanish when Mexican captives were taken in by the band, but I cannot read and write the language yet."

Sierra said, "I wish we had the time. I would love to teach you. My mother was Mexican, and I attended school in San Antonio where fluency in both Spanish and English was a graduation requirement. I am not looking to learn more languages, though. I sometimes slip back and forth between two. I don't know how I would balance five."

"And your parents are both gone, too?"

"Yes," Sierra said, "my mother took sick and died some years ago. My father was killed during a Comanche raid over a year ago."

"I'm sorry. You would not feel kindly toward The People, then."

"Wary, I suppose. But they killed both your parents, and yet you seem to think of yourself as Comanche. It is all complicated. Usually, I don't know what to feel."

"I understand. I hope we can talk about it, and that my choices won't get in the way of friendship."

"Oh, no. It is fine between us."

"Sierra," Rudy yelled, "have you checked the biscuits? They burn up, I'll see you get the credit."

"I had forgotten about the biscuits," Sierra said. "Can we talk later?"

"I would love to," She Who Speaks said. "After the meeting. And call me Jacl, if that would be easier. That was my birth name. Jael Chernik."

Chapter 32

AFTER SUPPER, JACK assembled Growling Bear, She Who Speaks, and a warrior called Throws Lance in front of one of the Studebakers with Tige, Jordy, and Sierra. Rudy had been invited but declined, admitting he probably would not hear a damned thing anyhow. Jack suspected his old friend was suffering from the latest assault on his scalp, aggravated by the work of putting together a banquet praised by Comanches and Lucky Fivers alike.

The sun was dropping over the horizon as they sat down on the parched earth in a loose circle. Jack spoke first. "She Who Speaks, I guess you will need to translate for us. I understand that my friend, Tess, told you about what we are up to here, but just so I am clear, I will explain. We plan to recover Sierra's horse herd consisting of more than fifty animals. There is a brand on the right side of every horse's neck or shoulder—with the exception of some of the foals at side. Sierra, while She Who Speaks explains to Growling Bear and Throws Lance, would you draw the brand in the dirt?"

Sierra got on her knees, placed the tip of her finger in the dirt and quickly sketched the image. "A turkey track," she said.

The Comanche warriors nodded their heads, as She Who Speaks told them what had been said.

Jack continued. "All we want is Sierra's horse herd. If you help us, you may take any other horses in the canyon, including those of the Comancheros. If there is anything else of value, you are welcome to take it. But there may be women or children there. They are not to be harmed in any manner. No scalps are to be taken, and we will kill only those who resist." He looked directly at She Who Speaks. "Make it clear that there will be no rapes of any women and that women and children are to be left unharmed."

"I understand, and I agree," She Who Speaks said.

She translated at some length to the two warriors, whose faces remained stoic and revealed nothing of their thoughts. Growling Bear nodded when she was finished, confirming Jack's suspicion that the young interpreter had authority to speak for the Kwahadis without anyone's approval. When she was finished, she turned to Jack. "We have ten warriors. I am proficient with a Winchester. Growling Bear must stay with me. Quanah's order. He will not leave me even if I instruct him to."

"But if we split your warriors, how will we translate?"

"That is why Throws Lance is with us. He speaks enough English that if you speak slowly and are willing to repeat sometimes, he will be able to convey your instructions."

"Very well. We can discuss this over the next few days as we travel, but here is what I have in mind." He went through the plan he had discussed earlier with Tige and then asked, "Do you wish to translate what I have said so far?"

"No, I will tell them about your plan later. What do you have in mind for us? That is what we really want to know," She Who Speaks said.

Jack said, "I mentioned that Sierra and some of our men will enter the canyon's west opening. There are no doubt other horses in the dead-end branches off the main canyon. The west end is too narrow to drive a mass of horses through without injury. Besides, we wouldn't have enough people there to contain and herd the horses once they broke through. All the horses need to be funneled to the east entrance where the rest of our people will be—right through the Comanchero compound. We'll sort and divide the animals once we're clear of Lookout Canyon and the Comancheros—maybe at Castle Gap after we have crossed the Pecos at Horsehead."

She Who Speaks said, "Growling Bear and I will take three other warriors with your crew to the east end. You do not have enough people there. We can help locate and round up horses, but how do we know when to head them out to the canyon's mouth?"

"As soon as you hear gunshots from our end. Try to hold the horses back till then. I know it will take a spell to get them out, but the sooner, the better, after the shooting starts."

"I understand," she said. "Our other warriors are at your disposal until after we have escaped with the horses. Throws Lance will see that the Kwahadi warriors do whatever you ask."

"Well, first thing in the morning I would like to have Throws Lance and Mitch Eagle Eyes ride ahead to scout out the canyon. It's a bit like Castle Gap, but it is much wider, I would guess a half mile wide at the east end, but it narrows sort of like a big funnel to the west. You and Sierra will be entering the downside of the funnel. The walls aren't nearly as tall as the gap, probably no more than 150 feet at the highest point. Steeper, though, with some cracks and crevices that would let a man on foot to work his way down. It's called Lookout Canyon because of two spire-like rock formations on each side of the east entrance, where the canyon narrows, that a man can easily climb and perch and keep watch over the desert for some miles."

"And there is no place for approaching riders to hide on this desert," She Who Speaks said.

Jack said, "Not with wagons. There are some ravines and gullies along the Pecos running north and west about a mile from the canyon's rim where men leading horses can move in close once they are past the lookout points. I would guess the canyon is between two and three miles long, whether you go as the crow flies or add in the twists and turns. It is about like the Pecos that way. Anyway, Mitch has a spyglass, and if he and Throws Lance can make it to the rim without being seen, they should be able to give us some idea of what we're riding into."

"So, how much notice will they have that we're coming?"

"An hour, or even more, if they have a telescope. We aren't going to surprise anyone from the east. That doesn't matter. As I told you, they are likely expecting us. You and Sierra will need to veer off a half day before we get within sight of the Lookout spires and circle around the hills that overlook the canyon."

She Who Speaks said, "I understand. I will tell my warriors what they need to know."

Jack nodded. It appeared there was no longer any pretense that the young woman was not at least the de facto leader of the war party. He suspected Growling Bear was charged with the protection of the young woman, but Jack figured She Who Speaks was probably quite capable of looking after herself.

Jordy walked up to Jack and grinned, "Jack, I don't think I've heard you spill so many words in all the time I've been with you. That lady coaxed you into doing all the talking."

Jack thought a moment, rubbing his chin thoughtfully. "Yep. Danged if she didn't."

Chapter 33

❝TELL US YOUR story," Jack said, when Eagle Eyes and Throws Lance rode in from scouting Lookout Canyon.

"Well," Mitch Eagle Eyes said, "no trouble working our way up to the rim. Got a good overview with my spyglass. Taught Throws Lance how to use it. When this is done, I thought I'd give him mine and buy a new one out of my bonus."

"I'll do you one better. I'll buy you a new one and won't charge it against the bonus if we get those horses back."

"I think you had it right, Boss, about where they're holding the critters. There are at least three dead-end branches off the main canyon toward the west end. Horses in all of them, almost twice what Miss Sierra's looking for. Couldn't tell which is hers. They got fences built across the openings to keep the horses in, but them fences ain't much. Take the whole works out in ten minutes but they got four or five men camped at that end, keeping an eye on the animals. That's besides two guards waiting to greet visitors that come through the passageway into the canyon."

Jack turned to She Who Speaks and Sierra who stood next to him in the shade of the Studebaker's canvas top. The young women had become fast friends in less than a day's time. "You're going to have a bigger task getting to the horses than I expected."

Sierra said, "We'll figure it out. But if we're going to wait for gunshots on your end, you will have a long wait before we join up with you. What if we hit first, collect the horses, and you wait for our shots? We will keep things quiet as long as we can, but with that many men, we're not going to get the horses without gunfire. And when that happens, it seems like the excitement is going to start up your way. You will have to start blazing a trail for us to get out."

Jack was silent for several minutes. "Yep. I think you are on to something, Sierra." He looked at Tige and Jordy, who were holding the reins of their mounts less than ten feet distant. "Tige, what does the soldier think? Say we pull in the wagons for the night as soon as we find a decent spot. That would give the west end bunch a good six hours of daylight to get to their entry place. They will have to spend the night somewhere outside the canyon. We pull out at sunrise. That should put us at the east entry by nine o'clock. To allow a little leeway, the others make their move about ten o'clock. When we hear gunfire, we start taking control of the compound."

Tige said, "Sounds simple. I don't have a better idea. You think this is going to be as easy as you're laying it out to be?"

"Nope. Not a chance." His eyes fixed on Eagle Eyes. "Mitch, what kind of a count did you get on folks at the compound?"

Eagle Eyes said, "Hard to get a count with folks going in and out of buildings and all. Me and Throws Lance figured there was more than thirty able-bodied men, maybe as many as forty. Had to be some that never showed their faces for us. Saw maybe a dozen women and a couple of kids. Women were Mexicans or Indians as near as I could tell. Likely slaves and whores, we figured."

Jack said, "Hopefully, they'll go into hiding when the shooting starts. I wasn't figuring on that many gun hands. Must be a Comanchero convention. Houses are mostly adobe, such as they are, as I recall, although there were a few stacked limestone outbuildings."

"That would be a fair statement, Boss."

"Best thing would be to drive them back to the buildings and open the way for the horses to come through. Probably hoping for too much. Okay, let's head up the trail and find a place to camp. Ladies, get your men together and see Rudy about provisions. From there, you are on your own. Mitch will be with you, so he should be able to find the west entrance of the canyon."

When the group broke up, Jack mounted the bay gelding and rode a short distance from the wagons to wait for the party to move out again. He looked off to the west, nearly blinded by the sun. The last time he had been this edgy was almost twenty years ago during his last visit to Lookout Canyon. He had a plan then, too.

There had been at least a dozen captive children held in the canyon, traded or sold by Comanches to the Comancheros for resale in Mexico at bordellos or as slaves to wealthy patrons. A spy, whose veracity Jack still doubted, had provided the location of the captives within the residential compound and assured his superiors that there was never more than a dozen or fifteen armed occupants at the compound, most Comancheros headquartering there being on trading or raiding missions at any given time. That made a certain sense.

He had intended to take twenty "armed to the teeth" Rangers into the canyon, leading extra horses for the children and heading directly to where the captives were being held, pick them up and fight their way out. That should have been easy enough. They were Texas Rangers, weren't they?

But they never reached the children. A force of twenty or more Comancheros faced them at the entrance, ready to battle, still not that difficult to dispose of, Jack had figured. But he had not counted on the attack that hit them like a lightning bolt from behind. A large Comanche war party from an obscure band known as the Bug Eaters had appeared like apparitions from an empty prairie.

The Rangers were pinched between two forces. The Comancheros stood fast, doing their shooting from long range, while the Bug Eaters rained arrows on the Ranger force before charging into the melee for hand-to hand combat. Chaos reigned that day. Jack took the lead slug he still carried in his back but remained mounted. An arrow lodged in Rudy's shoulder and another drove into his ribs. Jack had thought his friend dead when he saw Rudy stretched face-down on the ground, a warrior slicing at his scalp, ripping away the flesh that was covered by thick brown hair. The Comanche died when Jack's rifle slug dug into his temple, and the trophy disappeared beneath the hooves of the combatting horses.

Jack had finally rallied his remaining Rangers, including the walking wounded, and they dismounted and formed a circle back-to-back. With superior firing power, the Rangers began backing off the Comanches, who during those years rarely had rifles at their disposal or lacked the skills to use them effectively. The Comancheros had stayed at the canyon's entrance, wanting no part of the fight.

The Bug Eaters, their own ranks now thinned, had held back out of rifle range while the Rangers gathered up the horses that had not been killed or run off. The latter would be claimed by the warriors later. The Rangers slung the six dead, two by two, over horses' backs. Jack had been certain there was a seventh until he knelt by an unconscious Rudy and found him breathing.

By this time, Jack's own wound was throbbing painfully, but, strangely, there was little bleeding. Several other men lifted Rudy, his scalp and torso blood-soaked, into Jack's saddle and boosted Jack up behind him. Jack wrapped his arms around Rudy's chest, stretching to clutch the reins, as they moved the mounts out at a slow walk, battered and beaten, looking for a place to fort up, tend to their wounded and bury their dead. Jack had relived the nightmare many times over the years, but what really haunted him was that he had failed those poor kids.

Chapter 34

RUDY AND JACK sat on the wagon seat of one of the Studebakers as the splintered and misshapen stone spires that identified the Lookout Canyon entrance came into sight. From his aborted visit some years back, Jack recalled that the imposing rock formations that jutted from the earth like giant fangs were more than fifty feet high, one on each side of the opening to the canyon, which was sixty to seventy feet wide at the east end where they would enter. They had served as watchtowers for eons, Jack supposed, and ancients had carved steps and pathways to the summit where guards found outcroppings and stones that had been shaped into rugged crows' nests by early occupants of the canyon.

Rudy handled the mule teams, and Jordy rode alongside the wagon astride a bay gelding, having been unwilling to risk his injured buckskin in the fracas that might follow. Thor snoozed behind the wagon seat.

Swede Larsen drove the second wagon, the one constructed with the false bottom and loaded with backup weapons. Abel Burke joined him on the wagon seat, and Tige rode ahead a short distance within yelling range of Jack in the front wagon.

As they neared the canyon, Jack could see the flash of light off metal from the stone watchtowers in the early morning sunglow that promised blistering heat for the afternoon. Morning had already left an early balminess behind, and he found himself swiping beads of sweat from his forehead. Or had the pre-battle calm of old forsaken him?

Several minutes later, he was not surprised to see two riders headed their way from the canyon opening. Throws Lance and his warriors must have made it to the canyon rim without being detected, or there would be more than a two-man greeting party. "Company coming," Jack said to Rudy.

"Huh?"

"Riders. Do you see the riders?" he said, his voice just short of yelling.

"Hell, yes. You think I'm blind?"

"No, but you're damned near deaf."

"What?"

Jack said, "Pull up and wait." He pantomimed yanking on the reins to supplement his words.

Tige and Jordy reined their mounts up beside him.

"I'd say we're going to get inside," Tige said.

"Yep, it appears so."

As the riders neared, Jack recognized one of the men as Smack, the Comanchero scout they had released several nights earlier. His presence at least confirmed the man was who he claimed to be.

As they rode up to the wagon, keeping twelve to fifteen feet separation, Jack could make out Smack's face now with the sunlight's help. Clearly Anglo, the man might clean up well enough to suit a woman or two if he shaved a week's growth of whiskers that were split by a white furrow the full length of the left cheek, a scar that was likely a reminder of a long ago too close encounter with a knife blade.

The other rider was a stocky, barrel-chested man with dark skin that could have just been sunbaked or caked with dirt. He had shoulder-length black hair with a full beard that was as tangled as the unruly mane. Jack thought the man might be beyond cleaning up. A single eagle feather protruded from the band of a derby hat. Perhaps, the hat and feather were significant. Jack did not care. He just knew that this was not a man he would want to get hold of Sierra. Not for the first time it struck him that they might have embarked on a foolhardy mission.

"Good morning, Smack," Jack said.

"You're missing some men and a woman," Smack said.

"We came to trade. We don't need the young lady or more men to do that. We left the men and woman with the chuckwagon and extra mules and horses some miles back. The extra men were for protection against Indians. We figure they wouldn't be all that welcome here."

Smack was silent and then looked at his partner. "Make sense to you, Smiley?"

Jack figured the man's name must have been borne of sarcasm, for he had not seen a trace of cheer on his scowling face.

"Don't see nobody about. Boys in the towers will see anybody coming this way. Let 'em in. Their numbers ain't a threat."

Smack said, "This is how it works. You're going to follow me in. Smiley's going to bring up the rear to keep an eye on things. We will stop just inside the canyon, and you will meet more of the boys to help us check out your wagons to make sure you ain't bringing trouble with you."

Jack said, "We got nothing to hide. Everything in the wagons is for sale or trade."

"Well, if it all checks out, we'll go on to the village, and you folks can set up shop—after you give us your guns."

"Stop right there," Jack said. "That's the same as telling us to walk into that place bare-assed naked. Not going to happen. We'll just turn ourselves around and head for Fort Davis. The Army would buy some of what we've got. Trading post and tavern would take most of what we've got. We might have to settle for break even, but we wouldn't be handing somebody our lives."

Smack's grungy companion spoke with a raspy voice. "Hell, Mister Shit for Brains, you ain't got the numbers to be so damn cocky about where you stand. You ain't gonna outrun nobody with them wagons, and we got us a army waitin' in the canyon."

Jack replied, "I won't argue the point, Smiley. But we've got men that know their guns and fighting. You take us on, and it will cost you at least three for every one of ours. Now this fussing seems like a bunch of damned foolishness. We just want to sell some merchandise and be on our way. You are free to inspect the wagons, but you leave our guns alone."

Smack said, "Let's take them to the entrance, Smiley. Then, you can help with checking the wagons while I go talk to Potter."

"Who is Potter?" Jack asked.

"Amos Potter. You might say he's the overseer of the canyon. Folks come and go, but his bunch—I'm one of them—pretty much stays here and runs the place. Potter makes the rules and sees they're carried out."

"I'd like to meet the man who has grabbed that kind of authority."

"I'm guessing you will, if you behave yourself and don't get shot first."

Chapter 35

JORDY'S TRUST IN Jack's judgment was generally unwavering, but as the riders and Studebakers approached the stone watchtowers near the canyon entrance, his stomach clenched and gave him pause. Like Jack, he tended to be a planner, preferred to lay out a course and stick close to it. But he could make no sense of what they were doing here, taking their wagons into the middle of the Comanchero compound where they would be easy targets facing a force at least five times their own numbers. Hopefully, Jack had a plan in his head that he just was not talking about.

Smack signaled a halt as they came up to the watchtowers. Jordy looked up and saw that the lookouts were perched on ledges about halfway up the mammoth stone formations that were much broader than they appeared from some distance away.

Smack looked at Jordy. "You," he said, "come with me."

Jordy looked over at Jack, who sat stone-faced on the wagon seat.

Jack gave the slightest nod of his head, signaling that Jordy should follow Smack's order. Jordy nudged his gelding away from the wagon's side and fell in behind Smack. As they entered the canyon, they met three well-armed men emerging and walking toward Jack and the wagons. Jordy assumed the men were Comancheros who had taken on inspection duty.

Nature had painted the canyon walls the same variations of browns they had been seeing since moving into Chihuahuan Desert country, broken up intermittently with outcroppings of white and gray limestone. He noticed healthy splotches of green along the canyon floor, contrasting sharply with the drabness of the terrain above. Then he saw the stream rushing along the base of the northwest wall before abruptly disappearing into a black hole in the canyon, probably to exit from underground someplace and complete its journey to the Pecos. The stream extended back into the canyon for as far as eyesight would reach. This was likely the source of water for all the horses held there, more important in the short term than pastures, which were likely sparse. He hoped that after all this trouble, Sierra's horse herd was still here. Critters could not be fed under these conditions indefinitely.

No more than a hundred yards in, they came to a cluster of buildings and corrals that resembled a small village patched together without any thought of organization. The adobe structures were crumbling, many with gaps where clay mortar formerly bound the brick. A half dozen mud huts were backed up against the southeast canyon wall, roofed with thatch of some kind. The canvas tents near the far side of the village looked more inviting than the more permanent shelters. The few limestone buildings looked more stable but were obviously not constructed by craftsmen. They were the only buildings on the canyon's northwest side.

Most of the visible human life was gathered in the shade of a lonely cottonwood tree, which Jordy guessed had been around for a century or more. Some men sat on benches lining two weathered tables, engaged in card games, it appeared.

A few others napped on blankets nearby, and two men were yelling angrily at each other some distance from the others, but nobody was paying any attention to the dispute. His count placed fourteen men within the vicinity of the tree.

Smack pointed to the mud huts along the canyon walls. "That's where the whores do business. You play your cards right, Amos might let you folks take a pick and a poke. For the asking price, of course."

Jordy said nothing but thought he would not get within handshake distance of any woman who had bedded with this outfit. And still he was sorry for the women whose paths had led them to a place like this.

Smack veered off to the right toward the limestone structures set just in front of the stream and canyon wall. They dismounted in front of the larger of the two single-story houses. The Comanchero handed Jordy his horse's reins. "You stay put while I get Amos." He walked up the dusty path to the house, knocked on the door and disappeared inside.

He could hear angry voices through the uncovered window openings but could not make out what the speakers were saying. It sounded like several others were speaking besides Smack. Soon Smack came out the door, followed by two men, one a slight Mexican man with a thin moustache, cleaner and better groomed than any canyon occupant he had seen yet. He wore a black, low-crowned hat with a turquoise-decorated band. Matched Colts in fancy holsters at his side suggested the man fancied himself a gunfighter. The other man, about his own height, weighed a good three hundred pounds, Jordy guessed, and cleanliness was not his forte. A razor had not neared any part of his face for several years. One of these men was Amos Potter?

His question was answered when the dandy and the ox stepped off to the side of the path, and another man stepped out the door and walked toward him, getting within six feet or so before he stopped. He was a little man, standing no more than a few inches over five feet with his black, shiny boots on. A neatly trimmed, white goatee and moustache decorated his face, and his copper-colored skin hinted strongly at Mexican blood, although his appearance did not match the name of Amos Potter. Regardless, his bearing and the appraising dark eyes made it clear he was the man in charge of Lookout Canyon.

"Hablas Espanol?" the man asked.

"I read and write Spanish. But I don't converse worth a damn. The words go too fast for me."

"The reading and writing do you no good in this country." The man spoke with a slight accent.

Jordy shrugged. He did not offer his hand. "I am Jordy Jackson. I work for the Lucky Five."

"At least you are not a liar. I know who your boss is, too. He was a Texas Ranger, possibly the most hated when he was terrorizing us poor trading folks. And he is leading those who are bringing the wagons here. This makes no sense to me. Would you like to explain?"

Jordy did not like the direction of the conversation but figured it was time to test his lying talent. He hoped hanging around with Uncle Rudy had helped hone his skills. "Jack Wills hasn't been a Ranger for fifteen years or more. He's a businessman. I'm sure you are aware he has a good-sized ranching operation northwest of Fort Concho and San Angelo. But his most profitable enterprise is a freight outfit that moves goods all over Texas."

"That doesn't tell me why he came to Lookout Canyon. It seems like he would be too busy to come all this way."

"He's looking to grow the freight business. He thinks he could run wagons west to El Paso and pickup freight customers along the way. He wanted to see the country for himself, especially Castle Gap and Horsehead Crossing. Figured he could make a connection with Fort Davis easy enough. He already does a good amount of Army freight. He heard folks had sort of a town at a place called Lookout Canyon. He thought when he checked out the possibilities he would find out if there would be some business to be done here on a regular basis—maybe talk about setting up a way station here, make this a relay for wagons and merchandise. Jack says there could be some money in it for the right people with brains and ambition."

Potter eyed him suspiciously. "He's not making money on this run. Too many men and animals tied up in it."

"Jack didn't know what he would be facing out here. Ordinarily, he has a driver and a single guard or backup. Damn glad he brought a crew. Apaches hit us at Castle Gap, but the Indian problems are fading fast. He also figures that if he handles Army shipments, he might get some protection at the gap on scheduled days."

"I guess that makes some sense. But there is something not right about this. I don't know that I believe even half of your tale, but I have enough men to take you down quick if you make trouble, and I am curious to meet the great Jack Wills." He turned to Smack. "If the inspection doesn't turn up bad news, bring the wagons in. They can set up shop in the middle of the compound. And then you bring the great Jack Wills over here for a talk."

Chapter 36

JACK LISTENED TO Jordy's story of his visit with Amos Potter, as the Comancheros completed their inspection of the merchandise stacked in the wagons. With boxes covering most of the wagon floors and an aisle down the middle of the wagon box that a man could barely squeeze through, discovery of the false floor was a near impossibility. In the unlikely event the weapons hideaway should be discovered, however, Jack had a backup story. The guns were simply merchandise hidden for resale because they were particularly vulnerable to theft.

Jack knelt and scratched Thor's ears while Jordy talked, keeping his eye on Rudy, who limped around the outside of the two Studebakers, watching the Comancheros rummage through the cargo in the wagons and yelling at them when he thought a box was being handled too roughly. "You're damn well paying for it, if you break one of them whiskey bottles," he scolded.

Tige, Swede and Abel were huddled some distance away, seemingly engaged in serious conversation. Tige was key to getting the crews out of the canyon, so Jack figured the former horse soldier was rehearsing again.

Jordy said, "Amos Potter knows you by reputation, Jack, and I get the feeling you may have met up sometime. That worries me because, if you did, you weren't likely on the same side of the law. He wants to talk with you in private, I gather."

"I don't remember any Amos Potter, but names have a way of changing in Texas. You say he is part Mexican and wanted to speak Spanish? And on the short side? How old?"

"Hard to say. Younger than you by ten years maybe— sixty, give or take a few years on either side."

"Old from your perspective. Just a kid from mine. Years have a way of changing definitions when it comes to age. Some days, I admit to being an old dog, but most of the time, an old man is somebody that's ten years older than I am." Jack stood up, took off his hat and ran his fingers through his thick hair. "Hot enough to sunburn a horned toad."

Jordy said, "You don't think you know the man then?"

"Don't know. I'm wondering if it could be Alfonso Perez. Came from an old Spanish family that went bust and lost their grant fifty miles north of San Antonio not long after statehood back in '45. He would have been about your age then. He took up trading with the Indians, hired on a rough bunch that raided settlers. Got himself a reputation. He was sort of an outcast in his own family because he was born out of wedlock, and his father was an Anglo passing through—that was the story, anyhow. I picked that up from folks I talked to when I was trying to track him down."

"But you've met the man? You would know him if you saw him?"

"Can't say. My first meeting would have been twenty-five or so years back. He was a wily sort, and my company tracked his small Comanchero outfit for weeks. They were responsible for killing a man, woman and their two small children for no more than a bit of jewelry, some guns, and three or four horses. I'm sure it wasn't the first time. We caught up with them, and most of the bunch went down shooting, but he was careful to stay away from the gunfire and gave himself up. He was a well-spoken man, and at trial took the stand and claimed it was all mistaken identity, that he was just a simple trader."

Jordy said, "He was found innocent?"

"Nope. Jury's verdict was guilty, and I thought for sure he would hang. Judge said otherwise. Sentenced him to thirty years in prison. He never spent a week. Somebody broke him out of the local jail before he got sent off to Huntsville. If this guy is Perez, it stands to reason he would have changed his name, although why he would go with an Anglo name seems odd."

"It would throw off anybody looking for Alfonso Perez. They wouldn't expect him to carry an Anglo name," Jordy said.

"No, I suppose not. The man was well educated for these parts and was fluent in both Spanish and English."

"I don't like this," Jordy said. "If this guy is Perez, you are not looking at a grand reunion. It's more likely, the guy would like to kill you. He might even see it as a necessity once you have identified him. After all these years, he is still a wanted man, I assume."

"Nobody would be looking very hard for him these days, but, yeah, he wouldn't want to risk my passing on his whereabouts, which I would, of course."

Jordy said, "I'm sticking with you like glue."

"If we're forced to separate, you've got to stay with Rudy. We need every man we can spare with the wagons."

"Damn it, Jack, you can't go off to a dance with Amos Potter if he's who you think he might be. You might not be coming back."

"And he might not be who I suspect he is. And if he should be, it just might be Potter, formerly known as Perez, who won't be coming back. What I'm really worried about now is this damned inspection delay. We've got big trouble if gunfire starts at the west end before we get set up in the compound."

When the inspection was finished, Smack told the Lucky Five crew to fall in behind him. The man called Smiley continued to bring up the rear as the wagons rolled toward the compound.

When they reached the ramshackle buildings, Smack signaled for a halt on the trail midway between the canyon walls. Rudy reined the teams to a stop, and Swede rolled his wagon in behind as near to the front Studebaker as mule separation would permit.

"Who's got your inventory?" Smack asked.

"I do," Jack said, climbing down from the wagon seat. "Do you want folks to come down to the wagons and look over the merchandise and buy direct from us?"

"No, it don't work that way. Mister Potter will take everything off your hands. Then he will handle the divvying."

Meaning, Jack figured, that Potter would be selling to the other compound occupants at a tidy profit. "So where do I find Mister Potter?"

"I'll take you to him. He's waiting for you. Says you're going to celebrate a reunion of sorts."

Smack's remark removed any doubt regarding the identity of the Comanchero leader. Jack noticed that Tige and Swede were already starting to unload the second wagon and stack the boxes on the ground behind it. Abel was rushing up to the front wagon to help Rudy and Jordy unload, not that Rudy could do much more than supervise.

"Hey," Smack hollered, "what the hell you think you're doing? I didn't tell you to unload."

"I'll put 'em down," Smiley said, as he nudged his horse up beside the wagons and pulled a rifle from its saddle holster.

"Like hell you will," Smack snapped. "That's up to the boss." He turned to Jack, "Let's go, Wills."

Jack heard Thor growl and looked down and saw the big dog at his side, watching Smack and his teeth bared threateningly.

"My dog," Jack said. "I've got to have somebody take my dog." He called to Rudy, "Rudy, come get Thor, would you? You will need the leash."

"What?"

"Bring the leash."

"I owe this dog a bullet in the brain," Smack said, reaching for his pistol.

"You pull the Colt, and you are a dead man," Jack said, his own Peacemaker leveled at Smack's gut.

Rudy hobbled over carrying a short, coiled rope with a wide leather collar tied to the end. "You ought to keep him with you," he grumbled.

Rudy handed the collar to Jack, who knelt and fastened it about the dog's neck. Thor looked at Jack with sad eyes and whined as Rudy led him away. Darned dog always knew how to manipulate the guilt strings and usually get his way. Not today, though. He did not want Thor reacting more quickly than was prudent if Jack were threatened. Besides, a big dog would not likely be welcome at any meeting with the Comanchero leader.

Chapter 37

I T HAD TAKEN Sierra, She Who Speaks, and their party until well past midnight to reach the southwest end of Lookout Canyon and several more hours to locate the narrow entrance. They had found a fast-moving stream north of the rise that led toward the canyon rim before it went underground, apparently cutting through stone and sand to form a natural conduit to enter the canyon at the base of the wall. She suspected this was the source of the canyon's water supply, useful information for someone wishing to take up a siege against the occupants. She was just grateful for the nearby water. The desert fringes along the banks produced overgrazed grasses that would satisfy the horses for the short time they would be at the site.

They staked out the mounts and searched out spots for bedrolls. They could not risk a fire, but one was not needed for warmth. Blankets and bedrolls were tossed on the earth wherever promising resting places were found. Sierra and She Who Speaks, whom she now called Jael, huddled with Mitch Eagle Eyes and Growling Bear, who had ridden ahead and scouted the west entry to the canyon earlier.

Sierra said, "You are certain we won't be seen here?"

Eagle Eyes said, "I ain't never certain about anything, ma'am, but ain't much chance of it in my estimation. No way they see us from inside the canyon, us being behind the overlooks and all, and I can't figure why anybody would ride out of the canyon at night. Anyway, Roper volunteered for first watch, and I sure wouldn't want to be the man that run into him in the dark. He's one scary hombre."

She Who Speaks said, "Tell us how you see things in the canyon."

Eagle Eyes said, "Nothing much has changed since I scouted it a couple days back. Two guards up in the rocks just inside the canyon entrance. They won't see nobody coming, but they'd hear you before you got to them. Bad thing is, we got to go single file riding in. Guards are the key. I know the boss will want to hold off the shooting a spell, but I don't see how you get in behind them. Get the guards out—then you got time to hit them at the camp-site and take out anybody near the horses."

"Arrows," She Who Speaks said. "Growling Bear brought his bow. We just need to place him within shoot-ing range."

"Just," Sierra said. She pondered the challenge briefly. "Decoy."

"I don't understand," She Who Speaks said.

"I will walk through the opening into the canyon, make a fuss so the guards hear me coming. When they see I am a woman, their curiosity will get the best of them and they—or at least one—will come down to see what I am doing there. Growling Bear will be ten paces behind me and take them down with arrows before a shot is fired."

"You make it sound too easy," She Who Speaks said. "It is too risky. There must be another way."

"Jael, I can do this. I know I can. Tell me if you have a better idea."

She Who Speaks shrugged. "I am very tired. I am go-ing to my buffalo robe."

Sierra's plans were altered some the next morning. She found that Roper Hawley was a man to be reckoned with when her plan was explained to the others. "I will be with you, Missy," Roper told her, "and you ain't got a thing to say about it. Sergeant Tige said I wasn't to let you out of my sight. I go right along with you. You can hang onto my arm like you're sick or something. They won't think nothing about you having a black man helping you. Slave days are gone but not in the heads of men like these. They'll figure I'm your pet. I'll leave my rifle in the scabbard but have my Bowie knife on my hip."

"That's not necessary. I'll be fine."

"Ain't necessary maybe, but sergeant's orders. That's what I follow."

"You're not in the Army anymore, Roper."

"I still work for Sergeant Tige. I stick to my orders. Ain't nothing else to be said about this."

Sierra sighed. "Okay, you win." She admitted to herself that her resistance had been token. She had struggled with second thoughts about the previous night's plan. She took some comfort in having the towering man at her side.

A half hour later, Sierra and Roper headed into the entrance opening while Growling Bear with bow in hand and an arrow nocked waited for their signal to follow. The trail was set between limestone walls that tapered wider as they reached skyward, thus allowing ample light into the tunnel-like opening. Sierra guessed the entryway stretched at least twenty-five feet and suspected some of it had been carved out by ancients. It was wide enough that horse and rider could pass through easily, but it would have been awkward for two to ride abreast.

When they were halfway through the entry, Sierra waved for Growling Bear to follow. As they reached the outlet to the canyon, Sierra tossed her hat on the ground and grasped Roper's left arm. *My Lord, it is forged of steel*, she thought, when her fingers pressed into ungiving muscle. From a distance he looked like a scarecrow, but his appearance belied the sinewy frame. She tossed her hat aside and commenced sobbing and staggering as they moved toward the canyon proper. "It hurts," she screamed, "and I can't go any longer without a drink. Just leave me here to die."

"What in the hell? Who is it? Sounds like woman," came a man's voice from outside. "Cover me. I'll take a look."

Sierra and Roper had almost reached the outlet when a big, bearded man cradling a rifle appeared outside the opening.

"See anybody, Ferdy?" asked the other sentry.

"Georgie, we've got an honest to God female. You got to see this. And she's with the tallest nigger I ever seen." He turned his head back to the visitors. "What's the trouble, sweetheart?"

"Got lost. Our horses died. Hurt my ankle. Need water."

"Got water, sweetheart, but we'll have to come to terms on it."

"Anything. Please, anything."

"Now you're talking my language." He looked at Roper. "You, boy, bring her out where we can take a good look at the merchandise."

As Sierra and Roper stepped out into the open, a squatty, younger man came sliding down the rocks with his rifle in hand and gained his footing not far from his partner. "This is like an old time Christmas," Ferdy said. "A prize filly for the stable and a slave that can do two men's work. Boss ought to give out a bonus for this catch."

"We take our own bonus first." The big man, with tobacco drool at the corners of his lips, reached out to touch Sierra's breast.

His fingers never reached their intended destination. Quick as a cat, Roper stepped toward him, grabbed the man's arm and yanked him away before latching onto his neck with a vicelike grip. He then slipped his hand upward, grabbing the jaw with one hand, and held the hapless man steady while the razor-sharp Bowie blade raced along the fleshy throat. "Like that, boy?" Roper asked, releasing his hold and letting the guard tumble to the ground to bleed out.

Sierra looked wide-eyed at Roper, who was wiping the knife blade on his britches. She had already seen the man called Georgie go down with arrows sunk in his throat and chest. "I'll get my hat and tell the others to bring our horses and come on through." She could not help but be shaken by what had transpired and almost stumbled into Growling Bear, who was headed toward his kill, hopefully to recover his arrows. She would not insult him by reminding the warrior of the "no scalping" order.

When she returned, she found that the corpses had been dragged away from the entrance and secreted someplace. Growling Bear held the reins of two bay geldings she had not noticed previously. He was obviously claiming the horses.

Roper had slipped up silently beside her and startled her when he spoke. "He offered me my pick, but I turned it down. I'd rather be where I'm at than where he's headed. Figure he can make use of whatever he can cabbage on to."

She Who Speaks rode her sorrel gelding over to Sierra and dismounted. "Your plan worked flawlessly, it appears."

"Credit that to Roper and Growling Bear."

"What's your next move?"

"Do you have any ideas?" Sierra asked.

"Well, the horse sorting will come later, so we need to sweep all the critters from the canyon. But you will want to confirm that yours are here—or most of them anyway. What if we split up, and I take my warriors and try to quietly dispose of the men at the camp? There cannot be more than a few. We can collect their horses to take with us while you and the Lucky Five crew search out the branch canyons, take care of any guards and drive out the horses. We will join up with you to herd the animals out the east end when you send somebody to tell us you are ready."

"This will take us some time. As soon as there is gunfire, that starts Grandpa Jack's troubles at the other end."

She Who Speaks said, "That's the only way we get this job finished. We can't just call it off now. We will just hope we can hold off the shooting as long as possible."

"I know. I just wish I had called it off a week ago. Of course, Grandpa would tell me I can't rewrite the past. 'What's done is done,' he would say. Okay, I like your idea."

Chapter 38

SMACK PUSHED THE door open and nodded for Jack to enter and then stepped back out and closed the door behind the rancher. The room was dusky, but two unframed window openings admitted enough light to allow him to make out the occupants once his eyes adjusted. In the center of the room a diminutive figure sat at a desk, leaning back in his chair and smiling at the visitor. In one corner behind the desk stood an obese, scraggly-bearded man with his hand resting on a pistol holstered on a belt beneath his pendulous belly. In the other corner, a slight Mexican man leaned back against the wall with arms folded across his chest and a smug smile on his face.

"Hello, Alfonso," Jack said. "It's been a few years. I think of you every year or two."

"Oh, I think of you often, I assure you. It is beyond belief that fate would deliver you to Lookout Canyon."

"I am here as a businessman, not a Ranger."

"But if you leave, you will inform the Rangers where I am at, won't you?"

"Why should I care? I'm not a Ranger anymore. I am a businessman with merchandise to sell, and maybe a business proposition."

"You are, above all, a lying son-of-a-bitch. You didn't answer my question. Yes or no? Will you inform the Rangers of my whereabouts?"

"I would need to think on that. Depends on whether we make a deal or not." He stepped forward and tossed the inventory list on the desk. "This is what we've got in the wagons and the prices. Ten per cent discount if you take it all off our hands. Then we can talk about the canyon becoming a relay station for our freight business. You could turn your people toward making honest livings."

"What in the hell are you really here for?" Potter said.

Before Jack could reply, the echo of gunshots from downcanyon drifted through the window openings. The former Alfonso Perez would have an answer to his questions shortly.

A gun roared outside the building.

"What in the hell?" Potter said. "Jorge, see what's going on. Pronto."

The Mexican gunfighter slipped one of his pistols from its holster and broke for the door and opened it. He came tumbling back with a mass of black fur nearly swallowing him as he fell to the floor, his pistol clattering away out of reach. He struggled to grasp his other gun, but Thor's massive jaws closed on Jorge's neck and the dog's teeth sank into flesh and tore as blood spewed. The gunfighter cut loose with frantic screaming. "Kill him, kill him."

Thor kept biting ferociously, chewing up the man's shoulder and ripping open the hand that tried to push him away. The obese gunman stepped out, trying to aim at the dog, but Rudy's shotgun roared again at the instant Jack's Peacemaker cracked, and the man toppled forward and dropped like a felled oak on the floor.

Jack swung around and pointed his pistol at Potter-Perez, who already had hands raised above his head. Without turning, Jack yelled, "Thor, down. Down."

The dog's angry barking softened to a threatening growl, and he backed off. His adversary lay silently on the floor, breathing lightly as he bled out and a pool of blood formed about his neck and head. Out of the corners of his eyes, Jack saw Rudy loading his double-barreled shotgun.

Ron Schwab

Jack said, "Alfonso, you can save some lives if you walk outside with us and tell your people to stand down. In a short time, our riders will be driving horses through here—horses that you have stolen. Over fifty head came from my granddaughter's ranch since you wondered about my real reason for being here. Those with the turkey track brand."

"Boss, you okay in there?" came a loud voice. "Heard gunfire over here."

"Shit," said Rudy, who slammed the door shut. "Three men out there."

Thor barked and Jack turned and saw movement at one of the window openings. Someone was just outside the window. "Watch it, Rudy. East window."

Rudy swung around, ready to squeeze the trigger. A man stepped in front of the window with pistol raised to fire, but before either Jack or Rudy could react, gunshots dropped the would-be killer. Fire continued and seemed to be coming from above the canyon floor. "Throws Lance and his warriors," Jack said. "Rudy, I'm going to peek outside. Have your shotgun ready when I open the door. It's quieted some. Alfonso, just keep your hands high and stay put."

Jack walked over to the door, opened it just a crack, and peered out. "I assume you are the guy that shot

Smack. There's another dead man out front and two more running like jackrabbits away from here."

Rifle shots erupted again. Jack said, "Correction. Were running, thanks to Throws Lance. Our guys are starting to take some gunfire from the other side of the canyon."

"We need to get back to the wagons," Rudy said.

"Yeah. I don't see Tige and Swede. They must be in the wagon getting set up. Jordy and Abel are under the second wagon. Appears they're trying to draw fire. We've got to take our friend here with us. I don't know if he's worth anything in trade or not, but we can't leave him here."

Jack pushed the door shut and started to turn when Thor barked and simultaneously a gunshot sounding like a cannon in the small room sent a lead slug into the back of his upper right thigh. Jack stumbled forward but hit the wall and braced his hand against it and recaptured his balance. He realized instantly that Thor had leaped upon the shooter and driven Potter's arm down to thwart what would otherwise have been a back shot. Potter was screaming now as he tried to fight off the snarling, biting dog and struggled to stay on his feet, no doubt recalling Jorge's fate after he went down. Jack tried to get a shot, but Thor covered Potter like a blanket.

Potter held onto his pistol, got his gun hand free for an instant and squeezed the trigger. The retort was followed by yelp, but Thor held on, going for his enemy's face, his long teeth ripping flesh away and Potter's nose now hanging from one cheek. He dropped his gun, stepped back, his shredded hands grasping for what remained of his face. He went to his knees before he rolled over onto his side in a fetal position, moaning and sobbing. "Help me. Help me," he cried.

"Down, Thor," Jack commanded, as he pressed his back to the wall and slid to the floor. The dog backed away from Potter and limped toward Jack, who saw that his friend's thick coat was blood-soaked, but with whose blood he could not discern.

Rudy walked over to Potter who lay whimpering on the floor beside his desk. "Damn it, Jack," he said, "this never would've happened in the old days. No way would either of us have overlooked the likelihood of a gun in the desk drawer. Wouldn't have given him a chance at us for even a second. I'm sorry, Jack. I didn't have your back."

"Don't blame yourself. I told you to keep your gun pointed at the door."

"We're getting too old for these shenanigans, Jack. Look at us. You and me and Thor. Just three old dogs." He lowered his shotgun, squeezed the trigger and put Alfonso Perez and Amos Potter out of their joint miseries. "We won't run into him again, unless it's in hell," Rudy said.

Rudy hobbled over to Jack, who sat on the floor with his back leaning against the wall and Thor's head cradled in his lap. A war was raging in the canyon compound outside, but there was not a thing they could do about it right now.

"Let me see the damage," Rudy said, as he leaned on the shotgun and knelt beside Jack.

"Thor, first," Jack said. "He's hit in the upper left fore-leg. I think the slug went clean through, but he's bleeding like a stuck pig. We need to get a tourniquet on it. Give me that kerchief of yours. I can get it tied."

Rudy untied the kerchief that covered his neck and handed it to Jack, who reached down and worked the kerchief under the dog's leg and above the gaping hole, snugged it about the leg and tied it. The blood flow ceased instantly. Thor lifted his head and licked Jack's hand, and Jack rubbed the dog's ears.

"Let me see what you got," Rudy said. "It ain't killed you yet anyhow."

"Just like Thor. Upper leg wound. Back of my right thigh, no exit wound, so the slug is still there. Hurts like hell, but not that much blood as near as I can tell."

"Well, the dog's got to move so I can see what you've got. Where's your kerchief?"

"Sitting on it. Tried to wrap it myself but too much going on. And I couldn't see the damage."

"Nope, that's for sure," Rudy said, "unless you got eyes in your ass. Now get yourself turned around. Tell me if you need my help."

Jack gently lifted Thor's head from his lap, and the dog sat up on his haunches, holding up his injured foreleg, and watched while Jack struggled to lie down on his left side to give Rudy a view of the wound.

"I've seen a hell of a lot worse," Rudy said. "You're right. It's not bleeding a lot. That's okay right now, but bleeding would help clean it out."

Jack said, "Take my kerchief and bind the wound. Slice off some of my shirt tail if you need to. We've got to get back to Jordy and the others."

"Can you walk?"

"We'll find out, won't we?"

Chapter 39

JACK FIGURED THEY probably made a pathetic sight and prime targets, two gimpy old men and a big dog bouncing along on three legs as they departed the stone building and headed for the wagons. Fortunately, the Comancheros were congregated on the south side of the canyon where most of the dilapidated village lay. The Kwahadi warriors hidden behind rocks on the slopes had helped take out the enemy on the north side and provided some cover now. Jack looked over his shoulder and saw that Throws Lance and his warriors were slowly descending the sloping wall now, apparently with the intention of joining the crew at the wagons to provide support.

They needed help there, as Jordy and Abel could not hold out for long. What had become of Tige and Swede? The Comancheros were working their ways toward the embattled wagons.

Ron Schwab

Rudy had the same concern. "There must be trouble. Hope to hell Tige and Swede didn't take hits in there."

Suddenly, the canvas covering the wagon ribs on the near side began sliding up, and they saw Tige and Swede, each claiming one end, pushing the covering up the support rods from inside, revealing Miss Molly in her shining glory. As they approached, Jack let out a sigh of relief.

Tige had been itching to try the Gatling gun Fort Concho had dumped as hopeless. He had purchased the weapon, which had been judged seriously flawed by the Army, for a pittance and had been making modifications and repairs to the gun for better than a year and tested it briefly on a few occasions. The weapon, which often sat on wheels for ease of shifting directions, was today attached to a heavy steel base that would be manipulated by sheer muscle, thus requiring Swede's assistance. The gun operated with six rotating barrels moved by a cranking handwheel, and cartridges were dropped from a hopper to a carrier that fed the ammunition into the barrels. Properly operated, the gun would fire as many as two hundred rounds per minute.

Tige and Swede had been removing the gun's components from the wagon's false bottom and assembling the Gatling, which Jack figured Tige could do blindfolded. The plan was that Tige would handle the cranking and firing of the gun, Abel would feed the cartridges into the hopper, and Swede would handle any relocation of the weapon's aim. The gun would more than even the odds if it worked and if Tige was not disabled during the battle.

Abel scrambled into the wagon to take his place, and Jack and Rudy claimed spots near the gatling's wagon to defend the operators from blindsided attacks. Throws Lance and his warriors soon joined them and took up positions. The mules had been unhitched and moved to the sparse grass along the stream during the unloading of the wagons and were staked out there with the horses they had ridden into the compound.

Tige knelt on the wagon floor to speak to Jack. "I saw you limping, Boss . . . you and Thor. You going to be okay? What happened?"

"Thor and I both took bullets. We'll be fine. Got a slug in my leg. We can deal with that later."

"We're going to yank the rest of the canvas off the wagon. Unveil the Miss Molly, you might say. There's going to be a hell of a racket here in less than five minutes."

"It can't be too soon. It looks to me like they're gathering for a rush."

"Then I'd better get to it."

Jordy moved in beside him. "Jack, I heard the gunfire from the house over there. Since Rudy's shotgun was singing, I decided to stay put here, but I've been worried sick."

"Rudy and Thor thinned their ranks some."

"The leg?"

"Need a mite of patchwork, that's all."

The canvas dropped from the other side of the wagon, displaying the gun and its attendants to the southside Comancheros. There was almost a reverent silence for several minutes. Apparently, their adversaries were appraising the weapon's significance to the conflict. Jack held out hope they would back off, but during his years of chasing outlaws, he had concluded that most such men were short on brains, and he feared it would take a dose of reality to get their attention. At least the women and any children had apparently found some type of shelter.

Suddenly the Comancheros broke the eerie silence and began to fire their guns and move toward the embattled wagons. They had spread out some, leaving a good number outside the Gatling's line of fire.

Even with Comanche support, Jack figured his defenders were outnumbered three to one. Jack yelled, "Focus on the edges, boys. Let the Gatling take the middle." Throws Lance said something to his warriors, but Jack had no idea whether the senior warrior had understood his directive.

Now the Comancheros were racing toward them, yelling at the enemy as they charged. The Gatling began its rhythmic discharge and the center of the Comanchero mass disappeared as bodies fell. One of the Kwahadis groaned as a slug drove into his head and he fell backwards. The Comancheros were closing in on their left flank and he feared they would be overrun. Jack looked up when he heard a racket on the wagon. Swede, left side of his shirt blood-soaked, was lifting the Gatling and repositioning it. As soon as it was in place, firing resumed and more Comancheros went down, some dead but others worming away on the earth beneath the spray of lead.

At the sight of comrades in retreat, others wavered and soon followed suit. The charge was broken, and the defenders ceased fire without orders. Tige leaped to his feet and helped Swede down into the wagon bed. Jack started to move along the edge of the wagon bed where Swede sat until his head began to spin and his knees went weak. The last thing he remembered was stumbling forward and blackness overtaking him.

Chapter 40

JORDY AND RUDY tugged Jack's upper body under the wagon to capture some shade. Thor joined his friend and lay beside him, resting his head on Jack's shoulder, his nose just inches from the old rancher's face. Jack's eyes blinked and he opened them, but he seemed confused, Jordy noted, scooting back to check the leg again.

"Relax, Jack," Jordy said. "The bullet wound finally decided to give up some blood. I cut off your trousers' leg, and we've got it bound and the bleeding stopped."

Jack did not reply, and Jordy lowered his head, looked under the wagon bed and saw that his foster father's eyes had closed. "He's out again," he said to Rudy who stood nearby with his eyes fixed on Jack.

"Just as well," Rudy said. "He won't be moving that leg around if he's sleeping. And if Jack stays put, Thor won't be on his feet either. I'd say, let them be till they got to be moved."

"Jordy, you'd best take a look at this." It was Tige, speaking from the wagon bed where he was tending to Swede's shoulder wound.

Jordy got to his feet. "What?"

Tige pointed to a man standing less than a hundred feet away on the gentle slope that rose above the trail to the village. He was waving a stick with what appeared to be a woman's white camisole tied to it. "Guess somebody wants to palaver," Tige said.

"Do you want to talk to him?" Jordy asked.

"I'm still trying to get Swede patched up."

"How bad is it?"

"Not so bad," Swede said.

Tige said, "He's got a slug in his shoulder. Somebody's got to play surgeon later. But we need to talk our way out of this place first. I guess it's up to you, Jordy. That's best anyhow. I doubt if there's many among these people that would talk straight with a black man."

Jordy sighed and shrugged. "All right, I'll see what he's got to say."

He walked around the wagon and stepped out onto the open ground between him and the flag waver. The man took a step toward him, so Jordy reciprocated, and each started walking at a slow pace toward the other. As he approached the Comanchero, Jordy was surprised to see that he would be dealing with a young man about his own age, tall and lean with red hair and beard, both close-cropped from what showed beneath the hat brim. The man seemed nervous and wary, but Jordy supposed he might appear the same to his negotiating counterpart.

They stopped a few arms' lengths from each other. The Comanchero spoke first, "I'm Dan Flanagan. Most call me 'Red.'"

Why was Jordy not surprised at the nickname? "I am Jordan Jackson. Jordy."

"I'll get to the point. Where's Amos?"

"In hell, I'd guess. He is dead as a rock, along with Smack and a man I think they called Jorge and a big man. A few others on the ground outside the house, too."

"We saw them that was outside. Wasn't sure what happened to Amos and the others," Red said. "Can't say I feel sorrow about Amos. Some of us wanted to leave here, but he said we was dead men if we tried to ride out. I don't got any posters out on me, and Johnny and Taylor don't neither. We ain't been here long and was looking for any work we could find. And then I met Songbird here—she's Comanche, some north band. She was traded to this Comanchero bunch by her drunken husband and couldn't escape. She ain't what they used her for before I came. It took the last of my money to buy her from Amos."

"Why don't you get to the point?" Jordy said.

Red said, "Most of us have had enough of this killing. Songbird is with child. Mine, we think. Don't matter none. Baby will be raised as mine. We want to leave the canyon. Make an honest life. Johnny and Taylor want out, too."

"Amos is dead. You can leave anytime."

"But where to? We three want to ride out with you."

Jordy pondered the situation. "Are you speaking for everybody here?"

"Most plan to stay. With Amos dead and Comanchero days about done for, some might hang on for a spell, but the outfit will start breaking up, and everybody will go their own ways. It's sort of dog eat dog here, anyhow, friends in small bunches. Amos is all that held things together. Johnny and Taylor want to do what I do. And then my woman comes with us. Me and Songbird will marry up when we can find a place to make it legal."

Jordy found himself liking the young man. "It won't be long till some of our folks show up here from downcanyon with all the horses they could round up."

"There's a mighty lot of horses down that way."

"We can use some more wranglers to get the horses back to San Angelo. If you will help us, we'll keep you fed. If it works out, I might be able to find you a freighting or wrangling job with the Lucky Five. The other two might be considered, too, but no promises."

"You got yourself three wranglers, Jordy. And Songbird will help around the camp. We'll get ready to ride. We don't got much but our mounts. They're in the corrals up here. But what can I offer the others to stand down?"

"Their lives to start with."

"That's something, I guess, with that Gatling you got set up. But I'm hoping you can do something to cause better feelings, or they might not be so quick to let us go."

Jordy said, "They can keep all the horses in the compound's corrals. I'm guessing the men that we are leaving to bury had horses here for survivors to lay claim to, as well as guns and other valuables. I suppose Amos had a fair amount of gold eagles stashed someplace. They can have a treasure hunt. We won't be able to drive all the horses out of the canyon. Those that stay can divide the remaining horses. We'll leave behind all the foodstuffs, whiskey, pots, pans cloth and other goods that were unloaded from the wagons. That's the best we can do."

"I can make that sound like Christmas. But I'm betting a lot more folks will die before the dividing's done."

"We'll be long gone by then. You go make your pitch. Then get your friends and Songbird and be ready to ride."

Jordy watched as Red Flanagan headed back up the slope toward the clusters of Comancheros beginning to merge and gather as he approached. They did not move like men looking for more fight. Red seemed to have good instincts and brains that most of his comrades lacked. He was confident the new wranglers would be joining one of the Lucky Five crews soon. He had no second thoughts about taking on the extra hands. They could use twice as many getting the horses back to the Lucky Five, and Jack had been taking on strays forever. He would approve.

Chapter 41

THE WEST END of Lookout Canyon was a river of horses. Sierra, astride Dancer on a rise along the south canyon wall, waited for Mitch Eagle Eyes to return. She had sent Mitch ahead to check the status of those who had entered the compound at the canyon's north entrance. The gunfire coming from that direction had been horrifying, but all was quiet now. She had fired a few shots to warn Grandpa Jack they were coming, having killed or captured and bound all the guards without firing a shot, but the shooting had started too soon for her signal to have ignited the uproar that followed. It had sounded like several hundred men at war at the other end of the canyon.

Worst case, the Lucky Five crew members, including her grandfather and their Comanche allies, were dead or captured. She hoped for best case where the Lucky Five had defanged the Comancheros somehow.

She Who Speaks and the others were busy containing the horses while Sierra tried to evaluate what they faced at the canyon's outlet. She figured they had something over a hundred horses after clearing out the branch box canyons. She estimated those with Turkey Track brands made up close to half, so most of the herd had been recovered. The Kwahadis would claim the remainder, and the sorting would cost them a good day on the trail. According to She Who Speaks, she and her warriors would remain with them until they passed through Castle Gap. After that, Sierra's horses would be cut out of the herd, and the Kwahadis would take their bounty and break off on the Comanche War Trail, heading north to join their band, which could now be on the way to the Fort Sill reservation.

Sierra saw Mitch Eagle Eyes riding her way at a pace that did not seem frantic, so she hoped he was bringing good news. While she waited his arrival, she cast her eyes over the mass of restless horses that the Kwahadis and Lucky Five crew were trying to contain. She worried that if several broke away, others would follow and soon they would lose most of the herd and be forced to round them up again.

When Mitch rode up, he did not keep her in suspense. "We can take them out," he said, "I don't know what's going on. I stopped short of riding in, but there is a truce or something because nobody's shooting at nobody. We got a few down that's being tended to, but there's a heap more Comancheros being drug off the slope south of the trail. They got the worst of it."

"Let's move then," Sierra said, doffing her hat and waving it at the herders, pointing east toward the compound and the route that would take them out of Lookout Canyon.

By the time she and Eagle Eyes joined the others, the herd was moving along the canyon floor. It took little more than twenty minutes before the wagons came into sight. The wagon teams were being hitched as they entered the compound area. Sierra saw that the Comanches who were with Grandpa Jack were waiting to be picked up by fellow warriors to be reunited with their own mounts outside the canyon, although by her count they were one short. As they neared the wagons, Sierra saw Uncle Rudy standing near one of the wagons where he had apparently been hitching teams. It appeared everyone had frozen in place at the sound of the thundering herd coming toward the compound.

She saw Jordy and Tige kneeling in the bed of a coverless wagon bent over two other figures. When she saw Thor sitting not more than a few feet from Jordy, her heart skipped a beat, and her body went numb for an instant before she reined her roan mare away from the horse herd and angled toward the wagons. The horses and wranglers, enveloping the compound in a massive dust cloud, continued past and would soon exit the canyon and head toward the location of the chuckwagon and nearby water and patches of grass, where they would all rendezvous.

Sierra, struggling to find her way through the dust, came up to the wagon, dismounted, and hitched her mare to a wheel spoke. Wiping dust from her eyes and lips, she moved to the rear of the wagon bed where Jordy was crouched. Her panic eased when she saw Jack's hand reaching up and scratching Thor's head and floppy ears.

"Jordy, what happened to Grandpa Jack? Will he be all right?" she asked.

Jordy started and turned, "Sierra, I didn't see you. Of course, I can't see anybody in this dang dust storm you set off. Jack took a hit in his thigh. I'm rewrapping it now, trying to keep the bleeding staunched. But he's got a slug we ought to get out as soon as we leave this hellhole."

"Grandpa Jack," she yelled. "Say something."

"Howdy, Sierra. I'll be fine. I'm counting on you to do some doctoring on me and Thor when we get to camp. I don't know what fixing Swede needs. Tige has been working on him."

Grandpa Jack seemed in good spirits and a long way from dead, so she moved along the side of the wagon to check on Swede. "Tige," she asked, "how is Swede?"

Tige scooted closer to the sideboard. "Hi, Sierra. It would take more than a bullet to take this guy down. He says he's ready to get back to work. He got hit near the top of his shoulder. The slug passed through. I'd like to have you look and see what you think, if you wouldn't mind. I claimed four bottles of whiskey from our cargo, and I've washed the entry and exit with that."

"I'll fetch my vet kit from my saddlebags and hop in the wagon."

After she retrieved her kit, Sierra climbed into the wagon and knelt beside Tige. "I can't see much until the dust settles. It shouldn't be long before we can see the sun again. You've got the bleeding staunched it appears." The filthy rag that was pressed against the front of Swede's shoulder appeared to have everything but blood on it, but she admitted she would be hard-pressed to produce anything clean from her belongings after this many days on the trail.

She looked at Swede, who appeared quite stoic about his injury. "Are you in much pain?"

"Hurt? Nej."

She took that to mean "No."

Tige said, "He's drunk a half pint of whiskey. You could operate now if you needed to open him up, and he wouldn't feel a thing."

Sierra pulled back the compress that covered the shoulder wound, thinking she had never seen muscles like Swede's even on Jordy's stallion. "No terrible damage that I can see, but we will want to clean it when the light's better. I don't know about stitches. Can you help me get him on his side, so I can see the exit?"

Tige helped her push the giant on his side. Swede did not resist but did not help either. He did burst out in some unintelligible song, however.

Sierra removed the crude compress on the exit wound which was stuck by its own blood and fluids. "There is some tearing here. Might want a few stitches. We'll just have to look again when we get settled someplace." She returned the compress to the shoulder, using a bit of her surgical tape, careful not to waste it since it was hard to come by.

She crawled to the other end of the wagon bed, bumping her head on a huge gun that had been installed on the floor. Now she knew where all the racket had been coming from. She moved up beside Jordy. "Is there anything I can do now?"

"Jack's sleeping again. He does that off and on. Sleeps for ten minutes, awake for ten minutes. We've got to get ready to move out. We've recruited three new hands from the Comancheros. One has a Comanche wife. I was thinking we would move you and Jack into the other wagon, and the woman will ride with you. She might be less afraid if she was with another woman."

"Does she speak any English?"

"I have no idea. Her name's Songbird."

"What about Swede?" Sierra asked.

Tige said, "I'll be mounted near the wagon and keep an eye on him. In his state, I'd say he will enjoy the company of his bottle and the Gatling gun as much as anybody's."

Chapter 42

HE WAGONS PULLED in at the chuckwagon camp
more than an hour after the wranglers had arrived with the horse herd. It was midafternoon,
and, as far as Jordy was concerned, the priority was re-
moval of the slug from Jack's thigh. He did not check
with Jack. They would stay the night here. It seemed everybody assumed he had authority to make decisions,
and it had not occurred to him that he might not.

She Who Speaks came to him as he was unsaddling
his horse. "I understand Mister Wills was injured during
the fight at the compound."

"Yes. A slug must be removed from his thigh. Swede
took a bullet in the shoulder, too, but it passed through."

"I have medicines prepared by Healer's Daughter that
can be used in poultices."

"Talk with Sierra. She is with Jack at the wagon. I know she will welcome help. She needs to get this done during sunlight."

"I will find her. Kwahadi warriors will share night watch on the herd. Tell Throws Lance how many men you want and when."

"And I'm sorry about the loss of your warrior," Jordy said as she started to walk away.

She Who Speaks said, "Tall Tree was a good warrior, a kind man, but war does not pick its casualties for their character or lack of it. I am sad that we will be forced to bury him at this place, yet, it is nearer the homelands of The People than the reservation that is their destination."

Jordy sought out Rudy who was already organizing for supper, poor Nick Iverson having been pressed into domestic duties with Bram by reason of his mere presence. Jordy had no thought of interceding lest he find himself washing pots and pans. Rudy was inventorying his supplies when Jordy found him.

"Stew and biscuits tonight," Rudy said.

"What kind of stew?"

"Sonofabitch stew. You toss everything in the pot but the hide, hooves, and horns.

"Beef?"

"Not likely. Big damn cattle outfit and not an ounce of beef. I got a dab of ham you might find in it if you're lucky. Always got beans. I'll throw in whatever else strikes me, but you'd better send out some hunters tomorrow or no more meat."

"I just wanted to tell you I'll be over at Jack's wagon if anybody's looking for me."

"Slug's coming out?"

"Yeah. Sierra's going to do it."

"Tough gal. Smart as a whip. She's a Wills alright."

"She's okay, I guess," Jordy said.

"Just okay? That tells me she's too good for the likes of you. Sierra's more than a woman that's easy on the eyes, and if you don't know it, leave her be."

Jordy turned away. "I'm going."

"You let me know as soon as the slug's out, you hear?"

"I hear."

Sierra sure had Rudy wrapped around her little finger. The old devil had anointed himself her protector it seemed. He was headed for the wagons when Irish stopped him.

"Hey, Boss. I know you got a lot on your mind. Would you like me and Mitch to set up the night watches?"

Boss? "Uh, yeah. I would be grateful if you would do that for me. Have Mitch check with Throws Lance. They'll be working with us."

He was stopped several more times before he got to the wagons, but he was struck by something that he had not recognized before. Jack made ranch and freighting operations look like they ran themselves. That was because they almost did. Jack picked men who thrived on responsibility—hungered for it—and ran with it and got rewarded for it. Why had he not seen it before? Most of Jack's employees had endured lives of adversity, in some cases ups and downs, but mostly downs. Yet, they were the kind who did not look for somebody else to blame. They picked themselves up and persisted.

Jordy realized that he had been a beneficiary of Jack's philosophy. Since he was a kid, Jack had calmly drummed it into his head. Self-responsibility. Persistence. Don't count on somebody else to blaze your trail through life no matter how tough it gets. Jack always said he knew men who were blessed with windfalls along life's road and then pissed the good fortune away and spent their days whining because they had been unable to hang onto it. They had never learned to look after themselves, always waiting for somebody else to wash their dishes, take night shift, or as Jack would put it, "wipe their gluteus maximus."

By the time Jordy reached the wagons, Sierra had finished cleaning Swede's wound and departed the wagon where the patient rested. She Who Speaks was applying her poultices. He stopped to speak with the Kwahadi woman. "How is Swede doing?" he asked.

She shrugged and smiled. "He cannot tell you. He totally anesthetized himself. We must hide the whiskey bottles. My poultices will ease the pain, and I have other potions if he needs more help. Sierra is an accomplished surgeon. She found shards from his shirt in the wound and removed them with a forceps. They could have caused serious problems. She placed a few stitches in the exit wound. She says she is just doing what she would do for her horses."

"I'm glad you are both with us."

"Songbird is helping her with Mister Wills. She is of the Penataka band—the 'honey eaters.' She has learned some English from her man. I like her. You will, too, I think."

"I will see how Jack is doing, but I'll stay out of the way. Thanks for all you and your warriors have done. I'm afraid our effort would have turned into a disaster without your help."

"You are welcome, but we needed each other. The horses will be critical to the band as we go to the reservation."

The other wagon was no more than ten paces distant, and Jordy walked over to see what was happening there. He peered in the back opening of the canvas-covered Studebaker and saw that Jack lay on his belly and Sierra was hunched over his leg with a probing instrument of some kind clutched in her fingers. Songbird, the petite Comanche woman, held a cloth folded over various surgical instruments within easy reach and appeared to be focusing intently on whatever Sierra was doing. A pan of hot water for washing instruments sat on the wagon bed's floor next to her.

Jack was grimacing with pain and sweating profusely, but Jordy supposed the heat brought on by a fiery sun contributed to his misery. Unlike Swede, he suspected Jack would be cold sober. Jordy had only rarely seen Jack touch a drop of alcohol. Rudy always joked that he tried to drink enough for both men, and he likely achieved that goal. Jack was not a temperance proponent. He had been a serious drinker in the old days, Jack had told Jordy once. During his early service with the Rangers, however, he had awakened in a strange room one morning lying in vomit with an obese, wild-haired woman he could not remember meeting. He had decided at that instant the demon alcohol was not his friend, and his drinking since had been infrequent or "one and done." He was almost obsessive, Jordy thought, about remaining in control of his faculties.

Sierra was probing the wound with a forceps now, apparently fishing for the slug. She straightened up. "Grandpa, I found the slug, but it's pressed against bone at an angle, and I can't get a grasp. I need to make the opening bigger to get a hold on it. You should take a few swigs of the whiskey if I'm going to be cutting."

'No need," Jack said, "I'm going to keep it." His voice was weak and raspy but carried firmness.

"Just leave it in?"

"I already got a lead souvenir in my back. We'll just add this one to the collection. Old Razzie Wilson claims to have three. Of course, he's a lying old coot. Anyhow, clean the wound as best you can. Bind it up. I'll be walking in the morning, and I'll be riding again by the time we get to Horsehead Crossing and Castle Gap."

Jordy decided it was time to speak up. He startled both women when he spoke. "Jack, think about this. You always told me life was about choices. I had to choose to ride the white horse or the black horse, you said."

"Your point?"

"I don't like the horse you are choosing here. There's a reason the docs get the slug out when it's possible. This choice is one I think you had better be careful about. I know Sierra can get that slug out."

"You're always throwing an old man's philosophizing back at him, Jordy. Hell, I'm just blathering when I kick out my words of wisdom, likely wrong more often than right."

Jordy shrugged, "I just had to say my piece."

"Well, you sure did that. But I thought I had made a decision."

Jordy said, "Shall I give you the talk about changing your mind?" Jordy asked.

Jack turned his head to Sierra. "Maybe Songbird could pass me the whiskey bottle and Jordy could find me a stick to bite on. And, granddaughter, I wouldn't mind if you could make this quick."

After Jack drank more than a few swigs of whiskey and she had given the anesthetic a chance to settle in, Sierra asked Songbird for a scalpel and deftly made her cuts in the flesh about the wound. Jordy watched in awe as she entered the wound with the forceps and quickly plucked out a bloody lead slug. He wondered if Sierra knew she was the beneficiary of a gift that was priceless on the frontier. There simply were too few healers in the west, especially far from the big towns and cities.

"Jordy, I am going to stitch the cuts I made and do some more cleanout. Would you tell Jael I am ready for her to do her poultices?"

"Yes, ma'am."

"Songbird, would you stay with Swede until we get a bedroll laid out for him?"

"I do that. Bring me tools. I cook water and wash."

"Thank you. That would be nice."

By the time Jordy returned with She Who Speaks, Sierra had finished the stitching and was sitting next to Jack, wiping his sweaty brow with a cloth. She had removed the chewing stick from his mouth, and Jack had at some point escaped into the sanctuary of deep sleep. Whether he had passed out from the pain or the effects of the alcohol, Jordy supposed did not matter. The main thing was that he was not hurting for the moment.

Chapter 43

HOW ARE THE patients this morning?" Jordy asked, as he met Sierra on his way to check on Jack and Swede.

Sierra said, "Swede is fine. You wouldn't know he had taken a bullet in the shoulder yesterday. He can't drive mule teams yet, but he insists he's going to ride beside Abel on the wagon seat. He should have a fast recovery, but Papa said you have to worry about infections or putrefaction, as some called it, for at least three or four days. He told me about people who died from the tiniest cut. He claimed more men died from infections during the war than from the physical damage caused by their wounds."

"What about Jack? You wouldn't let me stay with him last night."

"I felt I should be with him and Thor. He wouldn't have been shot if I had stayed out of his life."

"You are putting too much of the responsibility on yourself. It's more complicated than that."

Sierra said, "Anyway, he seems better this morning. He slept through the night, which surprised me. He seems more concerned about Thor than himself. But Thor's wound didn't take much but some cleaning and a few stitches."

"And Thor's probably more worried about Jack."

She surrendered a small smile. "Oh, yes. I've had a few dogs in my life. I know about the bonding between a dog and its human. But this attachment between the two is the deepest I have ever seen. I swear they talk to each other in some secret language."

"I know what you are talking about. Can I help you with something? I was on my way to visit Jack."

"I am just going to pick up breakfast for the patients at the chuckwagon. I can take care of it. You go ahead and talk to Grandpa Jack."

When Jordy reached the wagon, he saw that Jack was in one of his pensive moods, lost in the clouds with his thoughts. "Good morning, Jack," he said, "got time to talk about getting the horses on their way?"

Jack was propped up against a cushion of blankets in the corner of the wagon bed and did not seem to hear him. Thor snoozed beside him, his head resting on his friend's lap.

Jordy waited in silence for a few moments before speaking again. "Jack?"

Jack looked at him, and Jordy thought his mentor had aged ten years. Dark hollows around the eyes, soft wrinkles turned to gullies overnight.

"These damned wagons are going to slow us down," Jack said.

"Not that much. We left most of the loads at Lookout Canyon. They'll be an easy pull for the mule teams. A single team could do the work."

"No, use both teams. The mules won't tire so much, and it will save switching teams so often."

"Anyway," Jordy said, "it's going to be hot as hell, we're short of grazing and even near the Pecos, the water's hard to get to. We can't be pressing the horse herd. It's better to take some extra days than lose horses. There are some foals to consider, too. Irish pointed that out."

Jack said, "We should be able to reach Horsehead Crossing and Castle Gap by the third day out. Then we've got to sort out the horses before we split with the Kwahadis. That will take a day or more. I figure I can cut three or four days, at least, if I pull out from Castle Gap right away. I wouldn't be helping with cutting out the critters, anyhow. I will be heading home. I've got to talk with Tess."

"Jack, are you sure you didn't take a bullet to the head and didn't tell anybody? That's crazy. You can't take off on your own. You can't handle that many hours in the saddle."

"I sure as hell can. It might pain me some, but I can stick to my saddle. Can't hurt any worse than my leg."

"But alone?"

"Thor's coming with me."

"He can't run a mile anymore, let alone over a hundred."

"Swede and I've been yelling back and forth about that. He's going to help me build a wagon for Thor."

"Jack, I'm worried about you."

"A two-wheeler. The Studebakers each have a spare wheel anchored under the bed. Thor might weigh 120 pounds. Swede says he can make a wood axle if we need to. We'll strip what materials we need off the wagons. I'll take an extra horse and whichever horse I'm not riding will pull the cart."

"You've thought this out. You are really serious about this, aren't you?"

"Never more."

"But the Studebakers might need a spare wheel."

"You and Tige will think of something. If you can't, leave one behind. I own the damn things. You got my okay."

Jordy could see he was not close to winning this argument. He could only hope Jack would come to his senses before they got to Castle Gap. "I have got to go, Jack. I'm going to have Roper and Possum handle the mule teams today. They will be hitching up soon. I'd like to pull out with the herd within a half hour. Horses are getting restless. They have eaten everything down to dirt and sand here. After you have had breakfast and Rudy has cleaned up the breakfast things, the wagons can follow."

Sierra came up with Songbird beside her, the latter holding two tin cups of steaming coffee. Sierra carried plates stacked with syrup-soaked flapjacks and strips of bacon on the side.

"Did you have a nice chat?" Sierra asked.

Jordy said, "No. We'll talk later." He walked away shaking his head.

Chapter 44

JACK'S APPETITE WAS healthy this morning, and he found himself devouring the plate of hotcakes and bacon. He had to credit Rudy. He could put out a decent meal with whatever he had to work with, although he tended to sop hotcakes with too much of whatever syrup concoction he came up with. He shared the bacon with Thor, although Sierra had assured him Rudy would be over with scraps for the dog as soon as everybody was fed. Now he was savoring the hot coffee, taking it in sips, knowing it would ignite his bladder and he would have to seek relief soon. He was not comfortable dealing with his new granddaughter concerning such issues, although she had offered "assistance" several times. He was not certain what that meant.

He knew that Jordy was miffed at him when he left. He admitted he would have been vexed if the circumstances had been reversed. However, he felt he had accomplished what he set out to do. They had recovered Sierra's horses, or most of them anyway. He had competent crews to finish the job. He conceded obsession had taken over, as it was prone to do with him on occasion, but he was driven to see Tess. The encounter with Potter-Perez had nearly done him in, and, once again it appeared that he had dodged the Grim Reaper. But it had struck him last night that at his age every day was a bonus that he wanted to share with the woman he loved. Besides, he had a promise to keep.

He could understand that others would think he was loco. Well, he had made more than a few mistakes over the years, a few he had even learned from. Some he kept repeating. He claimed no special wisdom about anything. He had always told the listener that his free advice was worth a little more or a little less than he paid for it. Jack set his empty cup on the wagon floor, and his eyes drifted shut and his chin dropped to his chest.

When he woke an hour later, the mules were hitched, Thor was gone and Rudy stood at the back of the Studebaker. "Where's Thor?" Jack asked.

"And good morning to you, too." Rudy said. "The pitiful hound is out here pissing on the wagon wheels, since we got no trees to water. I brung him some leftovers, and he made short work of them. Your granddaughter says she doesn't want you getting out of the wagon unless she's here to supervise. I brung you a jar if that will help."

"Not pissing in a jar while I'm sitting here. I'll get it all over everything. And I'm not having her supervise my pizzle business. So you can help or not, but I'm getting out of here. Let the backboard down, so I can skootch out."

"We're both going to catch hell for this. That little heifer's starting to take over things. It's just a matter of time before her and Jordy is butting heads."

Jack scooted to the back of the wagon and worked his legs over the edge. Stabbing pain struck the wounded leg, but his feet touched the ground as he slid forward and leveraged himself to stand with most of his weight on the good leg. Rudy moved up beside him.

"Put some weight on my shoulder," Rudy said. "We'll get you around the wagon, and you can wet what Thor missed. If you got to dump, keep it off the wheels."

"Just got to piss for now. Bad." He looked around to check for privacy and saw that the other wagons were gone. "Where is everybody?"

"They pulled out fifteen minutes ago, following the horse herd. You can see the dust ahead. I'm driving this wagon today. Possum's with Bram on the chuckwagon.

You was sleeping like a dead man when Sierra stopped by. She's helping with the horses right now. Songbird is riding in the other Studebaker with Swede. Sierra said she'd swing back to check on you from time to time, and if you need anything before, we should holler, and Songbird will come."

"I'll be riding horseback tomorrow," Jack said as he relieved himself a few feet away from the wagon. Thor limped over to supervise, moving surprisingly well, mostly on three legs.

"Just so you know, Jordy told me what you got in mind. You're going to have a tussle with him yet over your taking off."

"I'm sure you don't approve either?"

"Been scratching my head trying to remember if there's anything stupider you've done. Haven't found it yet."

Several hours later, riding in the back of the wagon with Thor, Jack figured the wagon must be moving at a good pace, the way the thing was rattling and shaking. He also figured riding a horse could not be more painful or uncomfortable. The unloaded wagon bounced and jostled as it rolled over the rough prairie, and every stone on the trail sent a shooting pain up his leg and lower back.

They had caught up with the other wagons now, and Jack hoped that might ease the pace some. No sooner had the thought entered his mind than the wagon rolled to a stop. He saw Sierra lead her strawberry roan mare to the back of the wagon where she hitched the critter and then climbed over the backboard like a graceful mountain goat. He doubted if he could have negotiated the climb that easily fifty years ago. Fifty years. A half century. He was measuring life in fractions of a century now. Darn depressing.

"Grandpa," Sierra said, as she sat down across from him. "How are you feeling?"

He was getting tired of that question and the cheery voices and smiles that went with it. Sierra Wills could be a charmer, but he refused to be charmed this day. "I'm doing okay," he said.

"You need to pee. Maybe you have other chores."

Chores. A refined word for shit. He would have to remember that. "I'm fine with my chores, and Rudy helped me and Thor out to pee before the wagon pulled out."

"He did? He didn't say anything to me about it when I pulled him over."

"Probably scared to. He's gutless when it comes to dealing with females."

She squinted her eyes and looked at him with annoyance, her smile having been replaced by tight lips. "Well, let me see if you did any damage." She crawled over next to his injured leg and began unwrapping the dressing. "It's bleeding and draining some, but I guess that's to be expected. It appears you didn't do great harm. I'll redress it before I go. We might need another of Jael's poultices. Flesh around the wound looks a little pink, but I suppose that's normal."

"I've got some spare britches rolled up in my possible bag. I think Jordy's got it with my guns and other personals. Would you tell him to bring it by tonight?"

She crawled away, apparently seeking out the little bag of dressing rags she had left in one of the empty boxes. She did not answer him until she came up with the bag.

"I don't think he will. Jordy told me about your scheme."

"Had no idea I raised up such a tattler. Nobody's business what I do. Tell Jordy I want my personal stuff. Tonight. Hanging onto my things won't change what I do one whit. If I can't have my clothes, I'll just ride out of here naked and bareback if I've got to. Like that Lady Godiva. Do you know about her?"

"Yes, I have read of Lady Godiva. She was a real person, but most scholars think what she supposedly did was more legend than fact. She was protesting taxes that her own husband, some earl, was levying on his tenants."

"I am impressed," Jack said. "Anyway, I hope you got my point."

"I do get your point. And I think you are a stubborn . . ."

Jack chuckled, "Old man."

"I did not say that."

"No. You reined in your words before you got there. But you are right, and you have just caught a hint of my stubbornness. Ask Jordy. Only I prefer to call it 'persistence.'"

Chapter 45

JORDY AND SIERRA stood a respectful distance away as Jack and Swede constructed the dog cart. Several Comanches watched with curiosity. Roper had volunteered to provide the muscle the two injured carpenters could not muster and had hewn an axle from a thick oak post that was one of the supports for a Studebaker floor. Floor planks had been scavenged from both Studebakers to construct a box for the cart. They had no saws, so the axe-carved edges would be rough, but a box some five feet long and four feet wide was starting to form.

Sunset would close the workers down soon, but they were well on the way to completing Jack's dog cart before the travelers and their horse herd reached Castle Gap. Insanity, Jordy thought. What was Jack thinking? And there would be no stopping him short of hogtying the ornery cuss.

"He is really going to do this, isn't he?" Sierra said.

"Yeah, he is." Jordy said. "I gave him his stuff. He plans to ride Pokey some tomorrow."

"That wound's not going to heal if he's jostling it on the back of a horse. I'm a little worried. I checked it before supper. There's more redness and swelling around the entry wound and a yellow discharge."

"Pus? An infection?"

Sierra said, "Till this trip, my doctoring has been confined to horses and a few cows and dogs. Some infection is sort of expected in open wounds. Usually, it goes away with time, but it is probably causing some extra pain. He hasn't complained, though."

"Of course not. That's not Jack. Uncle Rudy is in charge of complaining."

"I am going with him," she said.

"Me, too. But he will be madder than a rained on rooster. I don't think we should ride out with him. I was thinking of following a spell and then catching up with him after he's been riding a half day. We could take one of the mules and pack extra food and supplies, maybe some of those Army pup tents Tige brought along in case it rained. We might need some rest shade along the way. It's not getting any cooler, and the sun doesn't show any sign of giving in to clouds."

"You don't object to my going, then?"

"Would it matter if I did?"

"No."

"That's what I figured. I'm not up to taking on two with Wills blood. I'm going to go tell Tige about our plans. He will ramrod the rest of the drive. Do you want your horses to go to the Lucky Five for now? Plenty of grass and water until you are ready to move them back to your place."

"I haven't talked to Grandpa Jack, but he had made the offer early on. And I think I will take him up on it. I'll need to hire some of your wranglers to get them home."

"Jack wouldn't expect otherwise, and he wouldn't have you hiring anybody. And it has nothing to do with you being kin. That's Jack, too."

Chapter 46

THE COMANCHES AND Lucky Five wranglers reached Horsehead Crossing midafternoon of the third day out. They took the horses across the Pecos in groups of eight to ten to avoid injuries that might result from the crowded mass and to allow time and space for each bunch to drink their fill from the river. It was dark by the time the horse crossings were completed, and Jordy decided that the chuckwagon and Studebakers should wait till morning sunlight to make the river trek.

Jordy had spoken to Tige about taking over horse division and herding Sierra's horses to the Lucky Five if Jack took off like he insisted he would. Thor's dog cart had been finished late the previous night and tested before camp broke that morning. It had taken some ingenuity, but Jack and Swede had ended up with a creation that, attached by rope lines about a horse's shoulders, trailed the animal quite well. Jordy still had reservations, however, about what would happen at full gallop. He feared that poor Thor might be tossed from the cart or dumped on the trail.

He was sitting by the dying embers of the campfire when Sierra walked up and let herself down on the ground beside him. He turned and looked at her questioningly, glad to have her company but surprised at her joining him at the fire. She seemed to dodge those moments when they might be alone together.

Sierra was silent for some moments, staring at the soft glow of the fire's remnants. "We've got a serious problem," she said.

"Now what?"

"Jael's putting a new poultice on Grandpa Jack's wound, but she agrees with me. We were working in the lamplight and couldn't see as well as we would like, but the entire thigh is swollen, and there is a lot of pus and discharge coming from the wound. It stinks so bad I almost lost my supper. He's burning up with fever."

Jordy's stomach tightened, and he felt his heart racing. "What do you suggest we do?"

"Jael says we should get him to Fort Stockton. They would have a surgeon there. I talked to Tige a few minutes ago. He says that it would be a long day's ride, but with the wagon double-teamed and the light load, we could make it by tomorrow night if we started early in the morning."

"Don't sugarcoat it. What could a surgeon do?"

"He would likely amputate the leg. Tige was cynical. He said that is the first option for the Army's surgeons, not the last. But Jael thought there would be no other choice, and I am inclined to agree."

Jordy had not thought his stomach could feel any worse, but it did. "You won't sell that to Jack. Have you discussed going to Stockton with him?"

"No, I will, but I thought you might want to be with me."

"I don't want to do it, but you shouldn't have to deal with this alone." He got up, reached down and grasped Sierra's hand and pulled her to her feet. It was then in the moonlight he saw that her face was wet and glossy with tears. He tugged her to him and took her in his arms. He held her while she sobbed softly but could think of nothing to say that might comfort her, not when he could not even console himself, subdue his fear of losing the man who was his hero and surrogate father.

Sierra pulled away when she began to regain her composure. Instinctively, Jordy took her hand and walked with her to the wagon where Jack and Thor rested. She Who Speaks waited not more than a dozen feet from the wagon.

"I wish I could help more," She Who Speaks said in a near whisper. "He is a good man with a powerful spirit, capable of surprises. I will pray that whatever god watches over him intervenes."

"Thank you, Jael, for everything. You are a dear friend. I will talk to you in the morning," Sierra said.

Jordy walked with Sierra over to the wagon, which he noticed had the canvas top peeled back halfway, probably to give the fever-stricken patient some breeze. He saw that Jack was still awake, his eyes fixed on the star-spangled sky. He did not acknowledge their presence, but Jordy knew Jack was aware of their arrival. After waiting a few moments, Jordy said, "Jack, we think you should go to Fort Stockton tomorrow. You can see a surgeon there. Maybe he can help."

"You think?"

"I think it's worth a try."

"I respect your opinion, Jordy. I'm proud of the man you are. Your folks would be proud, too. It's odd how things work out. Your loss became my blessing."

"Fate blessed me, too, Jack, the day you came along and took me in."

Jack still was not looking at them but continued talking. "And you, Sierra. I got to see a bit of my son through you. And I am so grateful you came to me and allowed me to be a part of this adventure. You've got grit, young lady, and J. T. did himself proud raising up a fine woman like you. You are a treasure I never dreamed I'd find in this life. Now I'm getting all mushy-like. Let's all get to sleep, and we can talk about Fort Stockton in the morning."

Sierra said, "I can stay with you and bathe your head with cool water."

"Thank you, sweetheart. That's very kind. But I can sleep now, and you need your rest."

"I'll be under the wagon. If you need me, just call."

"I will. I'll try not to wake you during the night when I get up to water the cactus a few times. I can take care of that just fine."

"Well," Jordy said, "goodnight, Jack. We'll talk first thing in the morning." He turned away and started to leave. "Goodnight, Sierra. You know where I'm at if you need some help. I'm within a holler's range."

She walked with him a short distance from the wagon. "Thanks, Jordy, for everything," she said.

"Hey, we're practically family. You're like my little sister."

"Well, big brother, do you think Grandpa's going to let us take him to Fort Stockton?"

"Not a chance. But I don't know what the devil he's up to."

She sighed and turned away to go back to the wagon. "I guess we'll see what the morning brings. I could sleep on rocks tonight. Goodnight, Jordy."

Jordy watched her shadowy form slip away in the moonlight and then headed for his bedroll near the fire. It cooled down fast at night in the desert country and he would have tossed a few more logs on the fire if wood had not been so hard to come by out here. He rolled out his blankets, thinking about his calling Sierra his little sister. Well, if that is what she was going to be, he had better get rid of the thoughts that been teasing his brain whenever she was near.

Chapter 47

JACK WAITED UNTIL midnight before nudging Thor awake, dropping the backboard and slipping out of the wagon with his bedroll. He hoped that if he awakened Sierra, she would assume he was heading out to pee, which he did as soon as they were twenty paces from the wagon. He limped along, wincing each time he stepped down on the wounded leg. Still, since the whole damn leg hurt all the time now, it seemed you didn't notice an extra stab of pain so much.

Thor seemed to be adapting much quicker than his human friend, starting to put some weight on the injured leg already. Jack took some solace from the indications that Thor would make a full recovery. He was harboring some doubts about himself, but his fight was not close to over as far as he was concerned. He could tell from Jordy's and Sierra's reactions that they thought he already had a foot in the grave. Maybe he would surprise them—or, perhaps, he would not. Funny, such things did not matter so much when a man was hurting like blazes.

Jack and Thor took a deer path along the twisting river's edge to where he had staked the two horses and left the cart along with tack, possible bag, and guns. With the river's sharp turns, hiding horses and gear had not been difficult. Roper had helped haul the saddle and other gear and pull the dog cart to the spot. Everybody had been preoccupied with the crossings, and any that noticed had not given his actions any thought.

He had not been able to cobble onto much food without risking detection by Rudy's watchful eye. That did not matter, so long as he could remember the locations of water holes along the way. His appetite had disappeared yesterday.

He felt badly not saying goodbye to Rudy, his loyal partner of so many years. But Rudy would have objected again and would not have kept quiet for a minute. He hoped Roper would forgive him for claiming he just wanted his horses and gear collected for crossing the river the next day. It had not been a huge lie. He could rationalize that it was now the next day, but that would not wash out the guilt of his deception.

He found the horses and gear, partially hidden by brush that grew along the river's edge. With no small effort, he saddled Pokey and then with a series of knots and hitches anchored the cart to the docile sorrel gelding he had selected for the journey. The horse carried the Lucky Five brand, so Jack figured he was not a horse thief, but he was not certain who had been riding the mount or if it was one of the spares. Regardless, there were ample mounts, so no one would be left horseless.

He slipped out the sliding panel on the back of the cart. It took a bit of coaxing, but Thor finally hopped in, looking sadly at Jack when his friend replaced the panel. Hanging onto the sorrel's lead rope, Jack stepped into the stirrup, groaning as he swung clumsily into the saddle. He paused, waiting for the pain to subside, and then headed for the slope that took them into the river.

The crossing went off without a hitch. The Pecos was down from the earlier crossing, both horses had negotiated the crossing then, and, as Swede had promised, the cart was nearly watertight and skimmed over the water like a boat.

When he rode out on the north side of the river, Jack saw that the horse herd had been collected for the night some distance west of the trail to Castle Gap just as Jordy had informed him. The current plan was to identify the

Comanche horses here, sort them out from the Turkey Foot stock and herd them in small groups down the trail to the gap. Once collected, the Comanches would move their herd through the gap, connect with the Comanche War Trail and begin the journey to join up with their Kwahadi band.

As they climbed upon the flat, he noticed that one of the night riders patrolling the near side of the horse herd appeared to have turned his mount toward Jack. He could only make out the rider's silhouette but was certain he had been seen. He lifted his arm and waved, and the rider returned a wave and went about his business. Several hours later, he had passed through Castle Gap and reached a more hospitable and reasonably level trail.

He reined in and dismounted. He was burning up, and it was not the sun generating the heat at this hour of the night. He checked on Thor, who had seemed comfortable enough since Jack unfolded and laid out his bedroll in the cart box once they crossed the river. He adjusted the ropes that connected cart to horse, slackening them a bit to allow for the flatter ground. Jack pulled off one of the canteens that hung from his saddle pommel and dug a small tin pan from his saddle bags. He took the pan back to Thor and poured some water in it, placing the pan in the cart to allow the dog to drink. Only then did he indulge in some healthy swallows himself.

He could have emptied the canteen, but it was one of only three he carried, and he could not recall the nearest water source. He was confident he would recognize it when they approached it, however. Thor did not drink all his water, so Jack took the half-full pan, pressed it to his lips and drank what did not spill down his neck. He braced his hand on the cart's side and rested a spell, his eyes casting about the silent wasteland.

He rubbed Thor's ears and wet muzzle with the other hand. "You know, Thor, I think we will keep riding till sunrise. It'll be cooler and easier on man and beast. We'll keep an eye out for shade and nap after sunrise. We'll have to be on the move again in the afternoon heat, but we'll cross that bridge when we get there."

Thor licked his hand and whined.

Jack said, "Folks would think I'm crazy talking to you like this, Thor. I don't give a darn. I've had some of my best conversations with you, my friend. You just listen to what I've got to say. Never argue. Don't gossip."

Jack continued, "I can't believe we crossed the Pecos tonight. I've got to thank you for trusting me. Between you and me, that wins the prize for the dumbest thing I ever did in my life. Rudy will never let me hear the end of it. Goes to prove, I guess, we never get too old to out-dumb our last dumbest stunt. And I've got a collection during my lifetime, let me tell you. But sometimes I get it right. Took you in—and Jordy. Couldn't have got righter than that. Nope. And then there's Tess. I promised her I'd come back. Damned tired, but I guess we had best be moving on."

Chapter 48

SIERRA WAS HORRIFIED when she awakened and saw that the sun was starting to climb over the horizon. She had slept the entire night. She had not heard Jack get up to pee, and she could hear no movement on the floor of the wagon bed above her. Surely she would have heard him if he had called for her. What if he had died?

Struck by a wave of panic, she rolled out of her blankets, pulled on her boots and crawled out from under the wagon. She raced to the back, pulled back the canvas flap and peered in. He was gone. So was Thor. Of course, the big dog would not have allowed Jack to venture out alone. He was probably relieving himself away from the wagons someplace. But you could hardly get far enough away for privacy. How well she knew that. Her modesty had all but died on this mission. She stepped back and scanned the surrounding prairie, the spear-like rays of the rising sun blinding her when she looked east.

Sierra glanced back in the wagon. Jack's bedroll was gone. So were his guns and possible bag, which she could not remember seeing last night. She turned and headed for the chuckwagon, where the scattering of men who had remained with the wagons sat on the ground with breakfast plates in their laps. Rudy had sent along a cold breakfast yesterday for those who were going to spend the night on the other side of the river.

Then she saw Jordy and Rudy standing in the shade of the chuckwagon talking animatedly about something. She hurried toward them. Jordy saw her and waved her on. As soon as she came up to them, Jordy said, "We're having a serious discussion here. Rudy says that with the river down some, the chuckwagon can cross without the raft. I say the raft's still here, let's play safe and use it. Do you want in on this?"

"I want no part of that argument, but I would leave it to Uncle Rudy. We've got bigger problems," Sierra said.

"You are a wise young woman," Rudy said.

Jordy said, "What bigger problems?"

"I can't find Grandpa Jack. I overslept, and when I got up and checked the wagon, he and Thor were gone. His bedroll and personal things are missing, too, but now that I've thought about it, I think some of his stuff was gone last night."

Rudy said, "That old weasel. He's left us. You can bet on it. He's on his way to that woman he's got a hankering for. I seen more men than I can count with female sickness in my time. Their brains either drop to the pizzle or get lost altogether. No disrespect meant, Missy Sierra. Ain't your fault."

Jordy said, "But he couldn't have left. He wouldn't have tried the crossing in the dark."

"He done it. I'd bet on it," Rudy said.

Sierra said, "But last night we talked about going to Fort Stockton."

"He didn't make a commitment to do more than talk about it," Jordy said. "He knew exactly what he was going to do. Jack Wills is always several days ahead with his mind, but he's not inclined to share his plans with anybody who is not included. We were not. Rudy's right, he likely tried the crossing last night. I hope to God he made it. I can't believe he wouldn't have better judgment. Maybe it's the fever you were talking about."

"So, what do we do?"

"I'm going after him." Jordy turned and hollered at the other three men sitting near the fire with morning coffee. "Has anybody seen Jack since last night? Or know where he staked his horses?"

It occurred to Sierra that the cart was gone, too. How could he have ever got that across the river?

Roper Hawley got up from his place at the fire and walked over to Jordy. "Horses around that second west bend in the river. Boss Jack asked me to help him get the horses and that dog cart him and Swede made over there yesterday afternoon. Can't see much from here with the double twist and brush. I'll take you over there. Don't know why he would've moved them. Should still be there."

Sierra noticed Swede still sitting with his coffee mug in hand and walked over to him. "Swede, you haven't seen Jack?"

Swede stood up. "No, Missy. I sleep behind chuckwagon. Not so hard as wagon floor and some boards take away for cart."

"Would the dog cart float?"

"Ja. Boss and me fill cracks with cedar sap. Should work."

She remembered now that whenever Jack or Swede would see an occasional scrub cedar along the trail, Swede would go out and take a hatchet to it, or Jack would ask someone to cut it and throw in the wagon. None of the trees were more than six feet tall, and by the end of the day there would be a good number of small trees stuffed in the wagon. She had never understood how the trees fit into the project but never paid much attention to the cart because she had seen it as more of a distraction for Jack to keep his mind occupied. She had not believed that when the time came, he would really choose to take off on his own.

Sierra knew now what they would find as they followed that bend in the river. As if in confirmation, Roper said, "I'll be hornswoggled. All gone. Boss Jack ride out already, I think."

Jordy said, "Yeah. Like as soon as he figured everybody was asleep last night. Darn him. I'm going to check the crossing and see if there is any sign that he had trouble at the river. Then I'm going to get a few things together, saddle up, and go after him."

"I'm going with you," Sierra said.

"Not necessary. You should be here to oversee cutting out of your horses."

"Anybody can read a Turkey Track brand," she snapped. "Tige and Irish and the others will see that my horses are accounted for. And if you don't want to ride with me, you can ride some distance behind."

"Don't get your claws out. If it's that important to you, we'll go as a team."

She regretted getting snappish with Jordy, but she never had taken bossing very well. She decided to hold off with her apology until she accumulated more inevitable trespasses.

Chapter 49

SIERRA AND JORDY had an uneventful passage through the Pecos at Horsehead Crossing. On the north side now with their mounts and two spares, Jordy looked back and saw that the remaining crew members were preparing the raft for transporting the chuckwagon. The fuss with Rudy had been needless. Once he dropped the decision in the old devil's hands, he chose the wisest course. He had to remember that Rudy gave little credibility to opinions from anyone under the age of fifty, and that it was better to let him make up his own mind about things. He had to admit that more often than not the old guy was right about things that counted.

Jack's complications with the wound were worrying Rudy more than he let on, Jordy knew. Jack's disappearance during the night had put the old-timer on the edge of hysterics. Jordy could see he was angry and apprehensive, caught up in a crosscurrent of emotions, and frustrated because he could not endure the ride that would be required for him to join them. At least he was wise enough to recognize it, something that could not be said for the Lucky Five owner.

Jordy saw Irish astride a big bay gelding, picking his way through the milling horses and reined his mount toward the ranch's head horse wrangler. He raised his hand and waved, as Irish approached.

Irish tipped his hat when he rode up. "Morning, Sierra. You too, Jordy. Looks like you're heading out. Going to join the boss man?"

"You saw him pass this way?"

"Not me, but Possum said the boss waved at him when he came by last night. Thought it strange he would be making the crossing in the dark."

At least they could confirm that Jack had crossed the Pecos without mishap. "Any idea what time?"

"Possum said it was just before night-hawk shift change, so that would make it close to two o'clock," Irish said.

"That means he has a good seven-hour head start on us," Sierra said.

"You're looking to catch up with him?" Possum asked.

Jordy said, "That's the plan." He changed the subject, not wanting to furnish too much fodder for wrangler gossip. "Looks like you are about ready to start dividing the herd."

"Yeah. I don't think it will go so bad. Funny how the bunch with Turkey Track brands tend to hang together and don't stray too far from their own, sort of like family, you might say. I think the Comanches will have their horses and be on their way by early afternoon. I'd like to be able to move the Turkey Track critters into the gap and overnight them there. Won't take as many men for night watch. If we don't have any problems with wagon crossings, we can be on our way by tomorrow this time."

Jordy said, "We've got to be moving on. We're counting on you to get Sierra's horses to the Lucky Five, but we expect to be there three or four days before you are."

"We'll bring the horses in, Jordy. Count on it."

"And Irish," Sierra said. "Please tell She Who Speaks I'm sorry I didn't have time for a proper goodbye, but that I will be writing to her at Fort Sill."

"Yes, ma'am. I'll do that."

Jordy swung his buckskin stallion around and headed for Castle Gap, his spare mount following on the lead rope. Sierra soon fell in beside him, leading her extra horse. He wondered if she was making her point that she was with him, not behind him. It didn't matter. She did not realize how much he welcomed the feisty young woman's company. Rudy had told him Sierra was just a spirited filly but warned him that some could never be broken. Well, Jordy had no interest in "breaking" any woman.

After leaving the gap behind, Jordy and Sierra found that trailing Jack would be an easy enough task. The narrow span of the dog cart's wheels left distinctive tracks, falling in between the ruts dug by normal wagon traffic. They identified rest stops from big paw prints where Thor had likely been turned loose to sprinkle the dry earth some. One such spot was marked by a healthy mound of dog excrement.

Early afternoon they caught sight of one of the slow-flowing streams where they had stopped before and then noted that the cart tracks veered off the trail and angled toward the stream. They dismounted and led their horses to the stream to drink. Jordy retrieved some hardtack and dried fruits from a bag of rations that Rudy had collected for them, and the two sat down by the stream to share a meager lunch.

"This is what we will be living on for a spell," Jordy said. "No pots and pans. We have a coffee pot and a few tin cups."

"Maybe we can shoot a rabbit or, better yet, a deer and roast some meat."

"Maybe. Maybe not."

"You are sort of a pessimist, aren't you?"

"Expect the worst. Then you won't be disappointed."

"You poor man. That's why you are a moody sort."

"A moody sort?"

"Not always. But sometimes you are like Grandpa. You drift off someplace in your head and seem rather taciturn, shut out folks around you. Maybe it's contagious, you being with him these past years and all."

"Taciturn, now that's an interesting word," Jordy said.

"Well nobody's going to accuse you of being taciturn. You don't let silences last too long."

"I don't know if that's an insult or not."

"Whoa. Not an insult. I'm not looking for a fuss. I'm just saying that you are more likely to spill out what you are thinking. That can be a good thing."

"Or not," she said. "It all depends."

Jordy said, "If I've been quiet, it's because my mind is on Jack. I keep picturing him lying on the trail up ahead. Dying or maybe even dead."

"Now there you go, expecting the worst again. I'm sure he's doing okay but would do better if he had some company and a little help. He is determined to get to this Tess woman. I just want to see that he reaches her."

"We can agree on the goal."

Sierra asked, "Do you think we are gaining ground on him?"

"I can't say, but the signs tell us he is taking three rest stops for each one we take. He's dragging that cart, and that will slow him some. It's not the weight, but that thing, light as it is, won't trail very well if he goes too fast. Too much saddle time is murder to his back, and if the fever is still with him, he will have to sleep some. We don't need to push our mounts. If we keep riding steady, I think we can catch him tomorrow morning at the latest."

Chapter 50

JACK LAY CURLED up in a fetal position on the parched ground, the sun's rays baking him like heat from a kitchen woodstove. Maybe he had died and made the trip to hell. But he didn't hurt right now, so that was a fair enough trade-off. He would rather be hot than hurt like that. Then he felt the wetness swiping across his face. Was somebody trying to put the fire out? He was dead, so why should he care? Then he saw Tess with her hand reaching out, calling to him. And Thor, Jordy, and Sierra clustered around Tess.

He opened his eyes and found Thor licking his face and felt the unending bolts of pain running the length of his leg. He was off the edge of the trail, and Pokey stood by with the spare gelding's lead rope hitched to the saddle horn. He must have passed out and fallen from his saddle. How long had he been lying there? He rolled over on his back and looked skyward. The sun said it was mid-morning. If he recollected correctly, last night had been his second on the trail. He could not recall sunrise. He must have been here for some hours. Any horse but Pokey would have deserted him by now, but Thor, on the other hand, would likely have herded the mount back.

Suddenly, Thor swung around and bared his teeth, a low growl rolling from his throat. Jack could see that the dog's eyes were focused back down the trail they had just traveled. He pushed himself up to a sitting position, continuing to support himself with one arm as his head spun and blackness tried to take him down again. Finally, his head began to clear some, and he gazed down the trail. He saw nothing, not even a scattering of dust, but somebody was coming. Thor never lied about such things.

He thought about getting up and pulling his Winchester from its scabbard, but then thought better of it, deciding he would likely end up flat in the dust again. Instinctively, he touched the Peacemaker holstered at his side, knowing he was in no position to win out over a formidable adversary but figuring he would go down shooting.

He kept his eyes on the trail. Thor started barking at the same instant Jack saw plumes of dust rising from the ground. Thor continued barking and started racing toward what were obviously approaching horses. He seemed to be favoring the wounded shoulder only slightly, disregarding it in his excitement. The bark was a greeting bark, not a signal of attack. Jack could guess who was coming, and he felt like the damned fool he would have to admit he was. That feeling was worse than any pain the leg was giving him.

Jordy and Sierra rode up behind his horses and dismounted. Jordy took the reins and lead rope of Sierra's horses and stood by his buckskin stallion silently while she rushed to Jack's side. He could see that Jack was in bad shape, but he was sitting up, and he needed to think some things out before he stepped into any conversation. Thor came over to him as if to ask Jordy why he was not looking after Jack. Jordy knelt and rubbed the dog's ears and the back of his neck and accepted several face licks. He and the dog were almost brothers, he thought, having shared Jack for so many years.

"Grandpa Jack, what happened?" Sierra said, her voice trembling and telling Jordy she was on the brink of tears.

"Guess I must have passed out and fell off my horse."

"Are you hurt . . . outside the leg?"

"Pride hurts a lot to have you come along and find me like this."

She placed a hand on his forehead. "You're burning up."

"The sun. I've been stretched out here in the sun for a long time, I think. Since before sunup, I'm guessing. Don't know how long."

"Can you stand with some help?" she asked.

"Think so."

Sierra turned to Jordy. "Do you suppose you might help me get Jack to his feet?"

"Yes, ma'am. I can do that." He hitched Sierra's horses to Buster's saddle horn and joined her at Jack's side.

Sierra said, "Before we get you up, I am going to have Jordy steady you, while I pull your britches down for a look at your leg."

"No need. I can tell you it's not a pretty sight."

"There is a need. You will do what I say, or you can just stay here."

Jack rendered a sound that was someplace between a grunt and a snarl. Jordy moved in behind Jack to support his back, while Sierra unbuckled Jack's gun belt and let it drop off with the holstered pistol. She then unhitched the trousers belt and unbuttoned the britches, worming the legs down to Jack's ankles. When Jordy saw the wounded leg, he swallowed hard. The thigh was swollen like a balloon and had become a kaleidoscope of reds, blues, purples and yellows. Pus ran from the wound site and the lower leg was bloated so much it appeared the skin might burst. It had turned nearly scarlet.

As she worked Jack's denim trousers back up the legs, covering the sight Jordy did not need to view more of, Sierra spoke matter-of-factly. "It's nasty, Grandpa. I brought some dressing materials and some of Jael's poultice medicines, and I will redress and clean the wound when we find a water supply. Now, I have a question."

"I expect you are going to ask it whatever I say."

"You are catching on to how this is all going to work. My question is this. Are you still hanging onto the notion that you are going to Tess Wyman's?"

"Yep. That's where I am headed."

Sierra said, "Jordy and I have agreed we won't try to stop you. We will help you get there if that's what you want." She looked at Jordy. "Right, Jordy?"

Jordy said, "Yes. Jack, we're done pushing and fussing about this. You are the boss man, and you're mostly grown up. If you want to get to Tess, that's exactly where we are headed."

"I'd be mighty grateful for your help. I don't think Thor and I can do this on our own, to be truthful."

Jordy said, "I thought of something when I was talking to Thor a while ago. Listen to what I am thinking."

"I'm not going anyplace," Jack said.

"Jack, you're not going to be able to sit a saddle for more than a few minutes even if we can get you on your horse, but I think you and Thor can both fit in that cart. Extra weight would probably stabilize it some. The cart might be a little short for your stretching out, but we can get you in cattywampus or prop you up some. It would be a bit snug with Thor in the box with you, but you wouldn't be tossed about so much."

"Doesn't seem like I've got much choice. I've given up on preserving my dignity, and Thor's been trying to crowd me out of my bed for a lot of years now."

Jordy said, "I've got another thought. The wheel ruts on this trail don't make for smooth riding. I noticed from your tracks, you've been going off the trail and riding the edges a lot of the time."

"Your point?"

Jordy could tell that the conversation was tiring Jack. "I say we leave the trail and cut across country. I'm betting we could gain a good day. That cart should be able to make it through anything a horse can. I've been looking up that way and I see some green that says there's grass and maybe a few trees. Odds are that means water."

Jack's voice faded away. "Whatever you think." His head sagged and Jordy eased him back.

Chapter 51

THE DOG CART had been converted to a cozy nest, with Jordy and Sierra adding their own bedrolls to Jack's to cushion the floor. Jack mostly slept as the riders made their way across the prairie. The terrain would not be considered forested and the grass was not lush. Mesquite was plentiful and they did come across some scattered oaks and cottonwoods and even a cluster of willows along a stream where they were able to replenish water supplies and water the horses. By the end of the day, they had moved into some hill country, but the hillocks proved to impose no obstacles, offering sufficient gaps between them to permit passage.

They took a break late afternoon near a spring that erupted from a limestone hillside and trickled down the slope and ran off in a stream that was no more than a foot wide. Jordy built a small dam from dirt and stones to catch the flow in a little pool for the horses to drink and then filled canteens from the water's source. They agreed to nap and rest the horses for four or five hours, then saddle up for a night ride.

Sierra found some ground at the base of the hillock that had silted in over the years that promised some softness for bedrolls. Jordy assisted Jack out of the cart and helped him stagger off to relieve his bladder. Unfortunately, the urine came in drops and was colored a dirty yellow. They needed to get him to drink more water. Jordy had about given up on getting Jack to eat. Sierra had removed the bedrolls from the cart and spread them out side by side, hers next to Jack's, leaving room for Thor on the other side. Jordy's was next to Sierra's, but he noted she had kept a good yard between them. He did not care. A woman was the last thing on his mind right now. Well, sometimes when he watched her scurry about and move that firm fanny just so, his mind wandered where it should not.

Sierra did have some luck encouraging Jack to drink a fair amount of water before she let him lie down on his bedroll. They shared the hardtack and some dried beef with Thor before the dog returned to Jack's side. During another time, Thor would have chased down a rabbit or dug up some varmint to supplement his meal, but the dog never let Jack out of his sight now.

"I'll build a fire and make coffee when we get up, unless you want some now," Jordy said.

"Wait till we get up. That's when I'll need it. Could we walk a few minutes before we try to rest?"

"Sure. I doubt if I will sleep much anyhow," Jordy said.

Leaving Jack in Thor's care, they strolled a short distance away from where the bedrolls lay, checking the horses they had staked out nearby as they walked. Jordy was surprised when Sierra slipped her hand into his and grasped it.

"He is dying, isn't he, Jordy?"

"The odds aren't good for him. Every time I go to check on him, I worry he won't be breathing. He can't always talk, and when he does it's a whisper. Our best hope is to keep him alive till we reach Tess's. Maybe she can pull out a miracle. The important thing is that we get him there alive. We've got to do that much for him."

"Is Grandpa Jack a religious man?"

"I've been with him fifteen years, and I can't answer that. He thinks about religion a lot and he's got lots of books about different religions. When I was fourteen, he insisted I read the Bible cover to cover and quizzed me on it to be sure I wasn't just flipping pages. It turned out to be mighty interesting reading. He said I could pick what to believe, if anything, but an educated man in America needed to know and have some understanding of the Bible."

"So you didn't go to church much?"

Jordy smiled, "Nope. Easters with the Army chaplain after Fort Concho was built, then the Methodists after they organized a congregation in San Angelo. Jack did funerals and even weddings if he couldn't weasel out of it. He said he liked to go Easters to hedge his bets. Of course, he never discouraged me from going. But I was never much motivated."

"So he's not an atheist?"

"No. He would dismiss that notion out of hand. He always says religious folks cannot prove what they believe. It is a matter of faith. But Jack points out that atheists cannot prove otherwise, so they cannot arrogantly claim superiority. They just have faith in what is not, sort of a religion that denies the existence of God."

Sierra said, "I was baptized Catholic. Mama was devout, and while she was alive, I went to mass with her every Sunday. Papa was Methodist but he deferred to Mama on religious matters. After Mama died, I attended church with him until we moved out on the prairie where there weren't any churches. When he sent me to school in

San Antonio, I went to confession sometimes and went to mass quite often, but my behavior there was not angelic by any means."

"Now that might be an interesting story."

"Well, you are not going to hear it, so put that notion out of your head. Anyway, I am a Christian and firm believer, and I have been praying for Grandpa Jack."

They turned back toward the bedrolls. He was aware she had not released his hand, and he rather liked hers entwined with his. He attached no significance to it beyond that she had become comfortable with him, like a little sister. But he still was not feeling like an older brother.

Jordy said, "The only thing I remember about church as a boy was watching the preacher swat at flies one Sunday while he was giving a sermon. He had a bald spot round as a saucer on top of his head, and flies seemed to be throwing a party there. He would swat and swipe while he tried to deliver the sermon. I think he cut it short that day. It's funny what we remember. One of the hands asked me a while back how much I remembered before I was ten. He claimed most folks don't remember much of their lives before that time. Just bits and pieces."

"Well," Sierra said, "I'm not as old as you, but I think there might be something to it. And most of the things that come back to me, I can't imagine why I would even remember them."

"I remember the day the Comanches killed my family, more details than I would like to recollect. I was ten then, but most of life before that is a blur of generalities. And, like you, the specific events I recall make no sense. I feel badly sometimes that I don't remember my parents better, more than fragments. Jack and Rudy are my family. Jack is my father in all but name and blood."

When they returned to the bedrolls, Jack and Thor were still sleeping soundly. Sierra touched her fingertips to Jack's head and sighed. "He's still burning up, but I didn't expect otherwise. I'll keep the canteen near and see if I can get him to drink when he wakes up."

She turned to Jordy, and he could see the tears glistening in those hazel eyes, greenish tonight in the moonglow. "Jordy, I will feel we failed him somehow if we don't get him to Tess."

Chapter 52

SIERRA HAD BARELY dropped off to sleep when she heard Jack's moans. She tossed the blankets off and crawled out of her bedroll, grabbing the canteen and moving to his side. Thor whined as he nosed his friend's cheek. Jack was delirious, babbling non-sensical words. She heard Jordy's name and her own, but Tess's name came up most. Once, he said, "Hell no, Rudy."

She placed her hand behind his head and raised him up, lifting the canteen to his lips. She was encouraged that he took several healthy swallows of water. She wet one of her cloths and pressed it against his forehead as she lowered him and then bathed his face with cool water. "Grandpa, do you know who I am?" Sierra asked.

"Of course. You are my granddaughter, Sierra Wills." His voice cracked and was not much above a loud whisper.

"Yes, I am. And I love you, Grandpa. More than you can know."

"I love you, too, sweetheart."

Suddenly, he was lucid again, giving her renewed hope.

"Tell Rudy to get his fat ass over here, would you?"

"Uh, Grandpa, Rudy isn't here."

"Where the hell is he?"

"He stayed back with the horses and wranglers. Don't you remember?"

"What horses?"

It seemed pointless to explain, and he relieved her of further awkward dialogue by dropping off to sleep again.

When she turned away, she saw that Jordy's bedroll had been removed. She cast her eyes about their shadowy campsite and saw him with the horses. He seemed to be saddling the mounts to move out. She got up and joined him.

"What are you doing?" she asked.

"What does it look like?"

She thought he seemed a bit brusque. "Okay. It was a dumb question."

"Sorry. I had no excuse to be sarcastic. I couldn't sleep, and I got to calculating how far we have probably come and how much time we've saved by cutting off the main trail. If we head out now and push the horses some and switch mounts frequently, I think we could be at Tess's before dark tomorrow or not long after."

Sierra said, "We've got to try."

****

Jordy and Sierra had made a frantic race across the West Texas plains, winding through hills early on and finally reaching a straight run on the flat for some miles before connecting again with the wagon trail several miles south of San Angelo where the Middle and South Concho rivers converged before joining the North Concho at the town. It was only midafternoon, so they had beat Jordy's time estimate by some hours.

She reined in her mare, and Jordy followed suit. They both dismounted and went promptly to the cart. Thor looked up with sad eyes as if expecting her to do something. She stroked the dog's head and neck while she leaned over the cart and examined Jack. His breathing appeared labored, but he slept soundly, and under the circumstances Sierra considered that a blessing. Since leaving their stopover last night, they had stopped every few hours to rest the horses and to check on Jack and to try to get him to drink, mostly without much success.

She straightened up and looked at Jordy, not liking the whipped look on his face. "Do you think I should try to wake him to drink?"

"We're not more than an hour from Tess's. It has been a wasted effort the last two stops. His britches dry?"

"I checked. Yes."

"Then he hasn't passed water for almost a day. That can't be good."

Sierra said, "He was determined to see Tess. Let's move and hope she owns a magic wand."

Chapter 53

TESS WYMAN WAS standing on the front porch of her house when the party rode up to the hitching rail. She gave a quick wave, stepped off the porch and hurried to the cart before Sierra and Jack even dismounted. When the two joined her, Tess already had Jack's head cradled in one hand and was tracing the fingers of the other over his forehead.

She turned to Sierra. "Hello, Sierra. I am Tess. I have been waiting for you. I sensed an hour ago that Jack was on his way here and that he was terribly ill."

Tess's words sent a shiver down Sierra's spine. "We left the others behind. All Jack would say was that he had to get to you. He sneaked out and left on his own during the night, and Jordy and I caught up with him. We promised we would bring him here."

"And you have kept your promise. Now, please help me get him to my bed."

Jordy removed the sliding panel from the back of the cart. "I can hoist him under his shoulders and take most of the weight. Tess, why don't you take his feet and, Sierra, you support his midsection? Unless somebody's got a better idea."

"I fear that's the best we can do," Tess said.

Jordy dragged Jack, gently as possible, from his nest in the cart and then the two women took their positions. It was a struggle, but soon they had Jack on the bed where the covers had already been pulled back and a man's flannel nightshirt already lay. Thor sat at the bedside as if supervising Jack's care and Tess entered no objection.

Sierra found herself befuddled. How could Tess have known? And how did she happen to have a man's nightshirt? Well, she had suspected, but somehow could not accept the reality, that her grandfather occasionally shared this woman's bed. Tess Wyman was a striking woman whose near flawless skin and grace of motion suggested a woman much younger than her Grandpa Jack's age, but she knew that folks carried their ages differently.

Tess was unquestionably in charge now, firmly and politely issuing instructions that did not encourage disobedience. "Jordy," she scolded, "Jack would tell you those horses have been ridden too hard. Why don't you put them up in the pen outside the stable? There's a tank there, but you will likely have to pump and carry water. Hay in the barn and some grain in a barrel just inside the door. It all came from the Lucky Five, so use what you need."

Sierra could see that Jordy's eyes were fixed on Jack and that he was reluctant to leave. Finally, he wheeled and walked out the bedroom doorway.

"Help me get him out of these filthy clothes," Tess said. "We can't put him in a tub, but I have a pot of hot water simmering on the woodstove. We will clean him up and see what we can do for him."

Tess deftly peeled off Jack's britches and undershorts while Sierra unbuttoned his shirt and tugged the sleeves from his arms and pulled it away. In moments he lay naked on the bed. Tess's attention turned to the ballooning leg. "I have a drawer full of tea towels next to the kitchen sink and another of washrags. Would you grab a handful of each, Sierra? And then I will need the pot of water from the stove."

Jack was moaning and writhing on the bed when Sierra returned with the waterpot and an armful of towels and washrags.

"Stay with him," Tess said. "I have laudanum. I have to admit that works better for pain than any of my plant remedies." She came back with a bottle of brown liquid, a teaspoon and a glass of water and set it on the lamp table.

"He has calmed some," Sierra said.

"Good. We'll save the laudanum for later. Let's wash him up. You can take the upper body if you prefer."

Sierra preferred. She wanted no part of washing her grandfather's male parts. And she was ready to let someone else deal with the bullet wound that had become a rancid volcano of pus and fluids oozing from its depths.

While she washed Jack's face and torso, she watched Tess out of the corners of her eyes. The older woman's face was expressionless as she pushed Jack on his side, so she could examine the wound. She unwrapped the wound's foul dressing, squeezing the flesh some to excise some of the slimy fluid. She washed about the wound, rebinding it with one of the tea towels. Then she moved her washrag higher, starting to wash his genitalia.

Sierra started when she heard Jack's croaking voice. "Hey, woman, my old pizzle isn't open for business right now." Sierra stepped back, feeling her face flush and thankful again for her dark complexion.

Tess pulled the sheet over his lower body and moved to Jack's side, bending over, softly kissing his cracked, parched lips. She knelt beside the bed and took his hand in hers. "You've still got some orneriness in you. That's a good sign."

"I don't mean to complain, Tess, but I'm hurting like hell."

"I have some laudanum."

"Not yet. I need my head clear for a bit."

Thor had been watching quietly and at the sound of Jack's voice pressed in beside Tess, sticking his head over the side of the bed. Tess placed Jack's hand on the big dog's head.

Jack said, "I knew you'd be close by, old fella. We made it, Tess. Got here, by damn."

"Yes, you made it, and I'm glad."

"Will you marry me, Tess? I promised I'd be back to ask a question."

Tess kissed him again. "Yes, my love. I will marry you."

Jack gave the trademark crooked grin.

Tess said, "Sierra, go call Jordy. Hurry. Tell him to get here quick."

Sierra turned and raced for the door. When she stepped out onto the porch, she looked toward the small stable and saw Jordy in the pen with a pitchfork full of hay he was tossing along the fence line for the horses. She hurried to the end of the porch and yelled, "Jordy, to the house now. Tess says 'quick.'"

He set aside the pitchfork and scrambled over the fence. Sierra spun around and headed for the front door but stopped and froze when the mournful howling broke the late afternoon quiet of the isolated house. "No. No. Grandpa, no," she screamed.

Jordy came bounding upon the porch. "What is it? What's the matter?"

"He died. Grandpa Jack is dead. That's why Thor is howling. I know it."

Jordy took her in his arms and held her while she sobbed.

"I killed him," she said. "If I had not come to the Lucky Five, he would be alive and getting ready to marry Miss Wyman. He asked her, you know. He came back while you were with the horses and asked her to marry him."

"The barking has quieted. Maybe it was something else. We need to go in and see," Jordy said. He stepped back and took her arm and guided her into the house.

When they reached the bedroom door, she saw that Tess had pulled up the sheet to cover Jack to his neck, and he lay on the bed, his body totally still, no more rising and falling of his chest. Thor lay beside him, whimpering, his head resting on Jack's shoulder.

Tess evidently heard them and turned to face them, composed except for tears rolling slowly down her cheeks. "Jack's gone. I'm sorry. I thought we had just a bit more time."

Chapter 54

JORDY, SIERRA, AND Tess sat at the kitchen table discussing arrangements for Jack's burial. Thor remained in the bedroom with his old comrade. "Jack gave me instructions several years ago," Jordy said. "He wrote them down, and they should be in the safe at home. I'll double check, but I remember them well enough. For one thing, he said he did not want an undertaker messing with his body. That means we take the body back to the ranch tonight. Can we use your buckboard, Tess? I don't want to haul him in the cart, though he would probably have liked the idea."

"Of course," Tess said. "If there is anything I can do, please just ask. He will be buried in the ranch cemetery, I assume?"

Jordy was surprised at how calm and detached he felt. He could never love anyone more than he had Jack Wills, but real grief had not hit him, perhaps because there had been those days on the trail to prepare for what he had seen as inevitable. "Yes, he has a section all measured and sketched out for special burials. Jack the planner, you know. I can measure out where he is to be buried. There is a place for Thor on one side, and Rudy next to Thor. He plotted an adjacent area for me and any family I might have, but—this is difficult to talk about, Tess, there is a space on the other side of Jack for you, if you want it."

"You are serious? I've wondered where my remains might end up someday. No children, a brother many miles from here I have virtually lost touch with. Yes, I am making my reservation tonight." She gave a feeble smile and dabbed tears from her eyes.

Jordy said, "With this heat, he will have to be buried tomorrow. I'm thinking late afternoon to give us time to take care of the details. Jack didn't want the fuss of a big funeral. Just some of the ranch folks. I'll see if we can put out some kind of an outdoor supper for the few who would be there. I'm sure Josephina will take charge."

"Coffin?" Sierra asked.

"Stashed in the barn loft with another for Thor. Oak. Very simple. Jack had Swede build them when he was planning arrangements."

"Shouldn't we have at least a simple service with a preacher?" Sierra asked.

"We have a man who works for the freight company and preaches to the Methodists on Sundays, but he's likely on a run. I suppose I could check."

"I'll do it," Sierra said. "I would take care of the service."

He looked at her in surprise. "You would?"

"Short and sweet. You said there is a Bible in the library. I'll put something together."

Later, Jordy and Sierra shared the seat in the buckboard as Jordy drove Tess's borrowed horse team and wagon in the moonlight up the sloping road that led to ranch headquarters. They had ridden in silence most of the distance with Jack, now dressed in the nightshirt and carefully wrapped in a blanket by Tess, laid out in the wagon bed, guarded by his faithful Thor.

Sierra broke the quiet. "You weren't there when Jack spoke. You didn't hear what he said."

"No."

"He asked Tess to marry him. She said 'yes.'"

"Do you think that was what the rush to get back was all about? He wanted to ask her to marry him?" Jordy asked.

"I do. He knew he was dying. He had something important to finish. They obviously loved each other very much. It is so sad they were denied a married life together."

"But they had a love and a life for ten or more years that many never experience even with marriage. Let's be glad for that. I know that's what Jack would say."

"You seem so collected, almost businesslike, in dealing with all this."

He shrugged. "I can't explain it. Sometimes I think this is all a nightmare that I must get through. I suppose it seems cold."

"Strange, but not cold. I have heard that with some, grief waits, sometimes a long time. Do you hate me for bringing Jack to this end?"

He looked at her. "Hate you? Never. Dislike you? No. And I do not blame you. We have been through a lot together these past few days. I have no better friend than you. Get the notion out of your head. This was not your fault. Maybe it was just his time. I have heard some folks say that we've all got a time on the clock when it's all over. He could have died sitting in a rocking chair."

"You don't believe that?"

"Well, no. I haven't come around to that way of thinking yet. But nobody knows. Jack often said he was living on bonus time, that he should have died a dozen times over the past fifty years. He claimed he just could not quit challenging the rider of the pale horse. Biblical reference, I think."

"Death. Book of Revelation." She placed a hand on his forearm. "We're almost there. What happens now?"

"Most are still up. I need to go to Rusty Dobbs's house and give him the news. He will see to a lot of the details, notifying others and getting word to Tige Marshall's wife, Juana. She will tell the freight company workers. A lot of folks connected with the Lucky Five are going to take this hard. Jack Wills walked on water as far as most are concerned."

"And still, he seemed like such an ordinary man."

"That's why. He never held himself above anybody else. It was a natural thing with him."

When they pulled the wagon into the yard, Sierra said, "There are a few lamps on in the house. Somebody's there."

"Likely Josephina or Consuelo, or both. They might be looking for us to return any day and are getting ready to welcome everybody back. Are you up to giving them the news?"

"I don't look forward to it, but I will."

"Then I'll drop you off here and take the wagon and string of horses down to the big barn. Then I will roust out Rusty and give him the bad news. He can recruit a few of the hands to help. I'll have a few of the guys get the coffin down from the loft and we'll bring Jack up. I thought we would lay him in the library. Seems right somehow. Maybe you and Consuelo can round up some duds for Jack. Otherwise, I'll look when I get there. Whoever is at the house can get the rest of the Cortez family out to help with things there. It will be a late bedtime for everybody, but there won't be much sleeping at the Lucky Five tonight."

Chapter 55

JORDY STOOD WITH Thor at Jack's graveside. He was not certain Jack would have approved of the fuss made about his funeral this afternoon. Word had spread like wildfire about the Lucky Five owner's demise and burial plans, and an hour before burial was scheduled a literal caravan of people had descended upon the ranch, not only folks from the Lucky Five enterprises but from nearby ranch and farm families and town businesses. There had been a good number Jordy did not recognize that he figured Jack had done a good turn for at one time or another.

Even the Fort Concho commandant had showed up with a military funeral detail that had draped a flag on the coffin and provided a twenty-one-gun salute. The bugler playing taps had likely sent chills down many spines. Jack had been a veteran of both the Texas War for Independence and, later after statehood, the Mexican War, not to mention his long service with the Rangers.

True to her word, Sierra, stunning in a black dress with matching hat and veil that Consuelo had helped round up, had presided efficiently over the brief service. No sermon. A reading from Chapter Three of Ecclesiastes: "To every thing there is a season and a time to every purpose under the heaven, a time to be born and a time to die . . ." and then asking all to join with the singing of "Shall We Gather at the River?" But midway during the song the crowd had stopped singing, so awed were they by her beautiful voice echoing through the valley. She seemed not to notice she had become a soloist and had continued without missing a beat.

Jordy, heir to his mentor's ambiguity about religion, had been deeply moved by Sierra's performance. Finally, all had recited the Lord's Prayer. The flag that had draped Jack's coffin had been folded then, and when a member of the honor guard looked uncertainly for a recipient, Jordy had nodded toward Sierra, who graciously accepted the folded flag.

The female horse wrangler he had ridden with the past several weeks had left Jordy feeling a bit overwhelmed with her shifting roles, moving so easily to a poised, confident woman presiding over her grandfather's impromptu funeral. She had earned his respect this day.

Fortunately, most attending had brought food to contribute to a community supper, and hands had hurriedly requisitioned every table on the ranch to set out on the grounds below the house and cemetery. Jordy turned away from the gravesite. Attendees were now sitting on blankets and benches partaking of the feast that had appeared spontaneously. The sight would have pleased Jack, with the gringos, Mexicans, and colored ex-soldiers and families all intermingling comfortably on his ranch.

He saw Sierra and Tess working through the throng together, apparently greeting and thanking folks for their presence. He did not enjoy such things and would never make a politician, he thought, but he supposed he had some responsibility to express his appreciation. Before he walked away from the cemetery, he looked back and saw that Thor was not budging and was now lying on the mound of dirt that covered Jack's coffin. He decided to leave the dog to his mourning for now and return later with food scraps and try to coax Thor to the house.

When he stepped out onto the ground below the cemetery, he saw a mustachioed, impeccably dressed and suited man coming his way. He had never formally met the man, but he recognized him as Frank Bell Russo, the

San Angelo lawyer whom Jack had visited on occasion. Russo extended his hand when he came up, and they exchanged firm grips.

"Mister Jackson," Russo said, "I am Frank Russo, I was Jack Wills's lawyer. My sincerest condolences. Jack was a rare breed, and I was honored to do business with him."

"Pleased to meet you, Mister Russo. Just Jordy will do."

"And Frank for me, since we are going to become well acquainted, and I hope friends, during the months ahead. I won't take much of your time today, but I do require your help."

"I will help you if I can, of course."

"I am executor of Jack's will, and I would like to meet with all the major beneficiaries for a reading of the will Friday, three days from now, say one o'clock in my office. I would like to ask you to inform the beneficiaries, as I think you will be speaking to all of them."

"Sure, I could do that, if you will tell me who I need to notify."

He plucked a folded sheet of paper from the inside of his coat pocket, unfolded it, perused it a moment and handed it to Jordy. "Jordan Jackson, Rudolph Kilgore, Theresa Wyman, Tige and Juana Marshall, and Sierra Wills."

Jordy had no idea how everyone fit into Jack's arrangements. They had never discussed such things. It was none of his business, and Jack always held his cards close to the vest. "I will get word to them. Tige and Rudy are on a horse drive right now, but I expect them back by day after tomorrow. If not, I will just have to let you know."

"We could reschedule, but I think it would be desirable to make the will's contents known as soon as possible."

"Okay, Frank. I will see that everyone is notified."

They shook hands, and Russo disappeared.

Jordy again moved toward the clusters of people, who from their laughter, seemed to have turned the funeral supper into a festive occasion. He smiled. Jack would have liked that, too. Sort of an Irish wake. He wondered if he would always see things through Jack's eyes.

Before he reached the group he was headed for, Jordy was intercepted again, this time by Rusty. "Boss, I need to talk to you private-like for just a minute."

Jordy did not consider himself the boss, but he guessed he was making decisions because of the current void, so he did not correct the foreman. "What is it, Rusty?"

"Well, I didn't want to say anything because of all the funeral arrangements and all, and I know you've been hit hard as hell."

"Go ahead, Rusty."

"I didn't want to say anything, but when I was in town last week I stopped by Tobe's Tavern for a sandwich and a beer. There is something there you should see as soon as possible."

"I don't know what you are talking about, Rusty."

"Boss, I think you should just see for yourself."

Jordy sighed. "I've got to go into town tomorrow to talk to Juana at the freight office. I'll stop at Tobe's and have a beer." He avoided Tobe's generally. Tobe Marx maintained a dump, and the tavern was mostly a sideline to the whoring business he ran upstairs. But his interest had certainly been piqued. Curiosity would push him to Tobe's tomorrow.

Chapter 56

AFTER THE LAST buggy headed down the trail away from the house in darkness, Sierra entered the house and went to the kitchen to thank Josephina and Consuelo for their work in organizing an unplanned funeral supper. "Thank you for all you did today," she said to the two women who were finishing their cleanup. "I understand why Jack thought of you as a part of his family. This would have been a horrendous experience if you had not been here to take charge."

Josephina said, "You are welcome, but we loved Jack. Our hearts are heavy." She made no effort to brush away the tears that streamed down her cheeks. "He was watching today, though, and he would have been so proud of his granddaughter. That you carry his blood was never clearer."

Consuelo, also teary-eyed, smiled, "But I have heard Jack sing a few times, and your voice must have come from some other ancestor."

"You both have been so kind to me." She hugged each of them and stepped back. "And any voice I have was my mother's doing, I assure you. It did not come from the Wills family." She changed the subject. "Have you seen Jordy?"

Consuelo said, "He is in the library."

"I haven't spoken with him since the graveside service. I caught glimpses of him talking to different folks. I guess I will go see if he would mind some company."

Consuelo said, "I promise he won't mind."

When Sierra went into the library, she saw Jordy seated in Jack's leather upholstered chair, gazing at the wall of books shelved on the opposite side of the room.

"May I join you?" she asked.

Jordy turned his head and stood up. "Of course." He nodded toward his chair's twin on the opposite side of the lamp table, setting it at an angle more suitable for comfortable conversation before Sierra sat down.

"Are you a wine drinker?" Jordy asked.

"I am not a connoisseur by any measure, but I would try a glass."

"Jack didn't drink often, but if he did it was wine, and I guess he was as close to a connoisseur as we would have at the Lucky Five. He kept bottles and glasses in the cupboard behind the lamp table here."

Jordy put two wine glasses on the lamp table, which was within reach of both. Then he plucked a bottle from the cupboard shelf. "This is red wine. Jack preferred red wines. The label is French, so I can't tell you what it is."

"It wouldn't mean anything to me anyway, but if it is French it has got to be good, doesn't it?"

Jordy shrugged, poured two glasses, and set the bottle on the table. He handed a glass to Sierra and returned to his chair. "We should drink to Jack," he said, reaching over with his wine glass and holding it up. She touched her own to Jordy's. "To Jack Wills," she said. "A legend in his time."

"To Jack," Jordy said.

They both sipped at their wine. The liquid seemed bitter to Sierra, and she wrinkled her nose.

Jordy smiled, "The second will go down easier."

He was right. She looked about the room. "Thor. Where is Thor? He was always by your chair."

"He is still at the cemetery. It was the occupant not the chair that brought him here. I took him a pan of water and a big sack of food scraps earlier. He just sniffed it then. I'm hoping he will eat it later."

"What do we do?"

"Give him time, I guess. Maybe in a day or two we can coax him over. He used to sleep with me when Jack was gone. We'll think of something. I don't think we could drag him over here right now. He is where he wants to be."

"It is so sad."

"There is something I need to tell you. I talked to Jack's lawyer today. There will be a reading of Jack's will at his office in San Angelo Friday at one o'clock. He would like you to be there."

"Me? Why should I be there?"

"The only thing he said was that he wanted all the beneficiaries to be there."

"But Jack didn't even know of my existence until almost three weeks ago."

"You know as much as I do about it. Tess is to attend, as well as Rudy and Tige and Juana."

"I guess I will still be here. I should probably rest the herd a week or two before driving the horses back to the Turkey Track. If it is okay with you, I might leave Dancer here until Buster gets her bred. I might cut out a few more fillies for Buster's services. I would pay you, of course."

"I wouldn't dream of charging you a fee. It would be Buster's pleasure. But I think you should hold off any decisions till after the meeting with the lawyer anyway."

"It is okay for me to stay here then—in the house?"

"Of course, I don't even know how long I have the right to stay."

"Jack wouldn't have kicked you out of the house."

"I don't think so, but I don't know for sure. The Bill of Rights mentions nothing about the right to an inheritance, and I don't have any claim. Whatever Jack did would never change the way I feel about him. He prepared me to move on if that is the way it is going to be."

She had not realized she had finished her glass of wine while they sat there, but it had relaxed her some. She held out her glass. "I think I would like another."

She noticed that Jordy's glass was still half full when he handed hers back. He cautioned, "You don't want to drink this one so fast, string it out a bit."

She put the glass on the table and began to take off her shoes. "My feet are killing me. I am a boots kind of gal." She tossed the shoes aside and tucked her feet under her legs. Not too ladylike, she supposed.

Jordy said, "You did a fabulous job today. I had no idea you had such a beautiful singing voice, and you spoke so eloquently. I don't want you to take this wrong, but you were a stunning woman out there in that Texas sun."

She was a bit taken aback, but she sensed no disrespect in his tone. Besides, what woman wants to be told she looks like a dirty rag mop? "Thank you. I had never seen you in a suit before. You clean up good yourself. I guess we did well enough under the circumstances."

Jordy said, "I need to ask you something."

"Yes?"

"Would you prefer I move to the bunkhouse during your stay?"

"Why on earth would I want you to do that?"

"Think about it. There are just two of us sleeping in this house. We might get by for a night, but after that folks will start to talk. Our ranch people will just speculate, but by the time the story reaches town it will be fact."

"Are you dangerous?" She almost hoped that he was.

"I'm a man, and you are a tempting woman, but I would never take advantage of you. I'm not that virtuous, but all I would be able to think about was what Jack would say about my behavior. Heck, he would probably send a thunderbolt down to strike me dead if I got out of line."

"Then you will stay here. I don't want to be alone in this big house. That would feel creepy."

"Rudy might make me move out when he gets back anyhow. We will take it a day at a time, I guess. You must be tuckered out. I want to go check on Thor before I go to bed. You can go ahead and get ready for bed if you like."

"That's a long trip to check on the dog."

"Not that far."

"I want another glass of wine."

"Sierra, are you sure? I don't think you're used to this, and you've been drinking too fast. You're not drinking water."

"Never mind, I'll pour my own."

"No, I'll pour your wine, but you're going to have a headache in the morning."

She had almost decided to forego the third drink, but when Jordy tried to talk her out of it, she became more determined. When he handed her the glass, she could see he had shorted her some. That annoyed her, and she drank it in two swallows. Was that ladylike? Hell, who cared?

"I have to run in to town in the morning," Jordy said. "Anything you want me to pick up?"

"Do you want company?" When she asked, she thought she may have made another promise for the day, but she could not remember what it was.

"I've got private business. I'm going to stop at Tess's along the way and tell her about the meeting with the lawyer."

"Not wanted. Thas what you shaid. Leave me alone, She-aira." She knew she was saying something stupid, but her brain was not in control of her mouth. "Never liked me. But I saw your eysh. You wanted in She-aira's bloomers. Just like Carlos. I'm going to bed, and you keep your hansh and pishel to home."

She dropped the wine glass and it shattered on the floor. Then she struggled to get up, unable to get her feet from beneath her legs. She was aware of Jordy slipping his hands beneath her shoulders and lifting her from the chair. Her body collapsed against his, and she felt Jordy's arms slip around her and pull her tight against him. She lifted her head and pressed her lips against his, aware of his response when her tongue played with his lips. Suddenly, her stomach rebelled, and a wave of nausea swept over her. She pulled back, vomited down the front of her dress and on Jordy's suit before she fainted away.

Chapter 57

JORDY TOSSED HIS suit on top of Sierra's crumpled dress at the top of the staircase. Sierra could damn well explain it to the laundry women. He had no idea how the suit would be cleaned or if it could. Attired only in his undershorts, he walked back down the hallway to his room. He paused and peered into Sierra's room, where she lay in a dead sleep beneath a sheet and light blanket, snoring like a hungry hog. He had left her window open to air out the room, but the odor of vomit still lingered.

In a way, he was glad that the illness had intervened. His willpower had been fading. He would not deny he lusted for this woman, but if something ever happened between them, and that prospect seemed increasingly unlikely, he did not want it to happen like this.

He slipped into bed and dropped off to sleep instantly. Several hours later, he was awakened by an eerie howling sound drifting through his window. At first, he thought it was a lone wolf on the hilltop above the ranch house. Then he remembered Thor. He got out of bed and pulled on his denim britches and a pair of moccasins along with an old cotton shirt. He also grabbed a folded wool blanket from a chair in the corner of the room before heading for the stairway.

It was a balmy night with only a sprinkling of stars in the sky, but a near full moon furnished ample light as he rushed along the path to the cemetery. A stumble might launch him rolling down the slope to the ranch yard but would not plummet him to his death. Thor's howling was incessant and pitiful, and all the ranch occupants likely heard it. Hopefully, his presence would calm the dog. If he could not coax Thor away, he would stay the night.

When he arrived at Jack's gravesite, the dog heard him and turned, whining softly as Jordy approached. Thor sat on top of the loose dirt, Jordy noted. He checked the water pan. It seemed to be untouched, as were the food scraps he had left earlier. Now that he thought about it, the dog had eaten little, if anything, since he and Sierra caught up with Jack, and he was certain he had not drunk any water since Jack's death the previous night. It could have been a longer stretch. Jack had drawn their almost undivided attention.

He knelt and wrapped his arm about Thor and pulled him close. "Oh, Thor. I don't know what to do, old friend. I know the hurt is almost unbearable. But I love you. Others love you. Life can be good again. Not the same, but good."

Tears began to run down Jordy's cheeks, and then he started to sob uncontrollably. "Oh, Jack, I loved you, and I never really told you. I love you, Jack, and I'll miss you every day of my life." Thor licked his face as if trying to console him, and then he felt the touch of a hand on his shoulder. He turned his head and saw Sierra had knelt beside him. Still, he could not stop crying. She put her arm about his shoulders and hugged him softly.

Finally, he felt about cried out and began to get a handle on his emotions. Thor had slipped away and now lay on the grave again.

Sierra said, "I woke up and heard Thor howling and then you left. I collected my wits some, and even though I wasn't sure I would be welcome, I followed."

"It's okay. You're welcome. But I plan to stay with Thor tonight and decide to what to do about him tomorrow."

She held up a blanket. "I looked out the window and saw you were carrying one, so I found one, too. I would like to stay with you and Thor, if you will let me."

He saw that she wore a robe thrown over a flannel nightgown now, although she had made the journey barefoot. "We would like to have your company." He got up and spread his blanket out next to the grave, and she put hers on top. They crawled beneath Sierra's blanket, Jordy claiming the spot nearest the grave and Thor and rolling over on his side to face the dog, so he could reach out to pet and calm him should it be necessary. For the time being, however, Thor appeared pacified by their presence.

Jordy felt Sierra spoon up against him and throw her arm over his waist. She fell asleep quickly, and this time, thankfully, she slept with a soft purring, which was far better than the loud snoring and snorting he had heard earlier that night. *Nice*, he thought, before he dropped off.

He awakened before sunrise, having disregarded the hard ground and slept like an exhausted cat. Sierra was still asleep, snuggling against his back. He reached over and stroked Thor. He was not surprised. The old dog had joined his friend, Jack, during the night.

Chapter 58

I T WAS NEARLY noon and Jordy was astride Buster on his way to San Angelo. He had just left Tess's house after informing her of the lawyer's meeting. She had been surprised at the request and consented to have Jordy and the ranch participants stop by with Jack's double-seated buggy to deliver them all to the lawyer's office.

Tess had seemed sad but stoic and had brightened noticeably when she told Jordy she was expecting Sierra for a visit that afternoon. Sierra had not mentioned it to Jordy, but he was pleased that the two women seemed to be forming a fast friendship.

He and Sierra had spoken little since their vigil in the cemetery during the night. Just before sunrise, after wrapping Thor in one of the blankets, they had walked in silence from the cemetery to the house. Sierra had suggested he shave and wash up first, since she was going to talk to Consuelo about hot water for a bath as soon as she arrived. Sierra was obviously self-conscious about the previous evening's drunken episode and anxious to wash away her sins. Their soiled clothing had mysteriously disappeared from the hallway before he went downstairs for breakfast, so he figured Sierra had assumed responsibility for the garments.

She had been bathing when the Cortez family and Rusty gathered for breakfast. Rusty had nodded his head approvingly when Jordy informed him that he would be going to San Angelo later that morning. Enrique Cortez volunteered to help dig a grave for Thor, and after breakfast they had retrieved the coffin from the barn and carried it to the cemetery.

When they were ready to place Thor's coffin in the grave, Sierra called from the path and told them to wait. She read a blessing for animals which she said was written by Saint Francis of Assisi, the Patron Saint of animals. With a sling of two ropes, Jordy and Enrique then lowered the vessel into the grave. While they were filling the grave with dirt, Sierra had vanished as quickly as she appeared.

When Jordy arrived in San Angelo, he stopped at the freight office to speak to Juana, who was busy at her desk when he came in. He had spoken briefly with her before the funeral at the ranch; he had been unable to locate her after he spoke with Frank Bell Russo, the lawyer. She had evidently returned to town immediately after the service.

Juana waved him to her desk when she saw him, gesturing for him to be seated in one of the captain's chairs in front. She finished writing something in a ledger book and then put her pencil down. "Sorry," she said. "Scheduling problems. We need the rest of our wagon crews back—and the mules. Business is booming."

"I'm glad to hear that. I stopped by to tell you about some time you've got to carve out for Friday." He told her about the lawyer's summons.

"How strange," she said. "I cannot imagine why Tige and I would be invited. Tige needs to get back to work. Vacation's over, and I intend to tell him that."

Jordy smiled. "You are a slave driver—whoops, poor choice of words."

She laughed. "He calls me that all the time. I tell him I won't sell him to anybody else, and I swear the way some of these women look at him, I think he'd bring a good price."

Juana obviously loved Tige fiercely, and Jordy wondered what it would be like to have a woman love you like that. They chatted for five or ten minutes about the freight operations before Jordy said, "I have another errand while I'm in town, and then I've got to get back to the ranch. Don't worry about the lawyer's meeting. I know nothing about Jack's arrangements, but he wouldn't have done anything that would jeopardize your jobs."

As he stepped out onto the boardwalk, he looked down the street toward the warped board front of Tobe's Tavern. Only a few horses at the hitching post in front. That was good. Of course, things did not wake up at places like Tobe's until at least dusk. He left Buster hitched in front of the freight office and walked down the boardwalk before crossing the dusty street. When he reached the front of the saloon, he paused a moment, took a deep breath and pushed through the batwing doors.

He stopped abruptly when he was greeted by the large painting of a stark-naked Sierra Wills hanging on the wall behind the bar for all the world to view. His eyes remained fastened on her image as he approached the bar and ordered a beer. When the young bartender placed a full mug in front of him, Jordy dropped two quarters on the bar, one for the beer and the other for the bartender.

"Where's Tobe?" Jordy asked.

"Upstairs, and he don't want to be bothered."

Jordy tossed a dollar bill on the bar. "Bother him. Tell him Jordy Jackson wants to see him and that it's about money."

The bartender picked up the dollar and headed up-stairs, while Jordy found a table in the corner of the tavern's small seating area. He pulled out a chair and sat down, his eyes still fixed on the painting. She had not been much more than a girl when she posed, but the subject was undeniably Sierra. He guessed the painting to be about six feet wide and four feet high, with Sierra's perfect form stretched across its width, resting on a background of colorful pillows, one leg lifted suggestively, and her hand tossed casually over her muff to allow only imagination to see the rest. She was leaning on one elbow, facing the observer as if caught by surprise while engaged in some obscene act. Her breasts appeared firm and taut, not large but well formed. The artist had captured the eyes perfectly, a kaleidoscope of hazel shades of greens, browns and blues appearing, dependent upon angle and light. And the eyes seemed to look directly and invitingly at the viewer.

The artist was extremely talented, Jordy thought, admitting he had no basis for judging such things. His lust was uncomfortably triggered by the painting and the thought that this perfect creature had kissed him the night before and later lain beside him chastely in the moonlight. He suspected it would be easy enough to lure customers to the business upstairs once they had viewed the painting on the tavern wall.

"What do you want, Jackson?"

Jordy looked up. It was Tobias Marx, wearing a filthy suit and shirt and three days' growth of whiskers. He was a tall, middle-aged man, lean except for a beer gut that looked like it carried a watermelon. Jordy had always been distracted by the nose hairs that crawled a good quarter inch from his nostrils.

"I want to buy the painting of the lady."

Marx sat down. "I bet you do. Everybody wants that picture. Have that to keep you company at nights, no reason to come to Tobe's for your pleasures. Take care of yourself in a minute. She's something, ain't she? Not for sale."

Jordy figured Marx did not have enough money to have paid a lot for the painting, and he could pick up plenty of cheap art in one of the bigger cities that would serve his purposes. It wasn't like he was operating an art museum here. "Fifty dollars."

"Nope."

"Everything's got a price. What do you want?"

Marx was silent for a long time, which told Jordy the painting was now on the market.

"I'd never find another like this," Marx said.

"What do you care? You can find others that would decorate your place just fine. Some drunk will shoot this place up sometime and fill it full of holes. Then what would it be worth?" Marx's lips tightened and his left eye squinted, telling Jordy that this was something the tavern owner had not considered.

"Maybe I'll have me an auction."

"Go ahead, but if I don't get it today, I won't be a bidder."

"Three hundred dollars."

Jordy had never placed a limit on what he would pay to get Sierra's painting out of the place, but he would easily have paid five hundred. He did not want the man backing out because he thought he could have gotten more. He doubted if Marx had any integrity about such things. "Two hundred dollars."

Marx was studying him now, like a poker player. Jack and Rudy had always kidded Jordy about being poker-faced. He hoped that was the face he was showing now.

"Ah, shit," Marx said. "Split the difference?"

Jordy rendered a loud sigh. "Oh, what the hell? It's too damned much, but let's do it. Take my bank draft?"

"I know where to find you if it's no good. Besides, you wouldn't want word to get around that you're both a deadbeat and a deviant."

"Deviant. That's a big word."

"Don't know what it means exactly. Woman called me that because of my business once. Stuck in my head, and I figured you earned it today."

Jordy pulled a blank draft from his shirt pocket, filled it out, signed it, and handed it to Marx. "Now let's take the painting down and go to your backroom and see if we can get it out of the frame." He was not about to carry the framed painting down Main Street for all the gossips to see. There would be enough of that anyhow.

They removed the painting from the wall and took some "boos" from the few tavern customers. In the storage room behind the bar, Jordy carefully detached the frame and rolled up the painting's canvas. Then he returned to the freight office and asked Juana to help him wrap it in the heaviest cover she could find. She suggested another layer of canvas and took care of the task, binding it snuggly with twine but not so tight as to cause a depression in the object. She had obviously been curious but asked no questions.

Later, as Jordy headed back to the ranch with a rolled and wrapped painted canvas tucked carefully under his arms, he pondered what he was going to do with the acquisition that had cost him the equivalent of ten cows and half of his bank account. He was not about to tell anyone what he had done, but he was certain word would get around. And if Sierra happened to stay near San Angelo, how many men would recognize her as the beautiful woman in the painting? Should he warn her? What had possessed her to pose for the painting? Were there others out there? He had a lot of thinking to do. He decided that his purchase would go in his bedroom closet for now.

Chapter 59

JORDY HANDLED THE buggy reins as the party rode to San Angelo behind a team of mules. Rudy sat silently in the front seat with Jordy, and Sierra and Tess chatted amicably in the back seat. Rudy had said little since his return midday yesterday with the Lucky Five crew and Sierra's horse herd. The wagons had swung through town, where the Studebakers had been abandoned near the freight company's stables. There he had received the news of Jack's death. Although he should not have been surprised, the old man had plummeted into a stupor, and when he did emerge, it was frequently with sudden outbursts of anger.

Ranch operations had turned to near chaos when the horses showed up. Jordy and Sierra had joined the wranglers in driving the herd to the selected pasture area along the river. Sierra had ridden Dancer through the herd, weaving back and forth as she selected fillies to be cut out in a week or two and taken to the ranch headquarters and corralled to await Buster's services. The area was not fenced off, but water was close by and grass was plentiful. Irish said he would arrange for wranglers to rotate in six-hour shifts to keep the herd from straying but he thought it unlikely the horses would be looking to stray after so many days of barely subsistence forage.

Rudy had appeared at supper that evening and picked at his food before exploding into a rage at Jordy for not waiting for Rudy's return before burying Jack. Jordy chose not to respond. Following supper, Rudy had accosted both Jordy and Sierra about sharing the house without a chaperone. He ordered Jordy to move in with him until appropriate supervision was arranged. Sierra had prudently remained silent. Jordy had politely declined.

The old man had stomped out and before dark returned with blanket and pillow and made his bed on the living room couch. Jordy had suggested Rudy move into Jack's bedroom. Rudy had replied, "You expect an old cripple to go up and down them steps? But I can get there if I hear any foolishness going on up there, and I'll be bringing Jack's old double-barreled." Jordy thought the old devil would not even hear the shotgun if it accidently fired downstairs. If Rudy's hearing was the only barrier to any foolishness, all bets were off on upstairs socializing.

After leaving the passengers at the lawyer's office, Jordy took the mules and buggy to the freight company stable and asked one of the stable hands to see to the critters. He did not have a notion how long the lawyer's meeting might take. When he returned to the lawyer's office he was shown into a room with a long table where Frank Bell Russo and the others, including Tige and Juana Marshall now sat.

Russo stood and shook Jordy's hand. "Sit down, Jordy." He gestured to the only vacant seat, which happened to be at the end of the table opposite the presiding lawyer. Tige Marshall sat to his right and Sierra to his left. "We have all had a chance to meet each other while we waited for you—and you are precisely on time, as Jack would have noted. Just to give you a bit of background, Jack came to my office the day before he left on the recent search for the stolen horses. He did not appear to have any sense of foreboding. It was just his nature to prepare, and there had been recent developments in his life that made it important to him to update his arrangements. He expected that passage of time would prompt further changes in disposition of his property, but fate intervened, and the will that I am going to review with you today will govern."

The lawyer pulled several sheets of parchment from the envelope and laid them on the tabletop in front of him.

He said, "Jack Wills was not a simple man, but he treasured simplicity in expression. I hope you will excuse my vulgarity, but he told me to 'spare him the legal crap.' Thus, I have never previously drafted a will that disposed of so much property in so few words. Now, I shall read: *Will of John Thomas Wills. I revoke any prior wills. I give my property as follows: One: I direct my executor to incorporate the business known as Lucky Five Freighting Company, including all real and personal property assets utilized in the business, and thereafter to distribute the shares of said company as follows: Sixty percent to Tige Marshall and Juana Marshall jointly, ten percent to Theresa Wyman, ten percent to Rudolph Kilgore, ten percent to Jordan Jackson and ten percent to Sierra Wills.*"

Russo paused. "Tige and Juana, as executor of the will, I will work with you in setting up the new legal structure for the business. However, you should be aware that since you will own the majority shares, you effectively control the business operation, subject to paying out a percentage of profits to all the shareholders. It is not as complicated as it sounds, and Jack assured me that Juana could easily take care of the bookkeeping."

Tige said, "I don't understand. He was more than our employer, and he gave us so many opportunities anyway."

Russo said, "I remember the day he signed the will, Jack said that he never did that much for people by way of money, but he tried to give them chances to do for themselves. I think he thought you had already proved you would take advantage of opportunities, so he wanted to give you a big one."

Jordy noted that the lawyer seemed uncomfortable with Juana's tears and quickly turned his eyes to the parchment sheet in front of him.

Russo continued. "*Two: I give to Jordan Jackson all the cattle, horses, crop inventories, equipment and other personal property used in the Lucky Five Ranch operation. Three: I give to Theresa Wyman twelve hundred acres of land adjacent to or surrounding her real estate parcel, the dimensions and approximate boundaries to be determined by her and exact property lines to be established by legal survey.*"

Russo paused again. "Tess, Jack's intention was that you could choose to either sell the land or lease it back to the Lucky Five Ranch. But no strings."

Tess said nothing, shaking her head in disbelief.

The lawyer continued reading. "*Four: I give any remaining real estate, being that property known as Lucky Five Ranch as follows: To Jordan Jackson, an undivided three-fourths and to Sierra Wills, an undivided one fourth, both devisees subject to the right of Rudolph Kilgore to live in his current residence on the land for his lifetime.*"

He looked at Jordy and Sierra. "I was not enthusiastic about this provision, but I am only the scrivener of my client's wishes. This means that neither of you can identify specific acres that he or she owns. If Jordy continues the ranch operation, you would need to agree to a rent share for Sierra's one-fourth interest in the land or agree to a price for purchase by Jordy of that interest. The owner of an undivided interest can also force a sale of the entire property if the owners do not come to terms. The best I can say for undivided interests is that they tend to generate a lot of fees for lawyers." He gave a wry smile.

Jordy said, "Jack owed me nothing. I am grateful for anything. But I think he was tossing me a challenge." Jordy looked at Sierra. Her sober face told him nothing.

"*Five,*" Russo said. "*I direct my executor to pay to all persons employed by either Lucky Five Ranch or Lucky Five Freighting at the date of my death the sum of two hundred dollars for each year of service completed prior to that date.*"

He turned to Juana. "Jack said you would have re-cords to verify time of service. He thought approximately twenty thousand dollars would cover this."

She smiled, "Jack had ledgers in his head. If that is what he said, it won't be far off."

"Finally," Russo said, "*Six: I give the residue and remain-der of my property to Theresa Wyman, Rudolph Kilgore, Jordan Jackson and Sierra Wills, in equal shares.*"

The lawyer raised his head from the papers. "This is called a residuary clause. It takes care of anything not covered in the previous paragraphs. That would include cash, which Jack said Juana would know about. We will make a complete inventory of all assets in the course of settlement, but Juana, if Jack's employee figures were close, do you have any idea what funds would be left in his accounts?"

"Maybe forty-five thousand dollars."

Rudy erupted, "That penny pinching old fart. He al-ways acted like he was on the edge of broke. Couldn't buy this, couldn't buy that. Too much money. I can't believe he had a fortune squirreled away."

Jordy had to admit that the numbers left him stunned, also. He had no idea that Jack had accumulated signifi-cant cash assets. He was always fretting about the profits and staying ahead of the creditors.

Russo finished reading. "The last paragraph of the will reads '*I appoint Frank Bell Russo executor of this will.*' It is then signed by Jack and witnessed by my law clerk and the barber next door. The settlement process will take as long as a year. I will be filing the will with the probate court Monday, and you will be kept informed as to progress. I will be needing to meet with some of you individually quite frequently. You may continue business as usual. I will start making the employee cash distributions in a month or so. The residuary amount will be held until we determine if there are outstanding claims. Then I will start partial distributions of that. I anticipate my fees will amount to three or four thousand dollars, so I won't let that get away." He smiled at his small joke, but getting no response, asked, "Any questions?"

Jordy could not think of anything to say. He could not quite grasp the reality of what had happened this afternoon. None of it was worth losing Jack, and he figured everybody else in the room felt the same way.

Chapter 60

SIERRA FOUND JORDY at the table in the library after supper. He seemed absorbed with some papers spread out on the round tabletop, so she said nothing and sat down in one of the chairs across from him.

He looked up. "Quite a day," he said. "Lots of things to sort out."

She said, "I'm embarrassed. I didn't know Grandpa Jack a month ago. I show up here, end up getting him killed and now I am an heiress. I don't know if I should accept anything."

"The lawyer told me if Jack had not made a will, you would have been entitled to the whole works. Everything."

"But that would have been challenged."

"By whom? There is no other blood kin. None of the rest of us were entitled to anything in the absence of a will. That's what Russo said. If you renounce—I think that's the word—your share goes to the state of Texas. He warned Jack about that and told him he should have a provision that said what happened if you died first or renounced. He just wanted a quick will, and he might not have wanted to give you an escape hatch. I sure as hell don't want Texas as my partner, and I hope you wouldn't do that to any of us."

"No, of course not. But I could give it to you or sell cheap."

"I would be insulted, but if you want out some day, I would buy at market. It will be months before things are settled. We need to let things play out."

"Well, I will have funds to pay off my ranch east of here. I wouldn't be forced to liquidate the herd."

"You could stay here indefinitely, at least till the estate is settled. You own a fourth of this house now."

"Are you serious?"

"I am. We get along well enough most of the time. We could fence off land for the horse herd." He smiled. "That would be a credit against my rent, though."

"We would continue to live like we are? It will be a scandal. And Rudy sleeping in the parlor all the time?"

"I think Rudy's starting to calm down. He is the only old dog left here. He needs to come to terms with it on his own first. I'll be able to talk sense to him in a few days."

"My head's spinning. I have so much to think about."

"I will give you some more to think on. There is a way we could resolve a lot of problems in this situation."

"There is?"

"Get married."

"Married? You and me?"

"Yeah. It occurred to me on the way back from town. You are going to be able to pay off the mortgage on your own land and then you might leave. I almost panicked at that thought. I couldn't imagine you not being here. It just wouldn't be the same without you. I've come to really care about you. More than that. I have fallen crazy in love with you."

He got out of his chair and stepped around the desk, took her hand and pulled her up to him. He put his arms around her and held her close before he pressed his lips to hers. It was a soft, lingering kiss, and she found herself returning it before she eased back and looked up into his eyes.

"You caught me by surprise," she said. "After I turned into a drunken slut the other night, I assumed you couldn't wait for me to get out of here."

He grinned mischievously. "You are not by any means a drunken slut. I have known a few and have not minded their company on occasion, I confess. But I would never tell one I love her, as I am telling you, and I most certainly would not ask one to marry me, as I am asking you."

He had just taken her breath away. This was moving too quickly. She took a few more steps back, almost stumbling over the chair. "Am I hearing you right? Is that a proposal?"

"It is. Will you marry me?"

"We haven't known each other a full month yet. And there is so much you don't know about me."

"You don't have to answer me now. Just stay on. Run your horse business out of the Lucky Five. If you decide to stay, you can sell your ranch or keep it and rent it out. Do what you want. You're not a prisoner here. Just give us a chance. I'm good with that for now. As to our living arrangements, I will be a total gentleman, I promise."

"You have always been a gentleman with me," she said. "I have failed to behave like a lady, I'm afraid."

"Wait here a moment. Sit down. I'll be right back."

He turned and left the room and Sierra could hear him taking the steps to the second floor, probably two at a time. Jordy had just overwhelmed her enough. She was not ready for another surprise. She needed to saddle

Dancer and ride off into the night and think about all that was being dropped on her plate. Her physical attraction to Jordy was undeniable, but from her experiences with Carlos, she had learned that a lifetime with someone would require much more. She felt she had already bonded with Jordy as a friend despite her disgusting behavior a few nights earlier. He had not even said a word about it and not many hours later had welcomed her at the graveside vigil. He was a kind and generous man—like Grandpa Jack. And why wouldn't he be, raised in the shadow of such a man?

When Jordy reentered the library, he was carrying a canvas-wrapped roll of something. He laid it on the table in front of her and sat down. "Yours," he said. "I bought it at the tavern yesterday. I thought of destroying it, but it is just too beautiful. I can't do it. I am giving it to you. Do with it as you wish. Burn if it pleases you but don't ask me to help."

She stood up and began to unwrap the canvas cover. Before she was finished, she knew what she was going to find. She just had no idea which one. She pulled the rolled-up painting from its canvas sheath. "Help me roll this out on the floor," she said.

They both knelt on the floor, rolling out the painting to its full length, each of them pinning one end to the floor. She studied her own form stretched out there like a lazy cat. She remembered the painting and the countless nights it had taken and those passionate moments in the studio each evening after work was done and then sneaking back into her room at school. What a wicked creature she had been.

"Let's roll it up and put it back in the wrap," she said. "For now, you can put it back wherever you were keeping it."

After the painting was wrapped again, she sat down again at the table, and Jordy took the chair beside her, taking her hand in his. She spoke softly. "I don't know what to say. You found this in a tavern?"

"Yes. Above the bar."

"I hope you didn't have to pay too much."

"I got a bargain price. The owner did not appreciate the treasure he had there."

"There could be as many as a half dozen somewhere. I suppose I should tell you about it. I had such bad judgment and now I am paying for it."

"Good judgment comes from experience, and a lot of that comes from bad judgment."

She smiled wanly. "That sounds like a 'Jack-ism.'"

"It is. But I don't need to hear the story. Someday, if you feel compelled to tell it, I would be glad to listen. But it doesn't matter. I will never tell you every story from my sordid past. If you decide to marry me, I like to think we will start with a fresh canvas."

Later, she tossed in bed, her rambling thoughts denying sleep. She finally swung her legs out of bed, peeled off the flannel nightgown, stepped into the hallway and pushed the partly open door to Jordy's room. She crawled into his bed, slipping in beside him, pleased to discover that he was also naked. He rolled toward her, "What the . . ?"

She pressed a finger to his lips. "Yes," she said. "I will marry you."

It was several hours later when she heard Uncle Rudy's cane banging on the staircase. "I hear you. Sounded like you got a mountain cat up there. Get back to your room and leave that young woman alone, Jordy, or I'm coming up."

.

Chapter 61

I T HAD BEEN a month since Sierra accepted Jordy's proposal. Everything that had happened since that time only reassured her that her decision had been a good one. This was a man she could walk side by side with to the end of the trail. Already, the Lucky Five was in her blood, and she, Irish, and Mitch Eagle Eyes would develop a major equine side to the ranching operation. Jordy would stay with his cows and try to expand farming on the bottomlands of the ranch.

She still shed tears sometimes because she felt cheated out of so many years with Grandpa Jack, but she felt he was with her most days on the vast ranch. And everybody she encountered had anecdotes to share about Jack Wills, so she came to know him better each day.

She had not told Jordy yet that she had missed her monthly last week. What would Grandpa have thought about the prospects of a second descendent arriving soon, one who whether male or female, would carry the middle name Wills?

It was late morning, and the Texas sun would have them baking in a few hours, but for now they enjoyed the shade of a few oak trees and a gentle breeze drifting off the North Concho. They had selected this spot for their wedding because Jack had liked to fish here. The only guests were employees and families of the Lucky Five businesses, and some of those were absent because of freight runs or livestock emergencies. She guessed that just short of thirty people were gathered to witness the brief ceremony.

An employee of the freight company, Wilber Chambers, who also happened to be the pastor of the Methodist Church in town, had agreed to officiate. He was a kindly, middle-aged man with a ruddy complexion and cherubic face. She liked him and thought she might join up with that tiny congregation. Their child would need to be baptized someplace, and Jordy was leaving things religious to her so long as she did not try to crack any whips at him. She had also learned that Grandpa Jack had quietly funded the small church building and that the pastor's job with the freight company was essentially a subsidy for a congregation that would have been otherwise too small to afford a clergyman.

There were no chairs, so the guests stood, leaving an aisle between them for the bride and escort to walk through. Consuelo had made the bride a nice, pale-green dress for the occasion, Sierra having self-determined she did not qualify for white. She looked at Uncle Rudy standing beside her all clean shaven, his store-bought teeth shining like pearls and fixed in a satisfied grin and wearing a new black suit and polished boots. No man was happier than Uncle Rudy today. She and Jordy considered him as family, and the responsibility assigned to him would make it official.

Pastor Chambers at the opposite end of the grassy aisle nodded, and she took Rudy's arm. They moved slowly because Rudy had abandoned his cane for the occasion. When they reached the front of the onlookers, she saw Jordy with Tige at his side and on the other side of the pastor, Tess, wearing a tasteful dark green dress. If only they could have had a double wedding today.

Jordy stepped over and took her hand, and they moved in front of the preacher. Suddenly she felt a strange presence, and she shivered. The ceremony was a blur after that. The vows were recited, but she could barely hear them. She hoped she said "I do." She heard Jordy agree to take her and saw Tige handing him the wedding band, which he almost dropped. The band somehow got on her finger. The pastor pronounced them husband and wife, and then she was awakened by Jordy's kiss, which she may have returned too passionately if the guests' applause was any indication.

They turned to face the guests, and that was when she saw them. The only cloud in the sky above them began to roll and break apart. Suddenly Jack appeared. He was on one of the cloud fragments, that crooked smile on his face, his arm tucked about Thor, bright-eyed and tail wagging happily.

"Jordy," she whispered. "Do you see Jack? Look at the clouds."

He complied. "What are you talking about? I don't see anything. Are you okay, love?"

She looked again. Nothing. They walked down the aisle to the awaiting buggies that would take the group back to the ranch house for a lunch and refreshments. Sierra remained shaken by what she had seen but jubilant, too.